# Pleasure-Dome

# BY THE SAME AUTHOR

FICTION

*The Beautiful Greed* (1961)
*Cassandra Singing* (1969)
*The Shadow Knows* (1970)
*Brothers in Confidence* (1972)
*Bijou* (1974)
*The Suicide's Wife* (1978)

NONFICTION

*Wright Morris* (1964)
*The Poetic Image in Six Genres* (1969)
*James M. Cain* (1970)
*Harlequin's Stick, Charlie's Cane* (1975)

EDITED WORKS

*Proletarian Writers of the Thirties* (1968)
*Tough Guy Writers of the Thirties* (1968)
*American Dreams, American Nightmares* (1970)
*Rediscoveries* (1971)
*The Popular Culture Explosion*
     (with Ray B. Browne) (1972)
*Nathanael West: The Cheaters and the Cheated*
     (1973)
*Contemporary Literary Scene*
     (with Frank Magill) (1974)
*Remembering James Agee* (1974)
*Creative Choices* (1975)
*Studies in the Short Story*
     (with Virgil Scott) (1979)
*A Primer of the Novel* (1979)

# Pleasure-Dome

David Madden

The Bobbs-Merrill Company, Inc.
Indianapolis   New York

Parts of this novel appeared in different form in "Traven," *Southern Review*, 1968; *Brothers in Confidence*, Avon, 1972; "Nothing Dies, but Something Mourns," *Carleton Miscellany*, 1968.

The author wishes to thank the following publishers for permission to quote from these songs:

"Are You Satisfied Now?" by Ted Daffan, copyright © 1946 by Hill and Range Songs, Inc. Copyright renewed. All rights controlled by Unichappell Music, Inc. (Rightsong Music, publisher). International copyright secured. All rights reserved. Used by permission.

"You Belong to Me," by Redd Stewart, Pee Wee King, and Chilton Price, copyright owned by the Ridgeway Music Co., Inc. All rights reserved. Used by permission of the publisher.


Published by The Bobbs-Merrill Company, Inc.
Indianapolis   New York

Designed by Rita Muncie
Manufactured in the United States of America

First printing

**Library of Congress Cataloging in Publication Data**

Madden, David, 1933–
   Pleasure-dome.
   I. Title.
PZ4.M1787Pl   [PS3563.A339]        813'.5'4        79-10664
ISBN 0-672-52553-4

In memory of
"Good ol' Jimmy," my father,
and C. P. "Bill" Lee, my teacher

# Contents

Is this a fancy which our reason scorns?
Ah! surely Nothing dies but Something mourns!

—Byron, *Don Juan*

# *Pleasure-Dome*

# 1  Lucius, Bucky, and Earl Hutchfield

Did I ever tell you about the time I tried to get my little brother off the chain gang? . . . Oh, I did? . . . Okay, I *will* tell it again.

But first, I need to back up a little. I got through a year at Cherokee College before I finally hit the open road. Straight to Greenwich Village. I worked atop the Empire State Building as a mail clerk and messenger, then the night shift for the White Tower hamburger joints all over the city, replacing whoever didn't show up. Spent every day except Sunday sitting in the union hall in Brooklyn, trying to ship out. When Eisenhower and Nixon were inaugurated in Washington, everything turned gray and I thought the atomic bomb would fall before dark.

But Christmas I signed as a wiper on the *Polestar,* with a cargo of mercy rations for earthquake victims in Taltal, Chile. But what excited me most was that we were supposed to go on to India. This was my first ship, and it was interesting for a while, but I was depressed because I'd broken up with my girl, Anna Livia, a few months before, and I was worried about the Korean War and my ass in the draft and whether I ought to go back to college, and I couldn't keep my mind on the reading or writing I'd hoped to do. Every day I thought about the bomb—that it might go off while we were way out there and us not know it, and the wind would blow the radioactive fallout over us slowly. I thought of Anna Livia, and my grandmother, and Momma, there in Cherokee alone where I couldn't help them when the Oak Ridge atomic plants exploded. And between Antofagasta and Taltal, Chile, I turned twenty years old.

In Valparaíso, which almost plunged into the ocean when a tidal wave hit it in 1906—a sort of aftershock of the San Francisco quake—the captain received a change of orders and we were told that we had to go into dry dock in San Diego for two months. The *Polestar* had overreached herself. Dangerously worn out. Just in time, because the crew had gotten mean and I was having trouble with nine or ten of them.

I had one fantastic night in Valparaíso making love all night long to Irana, till she had to go to school—a sixteen-year-old whore who begged me to jump ship, promised to support me if I'd stay with her. Two weeks later I signed off in San Diego with the promise I'd get hired on again when the *Polestar* was seaworthy in August. I'd set out for India, and that's where I wanted to go.

To save money I hitchhiked across the mountains, the desert, and the plains. Happened to pass through Hannibal, Missouri, and poked around where Tom Sawyer and Huck Finn became immortal, then remembered Jesse James and went out of my way to pay homage to him in St. Joseph. Then, like Huck Finn adrift on his thumb, I went on to Nashville, where Jesse James once tried to live like a respectable citizen, and where my big brother Earl was in prison and my little brother Bucky was in the reform school, and

Momma was working in a hotel, trying to get both of them an early release.

Momma got permission to take Bucky out of the reform school to supper and to see the Grand Ol' Opry, but he was still grieving over the death of Hank Williams.

Momma had just gotten back from a short trip to Cherokee and she gave me a letter from Raine, the girl I had loved before Anna Livia. It had followed me from New York to the *Polestar* in Chile and back to Cherokee to my mother's hands in the lobby of the hotel in Nashville. Raine wrote that she thought I might like to have the clipping from the Cherokee paper that showed Cathleen Blackburn at her wedding to an Oak Ridge chemical engineer. 'You were never lovelier,' I thought, staring at the smudged newspaper picture, and I never hurt so bad. Last summer, when Anna Livia (my nickname for Cathleen) wrote to tell me we no longer belonged together, she'd said, "You belong with Byron, Shelley, and Keats." "You mean," I asked her, "I should be dead?"

From Nashville I hitchhiked down to Mobile, signed on the seatrain *Louisiana* as a messman, bound for Edgewater, New Jersey. Eager to get back to the Village, I signed off the *Louisiana*. But the thrill was gone, and over in Brooklyn, shipping was terrible. I need to wander, I need to roam, but I wanted to be back in the mountains, homesick for Cherokee, which Earl calls the asshole of the world.

On the way, in Baltimore, the humidity was making me nauseated, and as I stood on the corner under the noon sun, a baby blue Buick Streamliner glides to a stop at the light beside me. "Could you give me a ride to the city limits?" I asked the young driver, whose wife sat beside him, three kids squirming on the back seat. "Hell," he says, "drive us home and you can *have* the damned thing for a hundred dollars." Because the brakes were bad and the speedometer was broken and he was desperate for hard cash. And I did have the hundred dollars to spare, but I had no license to drive and no insurance, and on the road through the Shenandoah Valley was where I really learned to drive.

The radio worked fine. When I hit the Cherokee city limits, Jo Stafford sang Anna Livia's choice for "our song":

> Fly the ocean in a silver plane,
> See the jungle when it's wet with rain,
> Just remember, till you're home again,
> You belong to me. . . .

Like the song, images of Anna Livia came when I didn't expect them, and it hurt—the way she'd suddenly smile when she saw me amble through the Market House, pretending to appraise the iced fish. To gaze upon Anna Livia as she sacked fruit in the Garden of Eden, her father's stand, I parked between two vegetable trucks outside the Market House and went in. Her father worked alone.

To touch base with another holy place, I coasted down Sevier Street past the Bijou, where I used to usher and where we used to meet, and where *A Lion Is in the Streets* with James Cagney as Huey Long was now held over from the Tivoli. I parked on River Street and walked along the bank, past my old tower, past the marble quarry, the brick kilns, to the sagging dock where Anna Livia and I used to sit, watch the river, and dream up our future. The dock was gone.

Driving across town to my room near the college, I took in the news on the hour: "Ike" had read a western novel en route to a long golf weekend in Augusta, where his trusty Negro caddy, "Dead Man," renamed "Cemetery" by the president, waited. And in Cherokee, I began to hear the old familiar sound of "the mind-forged manacles."

When I walked into my old room in the basement of a rambling three-story house on Sequoyah Avenue, my daddy, who'd moved in to hold it for me in case I go back to school, looked up from my lopsided cot and announced, "Well, bub, the biggest atomic bomb ever exploded in the U.S. was dropped yesterday from a B-26 bomber over the Nevada proving ground," and offered me a goober from a wrinkled white poke, like I'd finally come home just to get the latest on the bomb as of Wednesday afternoon, June 5, 1953.

Since he came back from the war in '46, I seldom saw him that he didn't ask me for fifty cents to get himself a shot he needed "bad."

"Son," he says, "I tell you . . ." So I forked over fifty cents.

After he was gone, I looked through my mail, afraid I'd find a summons to Korea. The draft board was frowning over my erratic career as a scholar. But they weren't after me yet. My agent, Mendell Sarett, returned two of my stories that she'd sent to twenty magazines, and quoted *New World Writing*'s words of praise, with the reservation that I sounded too much like Faulkner in one of the stories, "Imprisoned Light."

I unpacked my clothes and books and prints. On the wall of my room I tacked the prints I'd bought in the museums in New York and ones I'd taped to the bulkhead by my cot on the *Polestar:* Breughel's "The Harvesters" and Picasso's "The Old Guitarist" and Tchelitchew's "Hide and Seek." To the artistic nude photos, I added one of a girl from India. The leather jacket I'd bought in New York last December, when Anna Livia ended our six-year romance, to wear to Maine where I intended to die, was too hot for Cherokee or India, so I put it away at the back of my closet.

That night Daddy came in looped, and I helped him move his stuff back into his old room, snug by the coal furnace. I stayed up late in my room, full of books, records, pictures, looking through my fat notebook, with Lucius + Anna Livia still on it, full of stories, poems, sketches, reflections, plays in progress. I couldn't get back into my play, *The Idealists,* about two brothers, one an ideal capitalist, the other an ideal Communist, both of whom have fanatical schemes for using their deceased father's money to save the world, that I started in Maine, instead of dying, so I made a few more notes on *Children of a Cold Sun,* the epic story of Anna Livia and me that she once said we'd write together when she joined me in New York.

We all gathered, even Daddy, over at my grandmother's for Sunday dinner on Thursday because Bucky was due to come rolling in from Nashville on the Greyhound. On his eighteenth birthday they'd transferred Bucky from the reform school to prison, and now they'd released him early. From her post in the hotel near the Capitol in Nashville, Momma had finally broken through to the governor's heart. Not just for Bucky's sake, but, a month earlier, for big brother Earl's too. Earl had already quit the job Momma had gotten him—ushering at the Grand Ol' Opry—and had hit the dusty trail again, a traveling faith healer with a tent in a Mack truck, swooping down on small towns from sea to shining sea.

So to welcome Bucky home we were all over at

Mammy's house. Anchor to all our wandering lives, not just the little house, its trees, the old oak cut down as a threat to the new roof, its changing trees—mimosa and apple—but the woman in the house, who did not change. She remained the merriest and moodiest woman any of us ever knew. Who got her name from me when she sang "Mammy's little baby loves short'nin' bread," and I thought that was her name. Even as Earl and Bucky went in and came out of various penal institutions, to return to strange houses or apartments where Momma lived, and even as Momma herself roved from Cherokee to Saint Louis, to Chattanooga to Nashville, and as I began to roam all over the U.S., the one place that remained the same was little ol' 702 Holston Street and Mammy. One change, though, was in the Chief, Mammy's second husband, who set up the fire-fighting system where Oak Ridge rose out of the two-centuries-plowed ground in the hills of Anderson County, and who was forced to retire now because his legs were giving in to old injuries and old age.

Having put the green beans and shellies on to boil, Mammy says, "Lucius, they's something I want to show you," in a tone that set me up for a dramatic presentation. She comes back from her bedroom with something held behind her back. "Here's why your Mammy don't laugh at miracles."

The mayonnaise jar I'd tossed into the Gulf of Mexico a few months ago had turned up on the beach at Tampa. Feeling far from home, I'd got the urge to try something I'd seen some people shipwrecked on a deserted island do. I got a gallon mayonnaise jar from the chief cook and washed it out and wrote a letter to Mammy, telling her how important she had been in my life, the effect her storytelling had had on my own compulsion to tell a story. I'd put the letter into an envelope, addressed it to her, stamped it, and when nobody was looking, I'd tossed the jar over the fantail and watched it bob on the waves out of sight. I thought at the time, 'This is corny, but what if it reaches her?' And there I was, standing in her living room, taking my letter to Mammy out of its still-crisp envelope.

"Write a story about *that,*" said Mammy, confident that I could, and, given her advice, would.

"A lot's happened since I tossed that jar overboard," I said, and began to tell it.

But before I could bring my adventures on land and sea to a climax, Momma got into the act, telling us for the third time how she broke her leg stepping down from the Greyhound that brought *her* back only a few days ago so she could look for an apartment for her and Bucky, and maybe Earl, if he played out as a faith healer, and maybe me, if I got tired of "living alone in a sooty old basement in the rough part of town," and I was cringing before visions of having to taxi her all over Cherokee in my sleek blue broken-down Buick Streamliner—to the store, to the laundromat, to Dr. Summers, who had operated on me the summer of '47 to correct incipient clawfoot deformity—and Mammy, telling the Chief and me it was about time to go meet Bucky at the Union Bus Terminal, was just putting the corn bread in to brown when the phone rang, and Mammy said, "Lord alive, reckon that's Bucky, coming in on an earlier bus, and nobody there to meet the poor youn'ern?"

It was long distance from Greenbrier, in the mountains, and it was me that answered.

"Lucius, they gonna throw me on the chain gang," Bucky said, in a whine vibrant with outrage.

Hell, it made *me* mad, too. After Bucky's year in the

reform school, looks like the other states could forgive and forget. But no, they were out to clear the books of those old charges.

"Prosecuting attorney said he might can drop the charges," said Bucky, "if the people I passed them checks on will settle for what they call res—restitution."

"Hello, Lucius?" somebody said, in a deep, lush drawl, "your little brother could use a little he'p." Turned out to be Frank Covington, the prosecuting attorney.

I asked Covington how much it all came to, and he said about one thousand dollars. Knowing I couldn't get a spark with two nickels, I said I'd see what I could do.

He says, "One problem."

I said, "What?"

"They all want Bucky's ass. They wanna be able to take a Sunday drive down the highway and see where Bucky's cut the grass."

"Didn't I read about some boys on that chain gang busted each other's feet with sledgehammers because they'd had more than they could take of that kind of life?"

"They run that story all the way up yonder?"

So I asked him what I *could* do, and he said, "Those people he passed the checks on—they're human. Bucky says you're studyin' to be a teacher and all—respectable citizen. Maybe if they got a look at his brother and talked to him . . ."

I said okay and told him I'd see him, and got Bucky back on to tell him to take it easy, I was on my way.

After I hung up, I wondered what the public prosecutor was doing, trying to keep Bucky *off* the chain gang. Then I remembered that it was Bucky's talent for charming his way into people's confidences that got him *into* this fix—a talent trained to performance by our big brother Earl.

Toward the thousand dollars, all I could scrape up was a hundred to show good faith. Since the Thirties, the Hutchfields and the Burnetts have spent most of their lives dodging the shadow of the dole, of welfare. All Mammy and the Chief and Momma could fork over was the gas money. Daddy got Momma to turn loose of a dollar, and threw that in as *his* share. And I was broke, after buying the Buick, paying the rent and other expenses, and by the time I could gather that thousand, Bucky'd have shackle sores on his ankles.

For the hundred, I crossed over to our kin on the other side of the Tennessee River, over in South Cherokee, who—I can't ignore the pun—are rollin' in dough. Hutchfield Bakery is still the local sponsor of the Lone Ranger.

I never cared much for money myself, but I always wanted to meet those rich Hutchfields on an equal social basis—they standing on their bankbooks, me standing on a Pulitzer Prize. But now I had to jump the gun, go to them begging, like I was just another poor white trash Hutchfield and not the writer the world would soon know as the author of *Children of a Cold Sun*.

Kitty, whose Platonic "marriage" to my father for the past ten years has kept Daddy *out* of the county workhouse more weekends than *in,* showed me right into Great-uncle Lucius Hutchfield's air-conditioned office, big as Mammy's backyard, and he didn't bat an eye when I reminded him that my daddy named me after *him*. But when I reviewed with him the story of Bucky's life, and showed him a childhood picture, which favored Daddy—the big Clark Gable ears, the buck-toothed grin that said, 'Aw, hell, all I need's a few bucks'—it wasn't long before he was taking me on a tour of the bakery, watching me wolf down cupcakes, as if Daddy hadn't taken me through and loaded me up many times before.

He must've thought all the men and women who recognized me and smiled were smiling at him. Really, we were just two reminders of the one they all loved more—Daddy, the lovable drunk that Uncle Lucius himself took pity on when his momma and daddy, who used to work there too, died of cancer within months of each other. So when I walked out the gates, I had a check for a hundred, and was gagging on devil's food cake with maple icing.

At the crack of dawn I put on a suit, and I, too, hit the dusty trail, riding to the rescue, and with each mile I put behind me, I felt I was moving deeper and deeper into the dark heart of the chain gang mythos, Carson McCullers's mournful words at the end of "The Ballad of the Sad Café" tolling in my head: "The soul rots with boredom" in the small towns of the South. "You might as well go down to the Forks Falls road and listen to the chain gang."

# 2

# "How Come You Ain't a Crook?"

Four flats and a new carburetor later, I'd passed through one of the worst rainstorms ever to hit the Smoky Mountains and was deep South, in Boone's Gap, the first town Bucky hit, with the names of his four victims in my pocket.

Nauseated from the humidity, I parked in front of the Boone's Gap Family Department Store, erected in 1813, the same feeling in my stomach I had when I played the old mayor in the Cherokee College production of *The Enchanted*. It didn't take long to see what they'd do to get a little business. They'd even take a check from a stranger passing through. Tempted to test that impression, I remembered I was there because Bucky already had.

Mr. Overby, the proprietor, leaned against the counter under a big, spread-eagle fan that hung from the high, pressed-tin ceiling. Mrs. Overby camped by the cash register, jacked up on a stool, her feet not touching the floor. As I imagine Bucky viewing this little tableau, *his* thoughts run through *my* head. Or were they Earl's? Because according to Bucky's version, his big damn brother Earl was the one got him into this.

Mr. Overby, fat, forty, with a voice like Froggy in *Our Gang,* wants to know if he can help me.

"Sir, my name is Lucius Hutchfield. I'm Bucky Hutchfield's brother."

Over by the cash register, Mrs. Overby stirs. "And here I was trying to match you up with some folks from around *here,* 'cause soon's you come in the door, I knew I'd seen a likeness of that face before."

Then Mr. Overby squints against the glare of noon sunlight coming through the door and lumbers around me so he can get me in focus, and when he does, says, "Bucky waltzed in here dressed fit to kill, tried on four suits and took one, and cashed a payroll check."

"But I bet you favor your mother," says Mrs. Overby, her black-and-white polka-dot rayon dress shimmering in the light.

"Folks say I *do.*"

"Because I think it was your walk more than your face. Something about the way little Bucky walked in here—kindly a lope—made you drop your guard and like him right away."

"I'm after his ass, myself," says Mr. Overby, inhaling fiercely through his nose.

"Otis, Daddy's old sign's going back on the wall if you don't curb your tongue."

"Well, it was the biggest I was ever took, and it just scalds my cheeks to think about it."

"I was in the merchant marines at the time, sir," I said, "to earn enough to go on through college, and now I'm about to start my sophomore year in the school of education or I would have been here sooner to let you know that I'll do everything in my power to pay you back."

"You gonna make a teacher?" asked Mrs. Overby, a plump woman with watery eyes.

"Yes, ma'am."

Mr. Overby squinted his eyes, suspicious. "That state investigator told me *you* was a con man too."

"That's Earl, my older brother."

"Well, how come *you* ain't a crook?"

I tried hard to fascinate *him* with an answer to a question most people seem to find fascinating.

Then they ask me if I'm a Christian, and when I tell them I was saved in a tent on sawdust, they invite me to supper.

For such a tacky store, they had a modern ranch-style house, but what Mrs. Overby puts on the table is bowls of good ol' country food.

We're sitting around talking, glancing at Eve Arden in "Our Miss Brooks," and I begin to tell about Bucky. "He's several years younger than I am, and Earl's two years older. So while I was looking up to Earl, I was looking down at Bucky. Used to have to take care of him while Momma was working in my gran'maw's café and Daddy was serving in the ambulance corps under his hero, General Patton. We passed most of our lives in movie theaters, soaking up dreams and nightmares.

"What I wanted to tell you is about stopping off in Nashville to visit Bucky on my way back home from San Diego. I'd just signed off this mercy ship that transported supplies to the earthquake victims in Taltal, Chile, and Momma'd moved to Nashville so's she could be close to Bucky, so I went out to the reform school to get Bucky to take him for one last look at the town before he turned eighteen and they transferred him to the prison.

"Watching the door for Bucky to show, I kept seeing him come through all the different doors in all the different places from the summer he was nine: the juvenile detention home, two different institutions for wayward children, in and out of the reform school. Well, here come Bucky through the door, grinning and waving, and he gives me a shake and a hug, and we talk about old times roaming the streets of Cherokee.

"We met Momma at the hotel where she worked behind the cigar counter in the lobby and we had supper at a little place and then went to the Grand Ol' Opry and I managed to get Bucky backstage to shake hands with Hank Williams"—I saw his picture on the Overbys' knickknack rack, but actually he died while I was still at sea—"and got him to autograph the white shirt that Momma had just bought Bucky at Penney's, right over his heart."

"All I ever got is a picture he signed and sent me in the mail," said Mrs. Overby.

I didn't tell her Bucky tried to sneak off from us in the crowd.

"It was so late, we had to take a taxi back out to Bordeaux suburb and the last I saw of him, he was standing under this weak yellow bulb at the front door, and I could barely see the guard behind him in the dark inside, but the pitiful look of forlornness on his face and in his sagging shoulders was clear enough to make my momma cry all the way back to the hotel, and it was so sad, it hurt me all the way to New York, where I signed on another ship to earn enough to get me through school, so they'd be at least one of us Hutchfields to graduate not only from high school but college too."

"Let's do without 'Our Miss Brooks' one time," says Mrs. Overby, twisting the knob. Mr. Overby sank into his own fat like he'd been mortally denied.

"So during one of my trips on the seatrain *Louisiana,* Bucky turned eighteen on Saint Valentine's

Day and they whisked him away from the kids and put him in with the grown-ups in prison. But you see, his attitude is like a thirteen-year-old, and his nerves got so bad they had to put him under the care of a psychiatrist. Then they decided he ought to learn a trade: how to make brooms. But before he got to fastening on the sweeping part, he flew off the handle and broke some guy's jaw.'' But I didn't tell the Overbys *why:* that the joker wanted to be Bucky's buddy after lights out. Bucky's got a hair-trigger temper. Good thing the only tools of his trade are a fountain pen and a book of blank checks.

"Momma told me it broke her heart to visit him, because they had him on tranquilizers, and it tore her up, because he moved and talked like a zombie. So with the help of the psychiatrist, Momma convinced the governor to get Bucky an early release in her care. What nobody thought of was that your county would want to prosecute him for the checks he passed down here, but when he stepped out the prison gates bright and early yesterday morning, there they were—the sheriff and a man from the state bureau of investigation.''

For one thing, Bucky had wanted to track down Earl and get even with him somehow. "My older brother Earl'd just come out of the same prison himself a few months before, full of religion, and somehow he's got hold of a Mack truck and a tent and he's gone on a faith-healing tour. I hope he's serious.

"You see, it was Earl that led Bucky astray. How it happened was this: Bucky had been out of the reform school for a year and doing all right, playing ball, in fact, and getting scouts interested in his pitching. He had one problem: an eye that was blinking out on him. How did he get *that?* One day when we were all little, the rain broke up our ball game and drove us indoors, so we were doing a dry run in the living room, with me pitching the imaginary ball, Earl swinging a real bat, and Bucky, age three, catching. Earl swung back and Bucky began to scream and hold his head and roll in a spreading puddle of blood. A week later, he slipped while walking a railroad track and broke the stitches. A month later, he fell off his tricycle and busted open the nearly healed wound. So he had a good pitching arm, but one strike against him: a bad eye. And the last I heard, he was going deaf in one ear. The prison psychiatrist promised Momma the chain gang would drive him totally *in*sane."

Before I could circle back to tell them how it was that Earl got Bucky into trouble, Mrs. Overby started to cry, I cranked up too, and Mr. Overby kept saying, in his deep-voiced, friendly way, "I'm gonna have his ass in a sling."

After Mr. Overby'd gone to bed, Mrs. Overby told me the story of her life, harping on the theme of childlessness, and she made me promise not to write her up in a story.

The next morning, Mr. Overby took me down to his favorite filling station and told them to fill me up on his credit card. I had convinced him I'd make full restitution in court Monday morning. I'd worry later about putting my hands on the money.

As I idled the motor, about to set out for Carsonville, he leaned on the window and said, "You tell that prosecutor okay, I'll settle for the money, and you tell Bucky it was just that it hurt mine and Mrs. Overby's feelings so much that he'd do us that way, after we took to him the way we did."

# 3

# *"And You Fell for It"*

In Carsonville, a truck full of fresh peaches was backed up to the curb in front of the courthouse. As soon as I talked with Mr. Crigger, proprietor of the Red Dot Café, I was going to get me one of those sweet peaches from just over the line—maybe two. I sat in the sweltering heat of the car and watched customers go in for the noon meal and come out again, and when I imagined the Red Dot was empty, I got out and went inside where Patti Page singing ''Mocking Bird Hill'' was on the jukebox.

The waitress behind the counter had a bottom like two clinging halves of a plump peach, and when I see homemade peach cobbler on the menu, I order it first. But what I bit into was Melba peaches from a can, and Mr. Crigger, thin as a hopeless T.B. case, is sitting on a high stool behind the cash register, looking right at me. Then he's staring. Then he gets down off the stool and lopes on his long legs out to the sidewalk and crosses the street.

But a few minutes later, Mr. Crigger comes back and sits down again and does a bad job of acting nonchalant, and a deputy, thin enough to be Crigger's twin, walks in and sits right beside me, no better an actor

18

than Mr. Crigger. The deputy seems aware his performance is weak, but he goes at it with a kind of aw-hell attitude. After I pass him the sugar he asks for, and he's got it thoroughly stirred up, he says, "You just passing through?" I give him the story straight and simple, and he gives Crigger a false-toothed grin and pipes in a high voice, "Hey, Ef, this here's that Bucky's brother!"

"Well, 'i God, I tell you, it was that walk that throwed *me*"—like a deep voice echoing in a sewer pipe.

"Ef thought we'd caught you. Hey, Ef, didn't I tell you they had Bucky in the Greenbrier jail?"

While Crigger leaned against the counter, a gleaming coffee urn behind him, I started in on them. But they were awful cynical and tough. After a while, I wasn't following the waitress's peachy bottom, I was sweating. I felt ashamed, guilty, and cheap, like the time I was thirteen, ushering at the Bijou, and I saw *The Razor's Edge* and it inspired me to strike out for India and I ended up in Asheville, bumming for eating money.

It picked up a little when I got to the part Mrs. Overby's tears had cut short—how Earl got Bucky *in*to this fix. ". . . so just when Bucky got the word that his physical defects ruled him out of a career in baseball, along comes Earl, just finished with a stretch in Montana. Momma's sick and has to have a breast tumor removed. She's in the hospital and it's Mother's Day, which Bucky never fails to observe, and she's lying up there worrying how she's gonna pay the bills, and Earl puts his arm around Bucky and starts in on what a hard life he and Bucky have given Momma. They owe it to her to take care of those bastards that's worrying her to death with bills."

As I run it up the pole, they salute the Mother-flag, and I realize I'm consciously trying to manipulate their responses, so when I got the waitress crying and Mr. Crigger says, "Jo Ann, you get back in the kitchen with that bellering! Can't hear what the boy's saying," I knew I had them.

"So," I says, "he tells Bucky about this perfect method of passing checks without getting caught, which he learned from some guy on his cellblock in Montana. He steals a check-making gismo from RCA, and they hit the highway. Earl's method worked fine for Earl. You didn't see *him,* did you, Mr. Crigger? No, he let Bucky pass the checks. So Bucky spent a year in misery, hating Earl's guts. Before that, all Bucky had done was refuse to go to school (because, as it turned out, he could hardly see or hear) and swipe a few things."

They all shook their heads, and there was good ol' Jo Ann, leaning in the service window, shaking hers, her long brown hair swaying on her shoulders.

"Jo Ann was here," said Mr. Crigger, "weren't you, Jo Ann?"

"Yeah, I was here. I been telling you all this time he wudn't a bad kid."

"Bucky caught me on a Saturday night just before closing and I just did have the two hundred fifty dollars to break his check," Mr. Crigger reminisced. "Said he had to get on home, 'cause his momma was in the hospital and he'd already missed Mother's Day, and a more pitiful sight, I never—"

"And you fell for it," says the deputy.

"Well, you needn't rub it in."

"What would it have to be 'fore you could smell what it was?"

I told them about the miniature copy of the little-lost-boy statue that my daddy brought back from the war. Long ago, in Brussels, a rich man's son was missing, and he vowed that wherever he found his son, he'd erect a monument on the spot, depicting him doing whatever he was doing when they found him. A life-sized statue of the little boy survived the war, showing him naked, taking a leak. "That little replica my daddy brought back always reminds me of Bucky when he was little."

I convinced Crigger that if he would withdraw charges in court, I'd make full restitution. He didn't pin me down to *when*.

"Listen," said Crigger, leaning toward me. "I almost died of the T.B. last winter, and I know what being shut up in a room is, so I say, turn Bucky loose. But not before I see that money. Who needs revenge? I'm like your momma, boy—I got hospital bills to pay."

The deputy went out with me and leaned on the parking meter while I got started, and as I pulled away, going toward Mount Galilee, I blinked at the red violation flag under the deputy's elbow.

# 4

# *A Blank Page,*
# *an Open Road*

In Mount Galilee, twenty miles down the line, I pulled into Pap's Service Station, where Pap, a toothless old feller with a crew cut, is eating a late lunch out of a turn-of-the-century lunch pail. I didn't think he'd mind if I took off my tie.

I told him I hated to interrupt his lunch, but that I was Bucky Hutchfield's brother and wanted to assure him that I'd make good the check Bucky passed on him a year ago. He didn't even let me get started on my little softener.

"A body gets what he deserves," says Pap. "Any son-of-a-bitch greedy enough to take in a big check like that from a stranger just for an oil change *ort* to suffer. Well, I did. I suffered two hundred dollars worth, plus the oil, plus the skin off my knuckles where the wrench slipped on that damned oil-pan plug. I learned *my* lesson, so I figure he ought to learn *his*."

"He *has* been, sir, for over a year. And the psychiatrist at the Nashville penitentiary told me that if Bucky went on that chain gang, it would kill him." Then I got it in about the threat of mental illness and how Bucky's right on the edge.

"Hell, let him *talk* his way off the chain gang. I

never heard such a line as that boy lassoed *me* with, and I ain't about to hear another one, because I ain't sitting still long enough for anybody's brother to get started." I'm leaning against the soft-drink box, absorbing the delicate chill through my fanny, about to break the silence by going, when he says, "Come in here grinning like he was my long-lost nephew. Why, if he'd wanted to be saddled with it, I bet he could have conned me out of the whole damned filling station, and my uniform throwed in."

While he laughs and slaps his crossed arms, hard, like he's giving himself a friendly whipping, I slip in the story of Bucky's life.

"And talk about filling stations, sir, something about them always drew him to them when he was little, I don't know what. Maybe *you* do. Loved to watch the racks go up and shoosh down, and push the button on the air hose. He'd sneak into car junkyards and play all day, trying out the drivers' seats and turning the moldy keys and looking through shattered windshields at imaginary six-lane highways.

"He wandered around a lot, up and down streets and alleys of Cherokee, alone, looking for buried treasure in the trash cans. And one time I was on a streetcar and I looked out as it turned the corner at the courthouse where this statue for the soldiers who fought and died in Cuba stands, and there he sat, like a little pigeon, on the soldier's iron hat.

"He was a lonesome somebody, till he met the first real bad influence on him—Emmett King. Four blocks over from where we once lived was the King family. They came down wholesale—every cousin and cretin of them—out of the hollers of eastern Kentucky. One of the men'd made big money in Cherokee in the knitting mills for a month and that lured the others, and at the end of the second month the one with work was laid off, and the others have been on relief, living in two shacks at the foot of Clayboe Ridge ever since.

"One of the sons, this fifteen-year-old lummox Emmett, who looked like Frankenstein's monster, minus the stitches and the electrodes, took up with Bucky, when Bucky was about six—just at the time when I stopped taking such close care of him, and let him run the streets more or less alone. So six-foot Emmett, with the big hands and the Charlie Chaplin feet and the slack-jawed stare, and little skinny Bucky, with the two cute front teeth, slightly buck, you'd see them everywhere, roaming the alleys and fields and creek banks together. Emmett wasn't an idiot, just vigorously backward. I used to take my guilt for deserting Bucky out on Emmett. Momma and I figured it was Emmett who kept enticing Bucky away from school and inspired him to steal candy and cigarettes." Years later, Bucky told me that he was himself the mastermind.

"So anytime Momma looked around and no Bucky, she'd send me out to track them down. I'd be on my paper route sometimes, and I'd see them in some alley, rooting in the trash cans, and I'd streak between the houses on my Western Flyer, chase them down the alley, gain on clomping Emmett, leap on him like Zorro from his horse, ride him down and beat him up. It never seemed to enter his numb skull that if he'd exerted a little of that bull-like muscular system of his, he could have broken me like a bird."

I told Pap about the two of them going to the reform school together and that Emmett was transferred to the state asylum after he nearly killed a guard for laying on Bucky's bare back with a bullwhip. And how I stopped off to visit Bucky between ships soon after Emmett

died of a brain hemorrhage, and they let me take him
to see Alan Ladd as *Shane,* and when I left him inside
the fence and walked back down the dusty road along
the fence to the highway, he kept calling in a sort of
laughing, sort of crying way, "Come back, Shane! . . .
Come . . . back . . . Shaaaaannnne."

Somehow, that part of the story got to Pap more
than the rest, and he says, "Son, I'll have me a talk
with that prosecutor, and if he convinces me Bucky's
got it in him to reform himself, I'll drop the charges
and settle for restitution. Now sit down and have a big
orange with me." Splits his peanut butter and apple
jelly sandwich with me, too. Then he points the nozzle
of his orange drink at me and asks, "They's just one
thing I want to get straight. How come your brothers
ends up convicts and you turn out a teacher and a
storywriter?"

I tell him all about it, and he hop-skips on his bum
leg back in out of the scorching sun from filling up cars
to turn me on again. When I tell him that a blank page
can be just as alluring and exciting as an open road,
and, provided that page doesn't bear the name of a
bank, you won't end up in a cell, he says, "Son, you a
card."

I'm in my car, the motor running, ready to head for
Greenbrier, and I tell him to keep an eye out for my
name as scriptwriter on some TV show, and when I
say it might well be a Western, he slaps the hood like
he's putting the seal of certainty on it. As I'm scatter-
ing gravel, he yells, "You get that boy out of there and
you bring him by here to see me, you hear?"

# 5

# *Greenbrier Jail*

Taking the manager of the Western Auto store in Greenbrier, where Bucky'd cashed a check by putting ten dollars down on a plastic rowboat and requested delivery to 2302 Sweetcreek Road, was difficult at first, but once I convinced him that he wasn't the damn fool he thought he was to swallow Bucky's story, it was smooth sailing. Louis Pineta was a bald, chubby bachelor who'd volunteered to take the store in Greenbrier and put it back on its feet, but he was homesick for the Bronx, and when I started going over the high moments in *Kiss Me Kate, Brigadoon,* and *Finians Rainbow*, Broadway musicals of the late Forties, he was fighting tears. When I showed up, he was closing the doors, so when we parted, it was in front of the drugstore, where I had a pineapple shake and he had a cherry smash.

By then it was twilight, so I drove around the square and saw the light in the barred windows upstairs over the jailhouse, catty-corner behind the courthouse.

Bucky must have been looking and listening for me all day, because just as I shut off the motor, he shows at the window, grinning, barechested, his pants hanging loosely on his hips, his navel black. "Hey, Lucius, where'd you get that carrrrr, good buddy?"

In the soft summer twilight, I guess that long baby blue body with the silver trimming looked like what he'd dreamed about in his cell, but in Baltimore broad daylight, I got *took* for a hundred bucks.

Bucky yells, "Come on up, Lucius!" like all I had to do was just walk in, climb up.

In the cool of the screened-in porch, a woman in a lavender, starched cotton dress, her hair in a bun, sat on a rusty glider, snapping and stringing pole beans, dropping them into a black iron pot clamped between her ankles.

"Majel," the woman says, "if I was you, I'd worry about them white streaks on the porch before your daddy gets back."

On the floor beside the screen door sat a girl of about fifteen in denim shorts and a pink rayon blouse that had a wing collar, billowed in the sleeves and fastened tight at the wrists. Two top buttons, unbuttoned, showed her white brassiere, and she was barefoot, but between her legs she was polishing her majorette boots white.

Majel hears me shuffling on the steps and looks right up at me over her shoulder, stretching that rayon over her breasts. "Momma, they's a boy at the door."

"Looking for the sheriff, ma'am."

"He's wandering over the county som'mers."

"When's visiting hours?"

"Who you a-looking for?"

"My brother, Bucky Hutchfield."

Majel jerks her head around, giving her long black hair a swirl'n'bounce, and looks up at me.

"Majel, it's Bucky's brother."

She sees I am.

"You come all the way from Cherokee, Tennessee?"

"Yes, ma'am."

"Well, you get yourself in here and go see your

brother. Poor thing's been hanging on that winder all day long. Majel, get up from there and show Bucky's brother where to go.''

Majel reaches back, pulls herself up by the screen door handle, and starts slapping off down a dark hallway on her bare feet before I can get the door open. I stepped over the boots and caught up with her.

"I bet you look cute in those majorette boots.''

"By God, I better, if I go all the way to Cherokee to compete in that baton-twirling convention, by God, I better look cute, and then some.''

In the dim hallway, all I can see are her pink rayon blouse and a silver-painted door that she stops at, and when she stands up on tiptoe to reach something on the top ledge of the door, a crescent of pink panties winks at me in the twilight that filters through the bedroom curtains across the hall. Then I smelled her.

"I bet you been practicing all day.''

"Now, ain't I?''

What she took down from the ledge was a long key that she shoved into the lock, and, like a baton twirler, Majel gives it a twist and yanks the door open.

She says, "Same key fits the one at the head of the stairs,'' and before I realize what she's doing, the key lays heavy in my hand and she's stepping aside for me. "And listen, tell Bucky to watch out for my daddy when he whistles while I'm practicing.''

"Don't you reckon it preys on his mind to see you leaping around on the lawn in that outfit?''

"Well, I gotta practice with a real live audience, don't I?''

"Why, sure.''

# 6

# *Fartso the Whale*

I went on up, and there at the barred door stands Bucky, posing for the millionth cliché photograph of the prisoner, hands clutching the bars.

I unlock the door, step inside, lock it again, and drop the key into my pocket.

Bucky gives me a big hug, then we shake hands. "Well, Lucius," he says, looking me in the eye, "they really out to get me *this* time"—with that tone of infinite injury. "They jumped me soon's I stepped through the gate. Damned man from the state bureau of investigation and Sheriff Thompson."

"Brought you some stuff," I said, and gave him a bag full of Lucky Strikes that Momma sent, a pack of Wrigley's Spearmint gum, a Milky Way, some devil's food cupcakes, and a *True*.

"Thanks. But I can't hardly read, I'm so nervous."

A fat man wearing nothing but a pair of overalls, his arm in a greasy sling, one eye puffed with insect poison, walked around, munching a Moon Pie, sipping a Dr. Pepper that he tucked under his good arm between sips.

Under the windows is a row of cots, and on one of them lies a scrawny kid of about nine, on another sits a lightnin' blond boy about eleven, who looks at me with mellow curiosity. "Hey, Bucky, that your brother?" yells the older one.

"Shot his mother," Bucky tells me, with a melodramatic look that reminded me of my old buddy Duke who shot his father *and* his mother with the revolver we'd planned to use to rob the manager of the Bijou when I was an usher. "Yeah, Tom, he's my brother." Then he turns back to me. "That's his little brother—Billy."

"You gonna get Bucky off the chain gang, mister?" asks Billy.

"I'm gonna try," I say, feeling silly.

"*I* heard they's going to 'lectrocute him," says Tom.

"I let him talk that way," Bucky says, his voice low, full of long-faced compassion, "to take his mind off what they might do to *him*. She wasn't really his mother. Foster mother. She's laying over there in the hospital, not expected to live. See, Tom and Billy's orphans—I mean, the court took 'em from their real mother, this o' two-bit whore, a little town down the mountain. So the county farmed them out to this ol' man and his young wife that run a chicken farm, and it was like slave labor. They'd get up at five o'clock and work till dark, and what they had to eat was scraps when the man and his wife got full. And least little thing, she'd burn 'em up with a belt.

"Fin'ly, Tom got tired of seeing his little brother covered with welts, so he slipped out one evening, climbed up on the chicken house roof, and told Billy to call the hateful thing out, and when she stepped out on the back steps, cussing, wanting to know what he wanted, Tom let her have it with the old man's shotgun."

"Blamed jolt of it nearly flipped me off the roof,"

says Tom, who's been straining to hear us. "I reckon she'll keep her face-slappin' hand *off* my little brother." His long, straight blond hair veiled a killing look.

Bucky tosses a pack of Luckies between Tom's legs. Billy jumps up on his cot and dives onto Tom's, grabbing for the cigarettes. Tom holds the pack high over his head. "Ut, ut, ut, watch it, watch it, damn it!" Tom slides off the cot and slaps around on the concrete floor barefoot, dancing around, holding the cigarettes up out of Billy's reach. "Wait, just a minute, Billy, don't grab, Bucky ain't offered *you* nothing."

"Give 'im one," says Bucky, like he's watching two feisty alley dogs that's likely to end up snarling.

"Okay, stop, just stop pawing at me a minute," says Tom, and starts to take one from the pack, but Billy snatches it out of his hands and runs with it, slips in the slime by the open shower stall against the opposite wall before Tom can even push off to chase him.

Tom and Bucky laugh, but the man in overalls stops pacing and looks at me. "They ain't no peace and quiet in this place either," he says, like that's what *I* came for.

Billy starts bellering, getting up very slowly, the pack squashed tightly in his fist, cigarettes strewn around him. "Ha-ha, ha, ha-ha," sings Tom, "lit-tle Billy busted his buh-utt!" Tom laughs so hard he starts to stagger, then tosses himself onto the cot, giggles vigorously, and rocks, his feet kicking rapidly in the air.

Billy cries and picks up the cigarettes carefully, looking at his brother between each one. "You better hush," he keeps saying. "Better huh-ush."

Then Billy walks calmly over to the picnic table in the corner and picks up a Dr. Pepper bottle from a crippled Royal Crown bench and whizzes it at the cot and it shatters against the stone wall a foot above Tom's head. The glass I shake off the front of my shirt twinkles weakly in the dim light of the three bulbs, speckled with horseflies, that dangle from the ceiling.

Tom, his body frozen in mid-rock, looks at Billy in mock awe and astonishment, then slowly gets up. "All right, by God, all right, by God, *now* you're gonna *get it*."

"Well . . . Well . . . Well . . . Well, you made me slip and bust my ass, didn't you?"

"I'm . . . gonna . . . beat . . . the . . . living . . . hell . . . out . . . of . . . you!"

Tom chased Billy for about five minutes, *all over* the big bullpen. Watching such a burst of energy was so tiring, I had to sit down. The severely carved initials on the top of the school desk I sat on cut into my buttocks.

"They shoulda drowned the little bastards," says the man in overalls, philosophically, "the day they was borned"—and he goes into the toilet booth in the far corner, slamming the door.

When Billy slams into the partition, the man says, "I'm gonna *kill* me a couple a hellions d'reckly."

Billy cracks his knee against the iron frame of a cot and doubles over in pain, Tom catches up with him and starts slapping his head and face.

Bucky watches every movement, becoming so absorbed his mouth goes slack and his big brown eyes get bleary like when Mammy used to tell us stories and she'd time the climax for the split second when the spit drooling down his chin splashed onto his shirt, and then I realize the kids' performance has *me* hypnotized, too.

"I'll kill you, you son-of-a-bitching low-life bastard," says Billy, slugging into Tom.

Tom slaps Billy until his arms weary, and then he walks away, leaving Billy screaming on the cot, frail bones shuddering.

"Tom!" a woman calls from out in the yard below.

He goes to the dark window, panting, red from exertion in the humid air. "Ma'am?"

"Are you beating on Billy again?"

"Yes, ma'am."

"Well, quit it!"

"Yes, ma'am, I will."

Tom had the cigarettes again, lit one, offered Bucky one, then me, but I only smoke cigars, and then he tapped on the toilet door. "Hey, Pete, your momma allow you to smoke yet?"

"Better not get close't enough for me to smack you."

"She's coming over." He tossed one over the top of the booth.

Billy'd stopped screaming bloody murder, and shifted into low.

"Crybaby." Tom passes Billy's cot, lies down on his own and smokes.

Bucky was like a zombie from all the narcotics they'd given him at Nashville and from fear and nervousness. The charm he'd turned on his victims was deeply submerged. I told him what I'd gotten done that day, and he had a sullen, resentful, bitter word for each of his victims.

"Now, Bucky, they want to help you. Why shouldn't they want their money, too? *Before,* they just wanted your ass."

When it finally soaked in that their attitude could keep him off the chain gang, he sneered at their gullibility. That annoyed me. I began to defend them, reminded him of the visit the man from Western Auto had paid him.

"He said you just wised off at him." Bucky denied it, tried to blame Mr. Pineta, said he and the judge were friends, out to get him. "He said you called him an s.o.b."

"Liar."

"He said you did, now, Bucky."

Bucky looked shocked. "You'd believe a stranger 'fore you'd believe your own brother?"

We were sitting on his cot and he scooted down a little to register his shock more dramatically. He wasn't consciously conning me, just reaching for the available cliché. If he detected the slightest blood disloyalty—as he did then—he'd go into a profound sulk.

You could've sliced the silence with a jackknife, until Pete ambles out of the toilet booth and lies down in the forty-watt light and strikes a match for the bent cigarette Tom had given him.

Billy's whimpering, the crickets are starting.

Tom gets up and goes over and sits on Billy's cot and pats his knobby shoulder. "Poor ol' Billy boy, come on, honey, don't cry, come on now . . . You hear?" He lights a cigarette and leans over and tries to look into Billy's face, stroking him with one hand, offering the cigarette with the other, crooning, "Don't cry, little Billy boy, don't criiiii." Billy pulls the covers over his head. Tom goes back to his cot.

From under the covers, Billy says, "Wait'll I tell the judge. I hope they *do* 'lectrocute you."

"Didn't I say I was sorry?"

Bucky looks at me—that slightly buck-toothed grin. "Who they remind you of?" I pretended not to see it, because I didn't want to go over it. "Me and you, when we was little, and you used to beat hell out of me for something, and then . . ."

That started him off. So I sat at the head of his cot, my back against the stone wall, and Bucky, half-reclined on the rest of the cot, talked in a resonant, mellow voice about our childhood in Cherokee, still pronouncing certain words in the childish way he has. I was embarrassed to listen at first, because I am afflicted with a terrible nostalgia.

Psychiatrists would say we had a traumatic childhood, and I guess the broken home, the bad environment, and all that had the predictable effect on Earl and Bucky, but *I* remember none of it with anything but affection.

Earl was nine when Daddy started drinking and staying away three days at a stretch, so he didn't even have to live through the worst part, as a little kid, the way Bucky and I did. But we were Depression babies, and Earl and I had to carry our lunches in a lard pail, our own milk in a Mason jar, and it was supposed to be humiliating. Earl, anyway, realizing that a boy deserved something better, would steal cans of pineapple from the A & P, and at the lunch table he'd pull them out, and, with a taunting grin like the Joker in Batman comics, he'd open a can with a little stolen can opener and eat the pineapple, smacking his lips, while the well-to-do kids squirmed.

Even at age ten, Earl's face looked like a man's— the skin dark, the gray eyes objective, the hair black, full, thick lips crimped into a sardonic smile, and he would look straight at you, nodding his head—an ambivalent look—as if he didn't see you, or as if he saw you very distinctly, but only physically.

In every neighborhood we lived in, Earl'd let the bullies run over him, chase him down, beat him up, cuss him out, and he took and took it all those years, until one day he almost killed Sonny and Jim Bob, the

two biggest bullies. But even when they were pushing
him around, he had this look on his face like he was in
control, like he knew something they didn't, and like
something in *him* made every one of *them* nothing.

About a year ago, he told me his hero had always
been Adolf Hitler. I'd thought the fervor with which he
convincingly played Hitler in our childhood war games
was just natural talent. And Rommel, as Erich Von
Stroheim in *Five Graves to Cairo* depicted him, was
another hero. And I always associated Earl with
Bogart, and after *High Sierra,* the kids called him
Maddog Earl, and he was even a little like Tyrone
Power as Stanley, a con man, magician, circus barker,
who became a drunk and a geek on the midway in
*Nightmare Alley.* He married the daughter of an ex-
Nazi colonel, but didn't bring her home from
Germany.

In Cherokee High, when Earl was in a military
prison in Germany for selling army cameras on the
black market in Belgium, I started a story about
him—by the winter light falling through the many tall
windows in the auditorium study hall—beginning with
the time he showed up on the stage of the Bijou, a
fugitive from the reform school, singing "Mammy,"
and he won twenty-five dollars for the best imitation of
Al Jolson, a promotional stunt for *The Jolson Story.*
Nineteen forty-eight, and I hadn't seen him in three
years. After closing the Bijou, I caught the last streetcar and there's Earl, and he slept with me on the fold-
out cot in the kitchen and told me about his sad
life—past, present, and future—and when I cried, he
laughed and made fun of me. And the next morning, he
steals my gold-plated, radium-handed Elgin wristwatch
(the one I'm wearing now) and my new leather jacket
that made me feel like Alan Ladd in *China.* I never

finished the story. Nor three or four others I started later on.

In some ways, Earl takes after my daddy: get what you can out of people with as little effort as possible, but if things go wrong, don't blame anybody, don't feel malice, resentment, or hatred. Daddy took to drink and Earl took to the con game as ways of dealing with life, and both of them take things as they come. But Bucky takes after my mother, seems like.

Momma had a good life in Saint Louis when she was a girl, up till she was about sixteen, then the Depression hit my gran'daddy who was doing well working in the glass factory, and they started going down, and had to return to Cherokee, till one day he shot himself. My family told it as murder all the years of my childhood, until 1947, when Mammy casually said he wasn't shot by an enemy as he washed his hands in the glass company bathroom, but that he'd shot himself because he'd failed in Saint Louis, had had to return to Cherokee without any of the fine things he'd accumulated in the big city up North, and had had to take a nightwatchman's job in the glass factory where he'd once been a foreman.

I felt no resentment toward Mammy and Momma for having encouraged me to intensify the myth of his murder over the years, to handle the empty holster as if it had belonged to a victim, who, like Jesse James, had laid his gun down a moment to free himself to perform an ordinary human act—Jesse to dust a picture on the wall, Charlie to wash his hands. I merely saw, given that revelation, my gran'paw in a different light, and thus all the rest of us—Momma, Mammy, and Uncle Luke.

But when Bucky heard the truth, he resented the deception, as if it had somehow diminished him, as if it perhaps explained his own thwarted upbringing. To Earl, it seemed to make no difference at all, and I often wondered whether Earl had known it all along, even as the myth had been perpetuated, and that somehow helped to explain his cynical attitude toward people, his own isolation as a man whose survival justified his every act.

But not until now have I used that knowledge of my gran'daddy's suicide to try to understand Momma's approach to men and to the world. I often wondered what kind of life she dreamed for herself up there in Saint Louis, living a very normal, middle-class life in the Roaring Twenties, before her father lost everything, brought the family back to the past, shot himself, and she got stuck in Cherokee, married to a handsome, soft-spoken, charming, easygoing fellow from the hills of South Cherokee, a young man who happened to come into the drugstore next to the old Majestic Theater on Sevier Street where she worked one day and order a strawberry soda, who turned out not to be much count. So she ended up with the attitude that the world, men in particular, had betrayed her. I see now, without diminishing my exasperation with her erratic behavior, that the woman in the soapy kitchen of my childhood, of whom I expected so much, was only a child herself. Adults, parents, are only aged children, playing seriously, glumly.

I've spent most of my life as God's spy, witnessing the behavior of the family He thrust me into, one event somewhat related to but still separate from another, one crisis snarling at the heels of another, and then Mammy's casual admission gave me a means of reinterpreting the past, reexperiencing it. What else, I often wonder, do I not know? Am I an orphan, adopted by these people? Am I the son of some man other than the person I call my father?

All life seemed to be *my* raw material, broken down into intimations of the world, Cherokee, neighborhood, and the family. In those settings, I consumed the world's media: movies, magazines, comic books, radio shows, plays, advertising, circus, vaudeville, books. These I filtered through my own means of expression: daydreaming, in serial fashion; telling stories to Bucky and Earl, kids in the neighborhood and in the orphanage, to kids at school on a rainy day, to Mammy, to the Bijou ushers, to Raine, to Anna Livia; drawing, comic strips and pictures, enactments of moments in real and fictive life; writing stories, scenarios, poems, plays, radio dramas, movies.

The movies, advertisements, and other media inspired in us all our own versions of the American Dream, simultaneously providing the con techniques for achieving that dream. The effect of all those forces is clearer in Bucky's life. And I try to see my effect on Bucky's, and Earl's and Momma's and Daddy's and Mammy's. In our way of life, our deliberate and unconscious techniques, each of us influenced the others.

So Momma raised three boys during the Depression and the war, while Daddy was in the ambulance corps, and every chance she got, she played the angle that she was a poor little woman whose husband had more or less deserted her. It just so happens that she did put up a good fight, and Bucky loves her more than anything on earth. Just before he left Nashville, he almost went berserk, worrying about her broken leg, and they let him talk to her on the telephone to pacify him.

Well, the kind of childhood we had, you'd think you'd want to forget, but even when I was six years old, I used to fall asleep after a ritual in two parts: I'd review my life until I sensed I was about to go to sleep, then I'd stop—pick it up the next night like a serial— and then I'd talk to God in a chummy way, and that's how I'd drift off. So Bucky in his cell stirred all that up in me.

Bucky and I talked about Sonny and Jim Bob and other kids we grew up with on Beech Street where the Hutchfield boys were last together, and most of the boys and a few of the girls were in the reform school or the penitentiary now.

"And remember that time we went to the show at the Hiawassee and the ticket man grabbed me as I run in, and ripped my shirt off, and you picked up a cigarette butt urn and threatened to frail hell out of him?" says Bucky. "He thought I was going in without a ticket, but I was so eager to see the next chapter of Zorro, I just raced on in, and you screamed at him for tearing my only good shirt, and then when I wouldn't leave after the show was over, you started pulling at me and slapping me, and I was screaming in the lobby, and some man come up and said he was going to beat hell out of you if you didn't quit slapping that cute, sweet little boy—*me*. Ha! Remember?"

I'd never forgotten. On the *Polestar,* bound for Chile, I was kept awake one whole night crawling in memory around on the floor of the Hiawassee Theater, looking, with Bucky, who is looking for spilled popcorn, too poor to buy more than one sackful, not enough to last all day, looking for popcorn and something more. There's Momma, *Mildred Pierce,* on the screen, and there's Daddy in *The Lost Weekend*. Time to go home, I'd look all over the theater for Bucky, find him tangled in some woman's legs, and have to slap him to get him to come out. I was my brother's keeper, and Earl was taking care of an armless, legless man in a sideshow—maybe the one that crawled in the rain, a knife between his teeth, under the circus wagon in *Freaks*.

From our front porch on Avondale, where we lived

almost two years, we looked, when the leaves were thin in the fall or all down in winter, or sticky buds in early spring, at the glow, like a red-hot poker, of the Hiawassee marquee a mile away. Earl leads us along the WPA flood-control ditch that cut through the dense jungle across from the house, we hit the smooth path along the bank of Crazy Creek, and climb up on the bridge on Fairlane Boulevard, and throw grass, flowers, and other offerings over the rail to Fartso the Whale, who lived in the creek.

Earl told us Fartso was a mean whale (he's probably never read *Moby Dick,* but he cottoned to Monstro the Whale in *Pinocchio*) who had many helpers, like gremlins. But if you threw him presents, Fartso wouldn't hurt you. He might even help you beat up your enemies. Bucky believed so passionately in Fartso the Whale that I perpetuated the myth, after Earl ran away with the circus when he was eleven, as a way of getting Bucky to mind me. "Throw your popcorn into the creek for Fartso and his helpers and you might get a new Gene Autry pistol with a red pearl handle like Otto's got." And Bucky throws over the rusty rail the germy popcorn he'd crawled all over the floor under seats picking up, in the Hiawassee. From Fartso's bridge, we crossed the most dangerous intersection in Cherokee, the Hiawassee's neon marquee lights pulsing on our faces. As I stood On the Spot, a Bijou usher at thirteen, I felt steeped in the remembered aura of the Hiawassee.

I says, "Yeah, and remember"—trying to steer him my way—"that creek we always crossed on the way to the show?"

"Yeah. Fartso the Whale."

"The who?" Tom's lying on his stomach, his face propped in his hands, soaking it all up.

"Lucius used to tell me there was this whale named

Fartso that lived in Crazy Creek, and we'd throw flowers and popcorn down to him, and I kept trying to see him, and his little helpers like Seven Dwarfs. I fell for that one for about five years, believing there really was a whale that would give you presents if you were good, like Santa Claus."

"Hey, Tom," says Billy, peeling the blanket off his face, "you remember that ghost horse you used to tell *me* about, and you said it was going to come some night and take me and you away from the orphanage?"

"Shhhh," says Tom. "Can't you hear it? He's outsyonder eating Mrs. Thompson's morning glories."

Billy jumps up and leans on the sill and looks out through the bars. "Hey, where? Hey, where at?"

"Ahhhhhhh. The springs popping in your cot scared him away."

Tom made me see the two brothers and the white horse in one of my stories, "The Pale Horse of Fire."

"You ought to've heard the stories Lucius used to tell me and Earl when we was little. We slept in the same bed and we'd get under the quilts and Lucius'd tell us stories about Zorro and Jesse James and Frank James, like we was them—brothers—and he let me be Jesse James."

"We were more like the Marx Brothers, most of the time."

"And Straight-Hair and Fatsy—Laurel and Hardy. They'd forget to put on their clothes in the morning—Straight-Hair and Fatsy—and get on the streetcar and these old ladies would say, 'Eow! Butts and dodos!' "

"Hey, if I turn out the lights, will you tell *us* a story?" Billy's standing up on his cot, looking at me, eyes bright.

"Yeah," says Tom. "Tell us a story, tell us a story!"

"Yeah," says Bucky, "tell us a story, Lucius."

All my life that was a command that I, with my compulsion to tell a story, never could resist. "Hate to get started and have to go. It's dark outside, and I reckon they're ready to kick me out."

"Hell," says Tom. "You could sleep *here,* far as that goes. Folks passing through stay the night here all the time. Sheriff Thompson's a good ol' feller."

"Go ahead, Hollis," says Bucky. "Tell one, like you used to."

Giggling, Billy runs the length of the room, leaping into the air to catch the light cords until all three lights and faces blink out and only the bright moon looks in.

The room stinks of stale pee and clogged drains and dirty, fetid clothes and feet and beds, and more than a century of sweat and mustiness, and from the stove below comes the smell of kale simmering and coal smoke. It smells like poverty, the smell we grew up in, lulls me like dope.

Says Tom, "Make it a ghost story."

"Ouuuuu," says Billy, and jumps over Bucky's cot and climbs under the wool blanket with his brother.

I says, "Get ready for bed first."

They shuck off their pants and snuggle in. Pete's under the covers too, his hog-thick back like a wall. Bucky smokes the cigarettes I brought him, and I get set to tell it. I don't know any ghost stories by heart, so I recast "The Pale Horse of Fire" as a story of terror and the supernatural.

Billy and Tom are chewing gum, popping and smacking, till I reach a scary part, and they stop and the gum lolls out on the tips of their tongues in the moonlight.

"For the first time since they started beating him, the white stallion whinnied and slobbered. The other boys with bats and rocks moved in and swung at the horse. And then suddenly he bolted and ran crazily, zigzagging into the black woods. After the boys had gone home, little Robbie stayed, lying outside the circle of trampled grass under a bush, waiting for the horse to come back. Just before dark he heard a sound in the grass, felt a slight tremble in the ground under him. He raised his head and looked around. The horse was in his circle again, as if nothing had happened, plodding around and around like a robot. But as Robbie walked toward him, he saw green saliva hanging from the horse's teeth. The old stallion was walking more slowly than ever before, hardly able to make it around the circle, as Robbie, his hand held out, walked toward him."

Bucky stops smoking, a long ash on his cigarette, and Pete turns over and looks at me, his eyes glazed, and in the pause, we hear cars outside in the distance rumble over bridges, and off in the trees, dogs bark.

And I remembered that time with Gale and Brady and Elmo backstage at the Bijou, lying up on a stack of tow sacks full of raw popcorn, hugged up to the big black speaker behind the screen where Humphrey Bogart and Lauren Bacall were doing *The Big Sleep* while I told them a story I'd just finished writing, "Helena Street," about Billy the Kid meets the Tennessee Kid, who was me, in my imagination.

Near the climax, a key turns in the lock and slowly, taking his cue from moonlight and the hush and the smell that softens all his movements, the sheriff walks in. His head bumps a light bulb, and he's slender, a little bent, and wears a pistol, slack on his hip. I pause while we watch him amble to the foot of Pete's cot.

"Pete, I been a-lookin' all day fer that gun. I'm wore out."

"Well, Joe, I been studying that over. No use in you hunting and hunting. Hell, I mize well show you where I thew the damn thing."

"Okay, bright and early we'll go out there, and—"

"Shhhhh," says Tom, his finger to his lips. The sheriff turns slowly and gets him in focus. "Bucky's brother's trying to tell us the finish of a ghost story."

"Well, I *thought* they was somebody extry in the dark with you all."

"Let him tell it, Sheriff," says Billy.

"Well, *I* ain't stoppin' *no* body."

He just sort of dangles there in the moonlight, and I ease back into the story—"When morning comes, all three of you will be dead"—and the next thing I know, he's sitting on the foot of Pete's cot, listening.

Just as the older of the two brothers stops in the middle of the burning woods and feels in the ground the hoofbeats of the white stallion that stomped his brother to death, the sheriff's wife calls up the stairs for him to come to bed, it's late.

"You welcome to stay," the sheriff says, and I say, thanks, and he locks us all in, and as he's going down the stairs, he says, "Good night, Baby Sam," and a voice on the other side of the wall calls out, "Good night, Mister Joe."

"Good night, Baby Sam!" yells Billy.

And they all yell good night back and forth, and I figure Baby Sam is a Negro prisoner.

I took a cot, and Billy was asleep, curled up against his brother, who fell asleep just as I looked his way, and Pete was gone, and Bucky, the past like dope in him, said, "See you in the morning," and I said, "Night," and a few d'recklies later, night was in us all.

# 7

# *Drawing Out Frank and Lee*

Next morning, a backfiring truck woke me. Using the key in my pocket, I sneaked down to the square, and got a sack full of peaches, still dew-dappled. I left all but one on the picnic table, and quietly locked Bucky in the cell and put the key above the silver-painted door.

The white kitchen door stood open at the end of the hall, and Majel's bending over a round table, taking a last sip of coffee, already setting the cup down as she swings her hip out to miss the curve, and she comes at me fast, the fluffy pompons bouncing on her snow-white boots, the luscious ruffles on her low-cut, white cotton, freshly ironed blouse waving as she bounces, one arm out stiff, holding a blue suitcase, and I thought she was going to run me down, but she tucks the baton under her arm as she gets to me, gives me a glancing kiss and a flick of her hip as she rushes on, and what she tosses over her shoulder is, "I'd love to give you a *pre*view, but I'm about to miss the Greyhound to Cherokee."

When I get to the porch door, she's aiming for the open door of a bus, twirling her baton like a buzz saw.

I started out walking, to look for the county prosecutor's office. Somebody directed me down a steep hill from the square to an old white wooden house.

Weeds stood high in the front yard and grasshoppers flew up as I went along the walk. Two black-and-white-spotted dogs on the porch lifted their heads, started raising hell.

A window shoots up to my right and a woman sticks out her head, says, "Ace, I reckon you and Hoppy want Frank to dump another spittoon on your heads! Now hush!" her voice louder than the dogs.

Inside, a man raised out of a deep sleep mutters, "What's that racket, Lee?"

She turns her head back in and says, "Go back to sleep, it's only eight o'clock." Just as I was thinking it must be somebody's house, not a lawyer's office, Lee says, "What *you* want so early?"

"This where Frank Covington's office is?"

"It's his bedroom till the office opens."

"You Mrs. Covington?"

"You looking to get slapped?"

"Well, when's office hours?"

"Come on in."

I was certain she meant the window, but I looked for a door, just in case, and then I guessed there'd be one around the corner of the porch. There was, and she was holding it open.

She was taller than I am, and wore a blue skirt, a white sleeveless blouse, spike heels, and stockings with a lustrous sheen in the dewy morning light. She had long black hair that took me back to the Forties. What I walked into was everybody's picture of an old-time law office, full of old-fashioned furniture.

"You're a week too early," she said.

"How come?" I was about to get sick at my stomach.

"The judge is out on the circuit till next Monday. Bucky goes before him at eight o'clock, a week from Monday."

"Oh, you know who I—"

"With that face and that walk?"

"Never knew I *had* a face or a walk till I come down here."

"They all described him by his walk, and when I saw him amble into the courtroom with Sheriff Thompson for the arraignment, I knew why. Half cocky, half friendly, half better-look-out."

"But Mr. Covington said over the phone that the hearing would be this *coming* Monday."

"Mr. Covington would forget the date of doomsday, if I'd let him."

"Tell *me* and we'll *both* know."

"Listen, I ain't in the mood. Just sit still and wait."

She had a loud cigarette-rasped voice, and when she spoke, her whole body got off little expressions that you noticed, but I saw right away she had misty eyes, and that does it for me. She was about thirty-three, fourteen years older than I was, but she had a hard-life prettiness, you know, country-come-to-town. I liked her, and she seemed to know right off I didn't mind her brassy manner. So I sat on the old cracked leather couch and looked around.

"Lose something?"

"Got anything to read?"

"Bucky said you was a writer."

"I like to read, too."

"Read? This early?"

"Then loan me a sheet of paper."

She hands over the one she was about to stick in the typewriter, then reached for another. I used a lawbook for a prop and started drawing her picture while she typed.

"What the hell?"

"Type and talk." I sketched along awhile, then asked her, "What's that my stomach smells?"

"Coffee. When it quits perking, I'll wake him up. He wants to meet Bucky's brother."

"That's good."

In a short while, she got up and opened a door and said, "*Oh,* Frank! You wanna rise and shine? Coffee's waiting and Bucky's brother's here."

She went back to the typewriter, and when I glanced up again, he's standing there in wrinkled blue trousers and a white shirt open to his navel, showing a hairy pot, his black-streaked gray hair stirred up on his head, his face red as a beet, his eyes swollen, his lips whitish. As he bends over my shoulder to look at the drawing, the smell of him hits me below the belt.

"I thought Bucky said you was a writer."

"He's a little bit of everything," Lee said.

"How would *you* know? He just got here. And it looks just *like* you. Little young . . ."

He slouched into the bathroom, and when he comes out again, he has on a tie and his hair's combed perfectly, parted almost in the middle, with a wave on one side, and she has three cups of steaming coffee poured. Blowing on his coffee and handing me one, he lets his broad butt and potbelly sink into the leather cushion. He watched as I put the last curve onto her breasts, and said, "Son, that was five years ago."

"Let me see that thing!" She'd tried to hold back all that time, but now she swings around the desk and looks at it.

"Look at her blush!" says Frank.

"Steam from her coffee," I said.

A tall Negro boy of about seventeen showed up in the doorway with a sickle in his hand. "I'm about to cut, Mr. Frank," he says, very quietly and politely, and I recognized his voice—the one that hollered good night from the cell after my ghost story. Turned out, he was an orphan that they let sleep in the jail and do odd jobs.

Frank said, "You can't cut those weeds in this heat, Baby Sam."

"Well, Mr. Frank, I got done weeding the flower garden up at the house and Miss La Verne told me to get down here and chop down those weeds from in front of your office, so I thought I'd better . . ."

"Then you was supposed to go back up to headquarters, I reckon."

"Yes, sir. She said—"

"I can hear her plain as day. And when you get back up there, she'll put you through the third damned degree, won't she?"

"He don't have to answer that," said Lee. "*He* can't help it."

"Damnit, Lee, I know it. Well, listen, Baby Sam, you wait till the sun goes down, you hear?"

"I don't mind to cut it, Mr. Frank."

"You want to get him in trouble up at the house?" says Lee.

"I don't mind cutting it, Mr. Frank."

"You want him to get a heatstroke?" Frank asked Lee.

"I don't mind cutting it."

"You go up to the drugstore," said Frank, "and tell Doc I said to give you a jug of Coca-Cola with ice in it, and when that sun starts to boil, you get in the shade, you hear?"

"Yes, sir."

He went out, and Frank hopped to the window and said, "Tell her whatever she asks you, I won't get mad, Baby Sam." Then he turns to me.

"Want some more coffee?"

"No, thanks, sir."

"Frank. I'm Frank, and you're Lucius, and she's Lee, okay?"

"Okay, Frank."

"See all them books that's got you surrounded?"

"Lawbooks?"

"Full, chock full of stories."

So he took me on an hour's tour of legal documents containing vivid testimony concerning various sexual exploits, from mere exposure to rape, from 1821 to 1952, and then he shows me a revolver he used on a German prisoner near Buchenwald, and says, "Write a story about *that*." And running all through it like a thread is Bucky, and I imagined not only that Frank had done a production for *him*, but that I was merely an affable stand-in for a rerun.

Then I steered them straight onto Bucky, with Frank and Lee interrogating me about Bucky's background, till their eyes were misty.

"But don't depend on Bucky's sad story with Judge Stumbo. The first fact you got to face is that Stumbo's been to the end of the line and come back. The gooks chopped off his son's head in Korea, and he ain't got nothin' or nobody. And second fact is that he's *always* been mean, and he hates my guts almost as much as I hate his."

"Then I'm afraid even to ask you—"

"Asking's free."

"—whether you think he'll let me pay off these people a little at a time through the next year or so out of my seaman's pay."

Frank made an exaggeratedly incredulous face. "Lucius, we may as well kiss Bucky good-bye."

When Saturday morning people in overalls and work clothes started coming in to consult Frank, I told him and Lee I'd see them later.

# 8

# *The Thrill of It*

By the time I got back up to the top of the hill, I was dizzy with the heat. The sun glanced off cars and pickup trucks parked rib-to-rib facing the courthouse and in the outer square facing the stores.

I stopped in the drugstore and bought a paperback copy of *Knock on Any Door* by Willard Motley to help Bucky keep his mind off his troubles. In Nashville, Bucky'd read all the Thomas Wolfe he could round up, because he knew Wolfe'd been my hero when I was thirteen, and though I'd switched to James Joyce long ago, he always referred misty-eyed to Wolfe, as if we shared him.

He'd tried writing, too. War stories at first, because he was in the marines when he was fifteen and got kicked out, and he thought war stories would sell easy, and he asked me to send them off for him and we'd split the money. Later, he wrote some things about kids in trouble, and he knew it would make the best-seller list because it was all true.

As though duty-bound to authenticate the cliché, old men were parked hip-to-hip on the benches around the courthouse, talking, spitting, whittling, gazing silently out from the hub of law, order, tradition, and sloth,

sitting in the cool, under skyscraper oak trees that
spread out so lush at the top they covered the clock
face in the tower.

"Hey, there, Hutchfield, you got any more of them
ghost stories?"

Through the leaves of a low-hanging, spread-fingered
limb of an oak, there's Sheriff Thompson leaning on
the sill of a wide window, smoking, waving. I laughed
and waved, and he chuckled and glanced around to
somebody deep in the cave-cool dark of the office and
dusted his cigarette on the ground, where no grass
grew. His clothes were a little wrinkled and slouchy,
but he had the Gary Cooper look going for him.

Then to his side, suddenly, steps a stocky man in a
severely ironed and creased khaki uniform, and his
glistening leather belt and holster and slick yellow hair
give him a corseted look, and he waves me in.

"Come to get your brother off the chain gang,
right?" says the well-groomed state cop, as I came in
the door.

"To put it subtly, yes."

"I *told* you he was a card," says the sheriff.
"Hutchfield, this is Mr. McCoy of the state bureau of
investigation. Me and him was the ones went to
Nashville to bring back your brother."

"And me and Bucky," says McCoy, "were the ones
nursed this old coot back to life. Broke down on us in
Chattanooga and we had to sit around a hospital all
night before we could come on in."

"Sit around ever' Chattanooga bar and roadhouse
ever was, you mean, while *I* was *dy*ing."

"I never heard *this* story," I says.

So they tell it, together, with the precision, pace,
and thrust of a duet.

"But my advice to *you*, son," says McCoy, "is to

turn around in your tracks and go right back to
Cherokee. Number one, that brother of yours is an
habitual criminal. Guys can murder once, and stop.
They can rob, and stop, sooner or later. But you take
your check passer or your con man, they don't *never*
give it up. So you may as well give up on your brother,
now as later.''

"Well, I think there's hope for Bucky. I know what
you mean. Earl's like that, Mr. McCoy, but Bucky can
be saved. Earl can't. Bucky's in it out of
bewilderment—always getting the world's signals
crossed. But Earl's in it for love. And it's the *only* love
he knows.''

"This your older brother?''

"Yeah.''

"Ain't no love 'tween Bucky and *him*. That long
ride back, all I heard was how Bucky was gonna make
Earl pay.''

"We all got tickled, thinking up ways he could do
it,'' says the sheriff, "and it two A.M. on the highway,
and me sick as a hog in the back seat.''

"You know, I once asked Earl, since he never seems
to get away with it, why he does it—passes checks
and stuff.''

"It's the thrill of it,'' says McCoy.

"That's what *he* said.''

"Hell, I didn't have to *ask* him.''

"Way *he* put it was, 'You walk into a store and you
fox a man into your confidence and you charm the
money out of his pocket, and when I walk out,' he
says, 'I feel great. I'm in control. It's not the money.
Look,' he says, 'I take a chance. When I lose, that's
my tough luck. Next time, I'll know how to get away
with it.' He's never bitter toward— toward you guys,
or the people who bring charges, or the prison officials.
It's just tough, and that's his attitude.''

"I like a guy with a good attitude, don't you, Joe?"

"I pre*fer* 'em."

I didn't go into Bucky's attitude, how he's always, since he was little, felt the injustice of it all. Somehow or other, somebody has sold him out, led him astray; it's not his fault; he can't help it; it all started when he was too young to control it. The evidence in his favor is overwhelming. Besides, that's what he's been told all his life. And he believes everything he's told, by this authority and that—by me, and by Earl, and by books, and by ads, slogans, salutes, pledges, promises, all the home truths. But when he rams his hand into one of those Christmas stockings up to the elbow and the smell of what's in it hits him, he gets that look on his face of awed surprise and hurt. Like the time I, inspired by the disappearance feats of the magician who came to the Bijou, showed Bucky how to make a crayon disappear by sticking it in my ear, and he turned around and tried to fool that lummox Emmett and ended up in the hospital with it stuck in his ear.

I say, "Another thing about Earl. One time when he was just out, and I was a freshman at Cherokee High, we took a walk through one of the old neighborhoods and stopped in front of the house, one out of about twenty-five that we grew up in, where we lived the longest and had the most fun, foot of Clayboe Ridge—the house where he broke open Bucky's head with a baseball bat—but that's another story—and I says, 'Well, Earl, I hope you've given it up for good.'

"'Lucius,' he says, solemnly, 'I've learned my lesson, I hope to die. I'm through. I'd rather die than go back.'

"I says, 'You know, Earl, the thing that's always scared me is that when the FBI is tracking you, you might take to a gun, and—'

"By the streetlight, I saw the hurt look on his face.

'Lucius! You think your own brother'd do a thing like that?' He likes to keep *his* image in as sharp a focus as the next man.

"At the time, he had a job driving a truck to Memphis. It paid well. He even urged me to accept a little gift of twenty bucks. A week later, they caught him transporting whiskey from wet counties into dry."

Then I ask Sheriff Thompson and Mr. McCoy, "You wanna hear a little story about Earl?"

"I'd a sight rather *hear* about 'im than track 'im down," said McCoy.

"Stick around till dark, and this'n'll rip off a ghost story for you."

"One time, soon after he was released from prison—I forget which one it was—Earl was traveling for a magazine subscription outfit, and he was using the district manager's car, going up and over the hills of West Virginia, and it was late and he was fagged out, and he woke up in a bed, this state trooper sitting by his side, and behind the trooper, a book of phony checks stuck out of the inside pocket of his coat hanging from a hook on the open closet door.

"'Driving a little reckless, weren't you, Mr. Hutchfield?' says the trooper, noticing Earl's eyes open.

"'Guess I was, sir,' says Earl. 'Went to sleep at the wheel. I've been working pretty hard this week, and I was trying to get home to my wife and kids.'

"'Know what you mean,' says the trooper. 'I was on the way home to mine, too, just off duty, when I saw you writing your name on the landscape.'

"'Will I be okay?'

"'You *feel* okay?'

"Earl says he feels like he could make it on home. Trooper asks him where he lives, and he says, 'Bristol,

Virginia,' and the trooper says, 'Oh, yeah, got a good buddy, used to be a trooper, running one of those big rigs where they're constructing the U.S. interstate highway through Bristol.'

"'What's his name?' Earl asks.

"'Cling Coker.'

"'Cling Coker!' says Earl. 'Good drinking buddy of mine. In the VFW, right?' Earl asks, because taking risks is part *of* it.

"'Yeah,' says the trooper.

"So they chat about good ol' Cling Coker.

"About an hour later, Earl gets ready to go, and the trooper says, 'Sorry, but I got to take you over to the courthouse and fine you. Serious traffic violation.'

"'Sure. I don't blame you,' says Earl, and he goes to pay his hospital bill, and when the nurse says, 'It's twenty dollars,' Earl asks if it's okay to write a check, and she says, 'No, it certain-ly is not.'

"But when the trooper, who's known her since she was a baby, says, 'It's okay, Lily, he's a friend of Cling Coker, the check's okay,' she says, 'Then go ahead.'

"'Mind if I make it for a little over the amount?—'

"Ut, oh," says McCoy.

"—says Earl, 'so I can gas up my car and get on home?'

"The trooper says, 'It's okay, ain't it?' and Lily says, 'I reckon.'

"Then the trooper tells Earl he'll have to sit around the police station until ten o'clock—it's just seven— till the judge comes in. Earl says it's his kid's birthday and he promised him a ball game, and couldn't the trooper take the check and give it to the judge?

"Finally, the trooper says, 'Okay, but let's see how your car runs,' so he took him over to the filling station, and that pulled in five more guys, and they all had another hour of Cling Coker while they got the car to running, and then Earl wrote a check for the trooper to give the judge, and got change from the trooper's own wallet, and then wrote a check for fixing the car, and got change, and when he passes the city limits, he has one hundred dollars in cash, and a large charge, and three more years in West Virginia prison waiting for him.''

''And you'll be telling the same story about Bucky 'fore long,'' says McCoy. ''What your big brother's got is contagious and your little brother is infected with a full dose.''

''Bucky, hell,'' says the sheriff. ''What about *this* one? Here I ort to be out rootin' 'round a cornfield for that gun Pete used on his wife, and 'stead of that, I'm listening to bedtime stories at high noon.''

''What *I'm* trying to figure out is what you doing here in the first place,'' said McCoy, ''less you expect to work on Judge Stumbo . . . Hit it, didn't I? Well, forget it, son. You'd have better luck with that statue of Stumbo's great-gran'daddy about to fall off his horse in front of the courthouse. Am I right, Joe?''

''I'd *swear* to it. *You* all make yourselves at home. *I'm* riding,'' says the sheriff, like it was an all-occasion exit line.

''And not only that,'' says McCoy, ''what you got a lawyer for, if you're gonna do the tear-jerking on your own?''

''What lawyer?''

''The one up from Florida.''

''That's one more than *I* know anything about.''

''Maybe your momma hired him since you left Cherokee?''

''To get Bucky off that chain gang, she *could* have done *any*thing.''

"Well, this lawyer came to see me this morning down in Chattanooga where I'm based, and he was wearing a white Panama suit with a wide-brimmed Panama hat, driving a white 1942 Lincoln-Mercury Zephyr in mint condition. Fellow with black hair and a mustache and a cigarette holder. And carrying a shiny, shiny briefcase."

"That's pretty good, Mr. McCoy, pretty funny. You're not a bad con man yourself, but you don't expect me to believe anybody'd be seen in public looking like *that*, do you?"

McCoy laughs and slaps me on the shoulder. "You really *are* a card, ain't you?"

# 9

# *Momma on Crutches, Daddy Under Patton*

In the downstairs hallway of the jailhouse, where the smell of pinto beans and ham cooking was thick enough to taste, a young man with repetitious little waves in his red hair was talking to the sheriff's wife. He wore a flowery tie, held a red leather Bible, and sweat from his armpits molded his white shirt to his ribs. They blocked the silver door, so I stood to the side while they finished talking.

"Way I done, I went up there like I'd just come to see Bucky Hutchfield, because he sent word he wanted a visit from a preacher, but I seen it was a good chance to talk to them *boys*." He's very solemn, as though standing in a church he's built with his own words. "But I kinda drew them into it, and before I left, I had them all three down on their knees, giving their hearts to Jesus. Sister Edna, it was a blessèd thing. If they'd just let Jesus in sooner, maybe none of this misery would've happened."

"Well, law, when kids ain't got no mother . . ."

She smiled at me, then stepped aside so I could reach the key on the ledge. I went on up, ready to behold the angelic scene—Bucky, Tom, and Billy, on their knees, sanctified.

I unlocked and opened the steel door and heard cot

springs bouncing rambunctiously. At the top of the stairs as I unlocked the cell door, Bucky struck a pose, the slack jaw and drooped shoulders of Paul Muni, intoning, "I am a fugitive from the chain gang," title of a movie the three Hutchfield urchins saw together at the Hiawassee. And behind him, little Billy is humping his cot sixty miles an hour, yelling, "Give me some poontang! Hey, preacher, get me some poontang, pretty please, preacher!"

Bucky and Tom were laughing, doubled up on their cots like doodlebugs, and Pete's just fading into the toilet booth, slamming the door behind him, disgusted. "Heatherns!"

"Hey, Lucius, you missed it, buddy!" says Tom, running to me. He did a perfect imitation of both the preacher, who turned out to be a student from the seminary ten miles down the pike, and of Billy. He acted out the preacher working on Billy for ten sweating minutes, inviting him to get washed in the blood of the lamb, and Billy nodding his head, finally saying, "Yes, sir, preacher, yes, sir, I want to be worshed whiter'n snow." When he asked Billy if he could get him anything, Billy said, "Please, preacher, all I want me is a red Bible like the one you got."

And Tom acted out how Billy, as soon as the preacher shut the door downstairs, yelled out that he'd rather have some poontang.

That got Bucky and me into a long story about the three Brummett girls that Earl and Bucky and I used to play jungle with back in Cherokee, and how we'd take turns being Tarzan and Jane and Boy and Cheetah, and how there were always two left out—Bucky and "Bandpants," because they were too little. Then Bucky told how they'd give up and go off and play Tarzan and Jane all by themselves.

Bucky was pretty resentful about the young

preacher because he wouldn't promise to drive fifty miles down to Chattanooga to see Reverend Arnold, a preacher who used to visit Bucky when he was in jail down there, waiting to be picked up by the TBI to stand trial in Nashville a year ago. Reverend Arnold, he was certain, would drive up and try to soften Judge Stumbo.

Bucky'd lain on the cot, imagining me riding up on a white horse, getting him out of there bright and early Monday morning. When I told him what Frank had said about the judge being his political enemy, and that it was probably doing him more harm than good that Bucky'd got him on his side, he started to cry.

I lingered with them until almost dark, telling stories, and Bucky made me tell Billy and Tom what I told him when I stopped off to see him in Nashville, about visiting the house where Bob Ford shot Jesse James, and I had to tell them the whole story of Jesse James, and that made me nostalgic to see the movie again, with Tyrone Power as Jesse James and Henry Fonda as Frank.

Just as Beverly Taylor bestowed upon me her girl-hood collection of movie magazines and stills when she got married, I'd turned around and bestowed them upon a homebound movie-crazy girl with polio when James Joyce took hold of me and I turned loose of Alan Ladd, but I kept back the stills from *Jesse James* and a few others. I'd shoot you if you tried to grab the one of Jesse in a black hat and coat reaching up about to kiss Zee, his eyes closed, Zee in a wide, flowered white hat and billowy white dress leaning down to him from a carriage.

I went out and got Bucky and the kids some hot dogs and a big orange apiece, and when I came back, Bucky was watching Billy and Tom playing like they were Jesse and Frank, and Pete kept saying, "I'm gonna make you *both* wish you'd never heard of Bob Ford."

Then, to pacify Bucky, I put in a call to Cherokee to see how Momma was. She said she was doing okay, except that the cast was heavy and her crutches hurt her, and she wished she could go dancing. Then she asked if I thought she ought to come down to Greenbrier. I told her I didn't see that it'd do any good.

She said, "But don't you think if I come down there on crutches, they'd see how much Bucky's mother believed in him, and maybe they'd . . . Well, you know . . ."

I told her I knew exactly what she meant, but that I had that angle pretty well under control. Knowing Momma was doing okay and that she'd offered to come down and plead for him soothed Bucky.

I felt guilty locking Bucky and the kids in and going to the movies that night, but I was bone-weary, worrying about Judge Stumbo's personality.

I was about to open the door of the screened-in porch when Mrs. Thompson called to me from inside the house. She held the telephone out to me as I came into the room.

"It's your daddy—long distance from Cherokee. Barely make out your name, he's so sloppy drunk."

He was drunker than that. "Lucius" was about all *I* could make out, and I've had years of practice, trying to net the little silver fish that leap up out of the muddy flow of his drunken gibberish. The penalty for falling for the lovable drunk notion is that you've got to hold still for a lot of unlovely flotsam.

As he let it flow, I remembered the bright Sunday morning a cop car pulled up in front of the house and

Momma had to take her bathrobe out to it so Daddy could get from the curb to the living room without the neighbors seeing he had on only his shorts and a hangover. The cops had found him under a viaduct, stripped of all but his shorts, into which he'd peed in fright as the robbers were stripping him.

His voice rose and fell on the phone, crooned and crowed, and I remembered the year after he came back from the war and Momma had divorced him as hopeless—the nights when he would stand out in the streets in front of several different houses where we lived and call for me. "Lucius! Hey, Lucius! Ho, Lucius! It's your daddy, son!" And Momma'd finally say, "Go out and pacify him, Lucius," and I'd go out at two A.M. to pacify him, and end up gathering material for stories, because as the curb chilled my tail, he'd tell about the way it was when he served under General Patton.

One of his army buddies came through Cherokee one summer and told me about the time Patton's Ninth Division was crossing the Rhine into Germany and the general's jeep sideswiped the ambulance Daddy was driving, and Daddy jumped out and yelled, "Why the goddamned hell don't you watch out where you're going?" "I don't believe you know who you're talking to, soldier," said General Patton. "I don't give a rat's ass who I'm talking to—I'm carrying wounded and you almost killed 'em." "I'm General George S. Patton; who are you?" "Private Fred H. Hutchfield." "Well, you're one hell of a soldier." Daddy had a theory that Patton was really murdered, because so many people thought he was a son-of-a-bitch, and Daddy'd kill anybody that said he was.

Then he'd tell the story about sitting under a tree cutting his toenails with a bayonet and limping quickly over to the first-aid tent when he stuck himself, and starting back for his boots just as a mortar shell shivered the tree to bits, and somehow I always connected that with Patton not being a son-of-a-bitch. He mourned his failure to live up to such luck. "Bub," he'd say, "if I could write stories, we'd *all* be rich."

I have only one memory of us all together—simple, but not typical: Daddy taking me and Earl and Bucky walking on a hot Sunday afternoon to the ball park. His hands seem huge and soft and hairy and warm. "Grab my thumbs," he says to Bucky and me, and we cross the dangerous intersection, Earl holding on to his belt in back. Then just me and Bucky: Daddy, on furlough, comes to the large white stucco Saint Thomas Episcopal Orphanage where we stayed six months while Momma was in the hospital and walks with me and Bucky down the steep hill overlooking Cherokee, and it's Saturday and the country women coming out of the Cherokee knitting mills in a horde of green uniforms look mean and sexy and Daddy takes us to the Avalon Theater across the street to see Don Red Barry as Jesse James, Jr.

And then, just me and Daddy, sitting on the curb with the ghost of General Patton, while Earl and Bucky are miles away from home, locked up. I always felt guilty that I never tried hard enough to save them all.

Finally, Daddy passed out on the phone, and I hung up, and drove down to Tipton, the next town south, and saw *The Spirit of St. Louis* with James Stewart as Lone Eagle Lindbergh.

# 10

## To Tell the Tale

Coming back from Tipton that night, Joni James singing "Why Don't You Believe Me?" on the car radio, I passed a red convertible coupe with the top up, parked on a little island in the middle of the intersection of U.S. Highway 109 and State Road 54, right under the red blinker.

I parked on the shoulder and walked back through the mist and tapped on the window. The car's full of smoke that comes pouring out when Lee rolls down the glass.

"Can I help you?" I ask.

"Do what?"

"Well, I saw you stranded—"

"I'm parked, not stranded."

"Oh."

"I love to park at a busy intersection and read, but actually, it's none of your business."

"Well, listen, Lee, I love the whole idea."

"Then get in."

As I shuffle around the front, she barps the horn. I did a little startled dance, and got in beside her.

"Some people—well, most anybody around *here* would think I'm crazy." She lit a cigarette. "You know, me sitting out here in the middle of the night, sometimes two-thirty in the morning, mist fogging up my windshield."

"Let me see that— well, I'll be damned." It was *The Razor's Edge*. "I never read the book, but I saw the movie, and ran away from home, heading for India, but I got bogged down in Asheville. Had this same paperback in my jacket pocket and my first typed story in the other pocket. Left 'em both in a crack in the pillars under Thomas Wolfe's house so I'd have room to keep my hands warm. Wonder if they're still there?"

"Let's go see. I love to drive at night. You know? Just get in and drive, by God, down to New Orleans, if I have to. Get it the hell out of my system. Because if I didn't, I think I'm capable of doing a little harm."

"Look, Lee, I get it, hell, I get it. You're like us—me and Bucky and Earl. You'd like Earl. Always got to keep moving, us Hutchfields. Between us, we've covered every town in this country."

"If I was a man, I'd just walk out. But when you're the mother of a teen-age boy who thinks *he's* a man and that his mother's a stupid old bitch, what do you do? Oh, the hell *with* it!" Lee reaches under the seat and comes up with a fifth of Jack Daniel's. "Good for what ails us."

I took a swig, then watched her gulp it down. That's when her eyes got mistier. Ever since I was little, I've had this thing, that a pretty girl with misty eyes is good and sweet and pure, and I've got to be in love with her. And here was this woman, my elder, but all misty-eyed little girls of my childhood, a little wide in the hips, tender shoulders, slightly hunched from too much shuddery kind of crying alone in parked cars, and breasts like the first girl I ever made love to that I really loved, and a full sulky mouth, and black hair like

Hedy Lamarr, and a long, lovely neck, and a foot taller than I am. It hurt to look at her. The way she made me feel, more than her looks, she reminded me of Anna Livia. Will Anna Livia look like Lee when she's thirty?

I tried to pull us out of a long silence by asking her what her husband did.

"You mean when he's not laying out with other women?"

"That wasn't what I had in mind, but—"

"Why do you think I'm parked here, with *The Razor's Edge* in my lap? He ate the dinner I fixed for him in this suffocating heat, then he strolled down the porch steps to the street and he was gone. And then my son shows up riding on a motorcycle with some creep I never saw before and declares that he's going to the stock car races in Chattanooga, I says *I* be damned if you are, and we got to fussing, I screamed at him, he said he was going anyway, I said you'll get yourself killed, and as they roared away, he was crying, yelling, 'I hope I do!' They can say things like that to you and then wonder why you're so tore up most of the time. Hell, they don't need *me,* and they act like they can't *stand* me. I just drove around, till about ten o'clock."

I waited for her to start crying, but she didn't.

"Then when I got home, my husband was in bed, snoring, and when I dropped a shoe, he woke up, pointed his finger at me and said, 'Where the hell *you* been?' and 'By God, if I ever catch you out with somebody, I'll cut your head off,' so I told him to kiss my ass and drove over here. I wish I'd slit his damned tires, or his throat, one. See, he drives a Greyhound bus and I reckon he thinks all I got to do is lay up with men while he's on the highway."

As I imagine Majel, sitting on the front seat of the bus with her legs apart, lapping up the miles to Cherokee, Lee starts crying.

"I hate to see you cry like that, Lee, come on now, ease up . . ."

I saw a chance to really get to her for Bucky's sake. "Listen, did I ever tell you about the time Bucky gave his Roy Rogers boots to Fartso the Whale?"

That tickled Lee, and she shuddered, half crying, half laughing, till she bounced up and down behind the steering wheel.

So I told her all about Fartso the Whale until her tears dried up.

"One time Bucky and Earl and I were shooting marbles under the Indian cigar tree with a bunch of tough kids from up on Clayboe Ridge, our fingers cold in the autumn air, and somebody says to Earl, 'Okay, Big Chief Chew Tabacca, shoot!' Earl stands up, hitches up his knickers like Humphrey Bogart, spits tobacco juice bull's-eye into the ring, and says, 'You-all take it easy, hear? I'm going swimming.'

"We all laughed like hell as he walked down the street past Lilly's Pond, his pockets loaded down with everybody's marbles, into the damned smoky red October sunset.

"Thirteen years old. Struck out with only a dime to his name.

"I didn't see him again until two years later, in September, when I looked up from reading *Flash Gordon,* and there he stands at the screen door, a merchant seaman's cap cocked back to show his black pompadour, a halo of sunlight around his head, evoking far-off places, exotic episodes.

"'Shhhhh,' he says, 'wanna surprise Momma'—as if he didn't have a lifetime to do *that* in.

"People often ask me, how come *you* didn't turn out to be a crook like your brother? Well, Bucky and I were both influenced by Earl, just differently. Because when Earl told Bucky and me about the ships, the ports, the fabulous adventures he'd had, the way he told it had such an effect on Bucky that he too began to wander, and ended up like Earl, in all kinds of juvenile detention centers, the same ones Earl escaped from, homes for wayward children, and then the reform school, not far from where Earl was serving time himself in the state prison."

Then I slipped in a few sad stories about Bucky that I'd already told coming down the highway, till when she started crying again, it was over Bucky.

"What's the matter?"—one of Mammy's storytelling techniques to make sure you're really into it.

Lee says, "Nothing," and shoves in the cigarette lighter.

"You listening?"

"Don't stop. Does me good to listen."

"Momma didn't wind up in the insane asylum or at the bottom of the river where she always said she would. She holed up in a hotel in Nashville, cashier at the cigar counter, so she could 'be near my boys.'

"What happened was that Earl conned Bucky into passing a raft of bad checks across state lines, and they got him for it. They couldn't prove any connection between Earl and the checks, but they caught Earl in Oak Ridge selling pretty little necklaces door-to-door, that he claimed doubled as radiation detectors.

"Earl and Bucky both convinced prison psychiatrists that they were nervous wrecks unfit to do time, and to make that go down smoothly, they got 'saved' by visiting preachers, and that gave Momma something to work with when she tried to con the penal officials into paroling them into her custody. I used to imagine them all three in her tiny hotel room near the Capitol building, waiting for my money orders to reach them from India—which is where my ship the *Polestar* is finally going when she gets out of dry dock.

"What charged up the image of Earl at the screen door was the aura of all those sea movies we saw at the Hiawassee Theater when we were all little together: Errol Flynn in *The Sea Hawk,* Clark Gable in *Mutiny on the Bounty,* Gary Cooper in *Souls at Sea,* John Wayne in *Reap the Wild Wind,* Glenn Ford as Jack London in *The Adventures of Martin Eden,* John Garfield in *The Sea Wolf,* and later, Gable in *Adventure,* and Alan Ladd, my hero when I was ushering at the Bijou in 1947, in *Two Years Before the Mast.* Isolated from Cherokee in the mellow dimness of the Bijou, On the Spot, the background music always swelling behind me, I used to feel like I was standing watch on a ship in foggy waters, and I'd daydream about going to New Orleans and standing on one of those iron-lace balconies, and I'd write epic sea sagas, 'The Sea Remains' and 'The Yearning Heart,' projecting myself into the future, shipping out of there, partly, I suppose, because Earl did. I stayed home, and never surprised Momma (she couldn't read my mind), but I think the wanderlust was even more restless in me.

"I'd be wandering in India *now* if I'd made it that time when they kicked me out of Bonny Kate Junior High after Raine and I broke up, and I saw *The Razor's Edge* at the Tivoli. Tyrone Power as Larry Darrel inspired me even more than that image of Earl at the screen door, because I hopped a freight train to search for the meaning of life in India, and I kept seeing *me* in that last scene, standing on the deck of a tramp steamer, at sea in a storm, the wind and ocean lashing against me in my black raincoat, but I ended up in Asheville, breaking into Thomas Wolfe's house to commune with my hero.

"Cold, starving, and hurting to see Raine, I came on back to Cherokee on a Greyhound, my fare paid by Travelers Aid. Going through the mountains, a white horse in a field stirred my imagination, and when I got home, I wrote my first really serious story, "The Pale Horse of Fire," which *New World Writing* sent back with an encouraging word.

"I first laid eyes on Loraine (which I changed to Raine) Clayboe the Saturday morning I got hired to usher at the Bijou. She stepped out on the stage at the Bugs Bunny Club to sing 'Heartaches,' and I fell for her the way Alan Ladd fell for Veronica Lake in *The Blue Dahlia*, the movie that was on. The next night, I wandered into a tent full of Holy Rollers and there she was, singing 'Power in the Blood,' and the first day of school, she was right there in my American History class, dropping her textbook so I'd pick it up.

"After we broke up, I was roaming Cherokee in mortal agony when I come to this little church in South Cherokee, across the river, high up in the hills, and I sneak in—dark, nobody there—and pray to God to send me the-perfect-girl-for-me. 'And please let her be nearby right now.'

"A few days later, I walked into the Market House to get Momma some country butter and me some Concord grapes, and Cathleen Blackburn sacked them up for me. Working for her daddy in his fruit stand. It was one of about forty stands in the Market House, and he, out of his deep religious nature, called it the Garden of Eden. I found out she lived in the same block as that little church. I was still thirteen and she'd just turned twelve.

"I hung around South Cherokee till I got to know her. I loved Cathleen, but it was three years until I could look at Raine or think of her without pain.

"I was reading a collection of James Joyce a few years later and I came across a section called Anna Livia Plurabelle, so I changed my nickname for Cathleen from Eve, because she worked in the Garden of Eden, to Anna Livia. Sometimes I called her bitch, too—affectionately, because I enjoyed reversing the standard meaning of words.

"She loves her daddy, a big, good-hearted man, and doesn't want to hurt him, so most of the time she had to sneak out to be with me, because he lost his wife to heart disease and Anna Livia has a heart murmur too, and also he has strict religious attitudes, so he was very protective. Since I couldn't go near the Garden of Eden in the Market House, we found other little gardens—in parks and woods and up in the hills of South Cherokee—and later the Shanghai Gardens Restaurant, and under the dome of the Bijou, where I didn't usher anymore.

"What made her daddy keep stricter watch on her was the time she slipped off and met me at the top of the highest hill in South Cherokee, where about forty kids were sledding. What she didn't tell me was that her heart was acting up and she had a fever, but she wanted to ride down that hill with me, so I borrowed a sled. Going down scared the living hell out of both of us, and we wrecked and got slung about fifty feet, but got up laughing. The melting snow made us soaking wet, though, and that night she was in the hospital, and her daddy came looking for me. I liked him, but I was scared of him, so I hid out over at Mammy's house.

"The next morning, I tried to sneak into the hospital to see Anna Livia, but her daddy had the cops on the lookout, and they pushed me around and took me for a ride to scare me away. Her daddy found all my love letters, and it was a year before we could drift back together.''

Lee says, ''Lucius, would you take it wrong if I asked you to let me rest my head on your shoulder?''

''Shoot no, Lee, go ahead.''

Dark sky above, mist hovering outside, smoke thickening inside, we were sealed off from Greenbrier and the mountains.

''I love the sound of your voice.''

''That's good, because that isn't all there was to it.''

And as I told her more, I felt my voice resonate in my chest, imagining the effect on her of each stroke.

And she was having an effect on me, her voice and the smell and softness of her body up against me. I've got this purity complex about women that keeps me from going right at them when the situation seems to call for it. Oh, hell, I started when I was three, though nobody ever believes me, except the ten or twelve girls I did it to before I was thirteen and the boys we all ran around with in Cherokee. But I remember going with this whore in Antofagasta, Chile—I'd never met one before, hardly even glimpsed that mystery, and I was scared—and even as I watched her supple buttocks ascend the stone steps into whoredom darkness, my attitude was affected by a lifelong conviction that women are pure, are morally superior to, are the prize of men who achieve great things. I wanted to know what an older woman thought of that, but I didn't want to break the flow.

''Even in junior high school and on through high school, I felt I was different from everybody—my family and the kids I grew up with—because of my writing and the way I loved Anna Livia. Like in that poem by Edgar Allan Poe, 'Alone':

From childhood's hour I have not been
As others were—I have not seen
As others saw—I could not bring
My passions from a common spring.
From the same source I have not taken
My sorrow; I could not awaken
My heart to joy at the same tone;
And all I lov'd, *I* lov'd alone.
*Then*—in my childhood—in the dawn
Of a most stormy life—was drawn
From ev'ry depth of good and ill
The mystery which binds me still:
From the torrent, or the fountain,
From the sun that 'round me roll'd
In its autumn tint of gold—
From the lightning in the sky
As it pass'd me flying by—
From the thunder and the storm,
And the cloud that took the form
(When the rest of Heaven was blue)
Of a demon in my view."

Lee was amazed that I could whip it right off like that, and even I was surprised that I could remember it. To take my mind off the wall-throbbing boredom and heat and pain of painting the damned engine room on the *Polestar,* I'd memorized my favorite poems from an anthology I'd brought along—ironically, because I always refused to learn lines by heart in school. Above the roar of the engines I'd scream Poe's "Alone," and "Kubla Khan," and "The Hollow Men," "Ode on a Grecian Urn," and Dylan Thomas and Yeats and Pound. The only one I already knew by heart was "The Laws of God, the Laws of Man" by A. E. Housman, which I recited to the principal at Cherokee High when he asked my why I was the village atheist. The teacher had kicked me out of Bible class the first day because she heard I had refused to say the morning prayer and she knew I'd be asking questions all the time. The principal didn't even suspect that I'd become the village Communist too. But I didn't tell Lee about that because we were sitting right in the buckle of the Bible belt.

"And there's a line from 'Childe Harold' by Byron that expresses how I felt: 'I stood among them, but not of them.'

"I put in the time at Cherokee College for a year before I finally lit out last summer for New York. Most of my favorite poems I taped at the college radio station a week before I left Cherokee, so that while I was sweating it out high up in the Empire State Building as a mail clerk and later in the engine room of the *Polestar,* I liked to think of my voice, reading the great poets, going out over Cherokee, Anna Livia switching me on in the Market House.

"I'd set out for India again and it felt odd to think that Thomas Wolfe was no longer my great hero, and to imagine how it would be if I were living in his house, writing *Children of a Cold Sun* in Asheville, this novel about me and Anna Livia, if Wolfe's sister had said okay when I wrote to her and asked her for the job of caretaker for the old house on Spruce Street. She was very nice and offered to fix me a Wolfean meal when I called her, passing through Washington where she lived on my way to New York last summer.

"Every letter to Anna Livia was full of strategies, and worry about me going to prison for transporting a minor across state lines, because she intended to run off and live with me in New York. So she's back there in Cherokee, working all day in the Garden of Eden beside her daddy, who claims he's not a well man and needs her worse than ever, because he can tell by the way she acts, I guess, that something's up. And she goes to business school at night to learn to be a secretary in New York, and has to iron his clothes and keep house when she comes home all worn out.

"She sent me stories and poems she wrote about people that came into the Market House. And in her letters, she wished she could come on up to New York, instead of putting in the time until we had enough money to bring her up here and get married and put her in a modern dance class and have a life of East Side poverty, but happy writing and dancing and slowly getting famous.

"When it looked like I wasn't ever going to get a ship, I tried out for a part in *Bernardine,* this Broadway play. They needed some teen-agers. With my background in radio and stage plays in high school and college, I thought I stood a good chance, even though I'd played mostly old men. Why old men when people always say I look young for my age, I don't know.

"One day, I came home from the union hiring hall in Brooklyn to sleep from three till eleven before going back to work at the White Tower hamburger stand and there was my daily letter from Anna Livia: 'Dear Lucius, This is the letter you always said you were always afraid I'd write you.' I tell you, words *can* break your bones.

"I hitchhiked home to Cherokee in a stupor, so sad I was sick, so tired I hurt.

"All these years her daddy and I have put her through a conflict of loyalties, a life of guilt and confusion, torn, too, between his vision of life and religion and mine. And my moody, vicious jealousy doubled the hell she's had. So I guess when I lit out for New York, she got some relief from all that.

"I rolled into Cherokee at blazing midday and called

her at the Market House and persuaded her to meet me one last time in the Bijou, on the back row, across from my old station on the main aisle. Some horrible Betty Grable musical in the background, she told me I had killed her love with tales of my adventures in New York, and she knew she'd never become 'an intellectual,' never understand me or the artists I was making my life with, weird people like Samara, the Russian Jew, the beautiful, intellectual, existential painter who I hadn't even really met yet, but I'd written out my fantasies and sent them to Anna Livia as gospel fact. And going into the merchant marines would only make her image of me more unclear as time and space grew between us.

"When I promised to stay home, she said it was too late. And that's when I saw her daddy sitting across the aisle, pretending to watch Betty Grable.

"So I hitchhiked back up to New York and the White Tower and the Brooklyn hiring hall. But I was sick of New York because it had made me repulsive to Anna Livia. I longed for the place we used to call 'our paradise on earth'—Maine.

"So I hitchhiked to Ogunquit, Maine, to die. Instead, I started a novel about us called *Children of a Cold Sun*. Out of money, I came back to New York at Christmas and got a ship that was taking mercy rations to victims of an earthquake in Chile but that would finally end up in India, my spiritual homeland because of the way the images in not only *The Razor's Edge* but *The Rains Came, Black Narcissus, The River,* and on back to *The Jungle Book* with Sabu made me feel.

"But after Chile we went into dry dock in San Diego, and in about a month we'll sail for India again. That's why I went home, and that's where I got the bad news about Bucky. Shipping out was exciting, but not the way I thought it would be. I guess I saw too many movies that showed the old ways, and wrote and daydreamed too many sea sagas when I was little. 'Much have I traveled in the realms of gold'—and garbage. Even though I just turned twenty, I'm already beginning to feel as if I've done, seen, felt, read, *experienced everything*. Maybe in India I'll get reborn somehow . . . You go to sleep on me?''

"Sleep? Hell, no, I'm relaxed. Your voice soothes me something nice. Then what happened?'' she asks, which is what I wanted to hear.

Sensing that my own story was less bewitching than Bucky's, I backed up and told her about how Bucky's never really had a home, how he was shipped from one institution to another, half blind, half deaf, forsaken, forlorn, getting into trouble only because he's "despurt.''

When I climax it with a final anecdote, she says, "Is that all?''

"Ain't that enough?'' I put my hand on her knee. "You feel any better?''

She nodded. "Say, I like the hell out of Bucky, Lucius. . . . Listen, I got some dirt on Judge Stumbo that I've been saving up to use at the right time. Well, hell, I may as well shoot it on Bucky, and maybe I can even hit Stumbo with it again sometime. So stop worrying and just sit tight.'' The ruthless tone with the misty eyes excited me.

Lee took my hand off her knee and placed it over my heart, then reached and took another ear-ringing swig of Jack Daniel's. "Lucius, I'm going to tell you something I ain't never told a soul in this world.''

"I'm listening,'' I said, like it was the first time I'd ever said that to a woman.

"People think ol' Lee's tough, but except for that

snoring son-of-a-bitch in my bedroom, I'm a virgin. It's just the way I'm made. Even if you *do* have the most beautiful blue eyes I ever saw."

Then she bent over from the waist and put her fingertips under my ears and stroked along my jaws and looked straight into my "beautiful blue eyes" and said, "But listen, you curl up on the back seat of your big blue Buick and when you go to sleep, *dream* about me . . ." And she gave me one of the most lecherous smiles I've ever seen on man, woman, or child.

Then she started the motor and I got out into clearing mist and the dark. The smell of that red convertible's exhaust was sexy.

# 11

# *Getting the Picture*

The next day was Sunday, and all I did was lay around the jail. I drew a portrait of Tom, and because they got jealous, I had to do Billy and Bucky, too. I got *Lord Jim* out of the Buick, but the kids kept distracting me with their antics and their wild, rich talk, so, deciding like Henry James to be one of those on whom nothing, no, nothing, is lost, I shut up Conrad. I tried to keep out of my head the image of Anna Livia in the Garden of Eden, but did make a few notes on my novel about me and Anna Livia—*Children of a Cold Sun*. Then I wrote a long letter to Anna Livia, trying to explain why I am the way I am. Never mailed it, though. And started a letter to Dana, the son we'd long dreamed of having.

For five days I sat around Greenbrier until I had worked up a kind of pattern, moving from the jail to the drugstore to the café to the courthouse john, to the courthouse bench, to Frank's office, where I listened to the story of Lee's life, and now and then got snatches of Frank's.

And I'd walk around the town and sit in the small library and read a book about Bloody Williamson in southern Indiana where crooked politics, union strife, and the Klan brought about several years of bloodshed. That book cast a strange aura over the look and feel of things as I moved slowly about Greenbrier in the heat.

Late Thursday night I was driving around aimlessly, and passing Frank's office, I saw a light in the window showing through the mist. Craving company, I pulled into the driveway.

There was a warm fog in the street just below the white frame house, and on each of the three porches down there a dog slept. Passing the pulled shade at the window of Frank's house was the shadow of a woman. So I knocked on the door, real light.

"Ain't it past your bedtime?" Lee said.

"Not if all I do is toss and turn. You got any coffee on?"

"Well, listen, I don't know if it's proper to let you in at this time of night."

"Isn't Frank here?"

"What do you mean by that?"

"Doesn't he sleep here?"

"Sometimes. I reckon tonight he made it before his wife locked the prison gates."

"Well, if I ain't welcome . . ."

"Oh, hell, get in here. I've just been trying to catch up on some work. Lately, my house ain't been much of a home, so I come down here—when I know Frank's at *his* house, I mean."

"Certainly." I was looking at the desk.

She ripped the hood off the typewriter. "Guess I better get started or it'll be midnight. How's Bucky?" She had a nervous time finding something to do.

"He's just waiting."

"Aren't we all?"

"Huh? Oh, sure. Me, too." I sat on that awhile, and

she ripped into some make-work for about ten minutes until she thought she'd earned some coffee, and then she made us some. After she'd poured it, blinking rapidly at the way I was following her around with my eyes, she jerked her skirt down hard over her knees and lit in typing again. One time, she kind of glanced up with a sick smile and said, "You gonna draw me another picture?"

"I been trying to *get* the picture ever since I walked in here."

"Now what the hell's *that* supposed to mean?" On *"that"* she shoves the carriage, on "mean" I heard the bell.

She got up with *her* cup and said, "Give me that cup," and I gave her mine. I heard her dash the coffee into the commode, and then she goes to the shelves and feels behind some books and comes out with some Jack Daniel's.

We drank, and then she said she had to go, and she went past the three porches where the dogs slept, and I climbed the hill to the jail.

In school, on my paper routes, standing On the Spot at the Bijou, painting the engine room on the *Polestar,* I got into the habit of weaving long, involved autobiographical fantasies, projecting myself into the future. Interruptions were like the end of a chapter in a serial, and later I'd pick up where I left off, and sometimes weave the tale for months. That night I got one started about me and Lee, who seemed to be attracted to me, but I also suspected something was happening between her and Covington, and that just made it more interesting.

The fantasy was that maybe after I got Bucky off the chain gang, I'd put him on a bus to Cherokee, and I'd pick Lee up at the office one of those late nights, or maybe at the intersection, and we'd do like she suggested—go to Asheville, and then on down to New Orleans, and we'd live in a place in the French Quarter overlooking the Mississippi River, and I could finish my novel while she worked in some exotic garden restaurant, and one night I would answer a knock on the door and her husband would shoot me, then Lee would kill him, and she'd visit me in the hospital and tell me my novel had been accepted, because, impulsively inspired by her love for me, she had finished the last chapter herself and sent it off, and when I get out of the hospital, we're celebrating at the same restaurant where she used to work, because now we're rich, and then, just as we're about to get on a ship bound for India, Frank Covington, who reads about the woman who killed her husband in the slave's quarters of an old French Quarter house, is sitting in our room in the dark when we get home from celebrating, and I con him out of shooting me, and Lee and I nurse him back to health again, because all this time he's been wandering all over America searching for her, and he's a bum, a wino, and he's dying, and Anna Livia, who's been searching for me all over the world, finally tracks me down, and that's about where I am Friday night as I'm driving around up in the mountains outside Greenbrier, and I decide to cruise by his office, and there in the driveway, sure enough, is Frank's car.

# 12

# *The Underside of the Rock*

The inner door was open, so I saw Frank through the screen, his back to me. Hearing me, he turned, a bottle in his hand, his fingers about to twist the cap, when he saw me, saluted with the bottle. Suddenly the two bird dogs are at the door, standing rigidly, their noses to the screen, their teeth bubbling with spit. "Ace! Hoppy! Don't you eat that boy! Sit!" They wiggle-backed off and sat, and I went in.

"They teed off at me 'cause I give up hunting. Have a drink." Frank was already tight as a tick.

"Well, thanks."

In the middle of pouring, he stops, and sniffs. "You smell what I smell?"

"What?"

"Lee."

"She been here?"

"Yeah, catching up on back work. . . . Musk smell, know what I mean? Like a nigger gal. The onliest white girl I ever met that had it. Enough to drive you up the wall. . . . Sit down." I sat on the leather couch and he stood in front of me.

"So you want to know why I drink. I didn't *used* to drink." He sat on the other end of the long old leather couch and drank out of the bottle. "Lucius, ol' Lucifer, just don't drive in front of my house tonight, because it's glass all over. I had me a civilized game of golf, then I had me a civilized highball, then I went home to have me a civilized supper with this old army buddy of mine, and that WCTUing bitch started picking on me. I take that back. She's not a bitch. Goddamn it, Lucius Hutchfield, La Verne Covington is *not a bitch*. She's a lady. The only thing wrong with *her* is *me*. Know what I mean?"

His red face started working and writhing like a can of worms, glistening in the light with sweat, and pretty soon gushing tears and slobber. I was a little uneasy when the bird dogs started thumping and whining, glancing at me like it was *my* fault.

"The bitch! The bitch!" Frank jerks out his shirttail and wipes his face, and then he starts to laugh. "Damn arm like— like— what's that pitcher's name plays for— what's that team they got . . . ?"

"I don't know, sir. I don't follow baseball much."

"You don't—? Ol' Bucky could tell me. But what I mean, she took those bottles and pitched 'em right out into the street. Glad she's never *hit me,* with a throwing arm like that. Reckon writing invitations to teas and such crap works up a muscle on a woman? That's how come lately I been coming straight over *here,* and don't go no further, and bring along *these* gentlemen to watch me. *They* know what I'm up to before I do it.

"And you know that that woman actually sticks her nose up at that house I bought for her? Never satisfied! Do you realize how famous that house is? Well, I'll just tell you. It was the very house General Lee slept in when he come through here—the very one. So, I thought, now there's a house, there's a house for a woman like La Verne. So while she was in Europe

with her sister, I bought it, and when she came back
I'd sold that damn wreck her daddy left her and—
That was thirty years ago. Listen, Lucius, next time I
call her a bitch, you slug me in the mouth, hear? That
woman has went through hell.''

Well, he went on and on like that until four in the
morning, and he said he really admired me for wanting
to be a teacher, that he had once served on the
Greenbrier board of education, and he said he had to
get down on his knees (which he did, to illustrate) to
anybody that could write a decent sentence, much less
a whole story, because it was English that got him
kicked out of V.M.I., or else he'd be a general today,
but La Verne, he said, had read all the classics. ''The
Great Books of the Western World.''

''Hell, I rode the rails in the Thirties. If I wasn't tied
down to the law, I'd walk out, sail with the merchant
marines to Paris. But see, we lost our kid, and we
can't have no more, so I got to overlook the way she
treats me, don't I? Now listen, you the only one I ever
told this to, because you a poet, see, just like me, hell,
by God, I'm a poet, too. Hell, look at Edgar Allan Poe.
You listening?''

''I'm listening,'' I said.

''*I'll* give you something to write about. Hell, I'm a
character. Folks all the time say, and not to be funny
neither, 'You know something, Frank, you're a real
character.' Why, if I was to tell you my life story, you
wouldn't believe it.''

He told it, and I believed it. Because I had heard it
*before*—in Cherokee, in New York, on the road, at
sea. I reckon some people are born listeners and some
are born tellers, and some, like me, are double blessed
and damned.

But when he got on segregation, I tried to keep my

mouth shut, because I knew that if I antagonized a man that talked like that, Bucky'd be on the chain gang by sunup. One time on the streetcar this nightwatchman drew his gun on this Negro veteran because he sat down beside him, and when I got up and let him have my seat to make the nightwatchman feel shitty, he almost shot me. Frank got so rabid, the dogs pushed open the screen door and huddled on the porch. Plowing through the whole dictionary of vulgar expressions, he took off his shirt, dripping sweat.

He had struck me as a rather sweet, charming, middle-aged fellow, prematurely gray. Now he was showing me the underside of the rock. After the way he had talked to Baby Sam that time, I was willing to believe him when he talked about what good care he took of his own Negroes, how he was very fond of them, would do anything for them, get them out of jail, take a little sass now and then from the females. But what churned him up was integration.

I had listened to Bucky rave against the Negroes in prison, but with him it was an obvious matter of the prison guards and the cops not being enough to soak up his hatred, resentment, and bitterness. And he, too, witnesses will testify, was a charming, sweet fellow.

"It was you college people that first let 'em in the schools."

"I don't get it. You treat Baby Sam like a member of the family, but you'd die fighting to keep your relatives from sitting beside him in school."

"What makes you think I give a rat's ass whether you *get it* or not? Listen, I'm sick of looking at you, and I'm sick of talking to you." Frank's hands are tense in his pockets, as though he stuck them there to keep from hitting me. "Bucky sure got took when he drew you for his brother's keeper. And I can't wait to put him on the chain gang. They ain't nothin' I'd love more, 'cept to see your balls nailed to a post in a burning shack."

"I'm sorry I turned you against Bucky. Listen, Frank, it ain't *his* fault."

"You sure had us fooled. 'Shamed to say it, but I liked you. Lee's crazy about Bucky."

"Listen, I'm sorry, I was just expressing my own personal— Bucky hates Negroes too."

"And here I was willing to humble myself before Judge Stumbo, the biggest enemy I got in the whole state, and you turn out to be— a nigger lover. They ain't nothin' lower."

While he took a leak in the john, I eased out onto the porch. Getting into the car, I could still hear him raving.

Hanging from a tree near the screened-in porch below the jail, a truck-tire swing looked awful still in the streetlight, and I smelled the juice of the weeds Baby Sam had cut, and the honeysuckle vines clinging to the side of the porch.

As I stepped up to the screen, a voice says, "Look out! Here he comes, with another ghost story," and as he took a draw, the tip of his cigarette lit up the sheriff's face. I opened the screen and somebody was sitting with him on the glider, his face, his bare arms and feet pale in the filtered moonlight. "Me and Pete's having us a beer. Old lady's sawing logs, so we thought we'd sneak down a few. Bite the cap off one, Hutchfield."

I said, thanks, but no, thanks, and went on up.

# 13

# . . . and Other Great Prison Writers

I thought a trip to Chattanooga to visit that preacher friend of Bucky's would be good—keep me out of town, out of Frank's sight. Afraid Lee's blackmail of the judge might backfire somehow—especially with Frank against me—I decided not to call on her to use it unless I had to. So on Saturday, I went on up to Chattanooga, because if I convinced the judge to let me pay for crime on the installment plan, he would need something to show.

Preacher Arnold was a nice fellow, and he was convinced that if Bucky could just get the right kind of help, he'd turn out to be a saint. He wrote a letter to Judge Stumbo, and I carried it back to Greenbrier.

When I got back it was almost midnight, so I stopped beside the courthouse and lay down on the back seat and went to sleep.

I dreamed I was onstage at a college play opening night at the Bijou, and no lines learned, desperately lunging into ad libs. Why do I dream that so often? And carrying my papers on Clayboe Ridge three days late, and going back to work at the Bijou as an usher after five years?

But lights blinking through my front windshield

roused me. I raised up and the lights blinked off and on, and I strained to see a red Ford convertible with the top up, pointing straight at my Buick. So I got out and walked over to the window.

"Hurry and get in," Lee said.

Good thing I shut the door when I did, because with a squealing of tires, she took off like greased lightning. And before I could catch my breath, we were in the thick of some woods along a country road, with the lights out.

She gripped the steering wheel, but her arms and mouth trembled. "Goddamn you, goddamn you," she said, low, hissing, through clenched teeth. "*Where have you been?*"

"To Chattanooga."

"To Chattanooga?"

"Yeah, to Chattanooga."

"Then you don't know where *he* is either, do you?"

"Who?"

"Frank, you— you smiling jackass!"

"I'm not smiling. And I don't keep up with him, since he hates my guts."

"Oh, shut up. Shut up! You're never around when somebody needs you. A woman panics. It's the way they're made. I couldn't find your car *any*where, and Frank's office was dark, and I don't know where he can be. I needed somebody to talk to, Lucius. I got to crying so hard I had to pull over on the shoulder— I felt so deserted. First my husband packs up and leaves me, and my son went to visit his grandmother in West Virginia, and then no Frank and no Lucius, and—"

"Hey, you hear something, Lee?"

"What?"

I turned and looked behind us. "A car creeping up behind us with its headlights off."

"What we gonna do?"

"You got a gun in the dash?"

"You got rocks in your head?"

It was Frank. *He* had a gun, though. Even if he did carry it with a frightening casualness.

"What you doing with *him*, Lee?"

"I been looking all over for you, Frank."

"And you found me in the woods, right where I usually am."

"Well, you wasn't in the office. I got something awful to tell you."

"You tell *him?*"

"No."

"Then shut up. Get your ass in my car and go to the office. I'll follow in yours—after I nail this boy's balls to a sycamore tree. He raped you, didn't he?"

"Now, listen, I don't care if you *are* drunk."

"Well, I ain't drunk, and my aim is sober, too. You gonna get in that car like I told you?"

"Don't you hurt him."

"Lee, I don't want to see nothing but tire marks where that car's setting."

Lee gets into Frank's car, backs it, the lights come on, and she drives away. In the dark again, I notice lightnin' bugs among the trees.

I was almost certain Frank was just trying to scare me with that gun in his hand, and he did, even though I can hardly see it now.

"Okay, nigger lover, how come you trying to get my secretary in trouble?"

"Her husband's left her—but not over *me*."

"Who over, then?"

"I don't know."

"That's right. You don't know. But you know the way back to Cherokee, don't you?"

"Yes, sir."

"Where's your car at?"

"Beside the courthouse."

"Get in."

He made me drive Lee's car, and as I drove, he talked, the pistol he had used on a German prisoner near Buchenwald lolling in his lap. "Lee's begged me not to take it out on Bucky. They's other ways of fixing you. . . . You a writer, you a teacher. Now I'm gonna give you one that'll really tax your imagination. It's so good you can't help but admire it. Lee's been saving up some dirt to use on Judge Stumbo, and now's the time. I can go to him and dump that dirt in his lap and get him to dismiss this whole thing— providing you make restitution, and providing also you pay the court costs."

"I didn't have but a hundred dollars when I left Cherokee. And that's just to show good faith. I was going to promise to pay the rest out of my wages in the merchant marines this summer, and I'm willing to throw in an advance on my novel when it's accepted."

"Don't forget court costs."

"That's the least of my worries."

"You know how much court costs *are* in a situation like this?"

"Well . . ."

"Two thousand dollars."

I blinked at him. Then I saw what his face was saying. "Well, at least Bucky'll have his brother *with* him on the chain gang," I said. "Maybe by Christmas we'll all be together—Earl with us."

"Could be, could be. But don't *need* to be. Use that imagination of yours. Suppose you was to find a book of blank checks some drunk-ass fool let slip from his pants pocket? I mean, even *I* could be sitting in a car like this, not paying any attention, when all of a sudden my checkbook falls out on the seat.''

Sure enough, it did. He was right. It could happen.

''And what if you found somebody's checkbook, and meanwhile the prosecuting attorney persuaded the judge to set the hearing up another week, and whoever found that checkbook had time to cash all them checks up to two thousand? And the guy that dropped the checkbook is safe because the checks ain't personalized with his name or nothing. So the finder can write in any name he wants to dream up.

''Hell, I bet I could outwrite *you*, boy, when it comes to thinking up how things could turn out. Why, it don't take much imagination to see how everything would work out to a happy ending—except maybe if the one that found the checkbook got caught. But if he'd already sold out his own brother for niggers he don't even know, he might *deserve* to get caught.''

''Can't I take a while to think it over?''

''You better hope *I* don't take a while to think it over. I don't care whether you believe it or not, but I'm cherry on something like this. And I hate your guts for being at the right place at the right time with the wrong means to an end.''

I didn't stop to think how much I owed my brother (all I had to do was ask him), I just played the scene the way Frank improvised it.

He made me get out of the car at the edge of town, and I left him with the impression that I had agreed to live out the plot of his imagination. But before the showdown on Monday, maybe something would turn up in my own imagination.

I awoke Sunday morning on my cot beside Bucky in the bullpen, and where Lee fit into Frank's scheme nagged me until I had to get up and walk.

I didn't know where she lived, so I set out to roam up and down the fifteen or twenty streets of Greenbrier, looking for her little red convertible. If her husband had left her and her son was visiting his grandmother in West Virginia, there'd be little risk in knocking on her front door. Or maybe her back door. Since Frank had never worked such a blackmail scheme before—or so he said—perhaps Lee could shame him into dropping it.

The red convertible, its faded black top jauntily folded down, is parked in the driveway of a neat little green and yellow house, a pink plaster elephant in the front yard under a mimosa tree, a swing on the porch, morning glories climbing the trellis. Out from under the raised hood stuck two men's asses—one draped over each fender. The clink of wrenches and the drone of voices—a young man's mingled with an older man's—was pleasant on that leafy street, almost lyrical. Through the screen of what was probably the kitchen window, Lee spoke to them, the words blurred, but the tone distinctly hers.

Confused, I turned the corner and disappeared. But as I'm winding through the streets toward the jail, my eye on the courthouse clock, I see her cross at an intersection up ahead, dressed for Sunday, wearing a hat that made her look like a wife and a mother, thirty-three, maybe older. I caught up with her.

"Where you headed, Lee?"

Her long black hair swirls as she looks back at me over her shoulder and keeps walking. "To church," she says, coolly. In those high heels, out on that sidewalk, she looked taller.

"I thought you said your husband packed up and left?"

"Who says he didn't?"

"Your son still at his gran'mother's in West Virginia?"

"What difference does it make?"

"Plenty, if they're both working on your car right this minute."

Church bells start ringing nearby.

"You been sneaking around my house?"

"Hell, no, just looking for you— to talk with you."

"Well, listen, I got to get to church."

"You got the longest, fastest legs of any woman I ever saw."

"People always did make fun of me for being too tall."

"I ain't making fun. I just want to know what's going on."

She didn't act like she "loved" the sound of my voice. I let the silence become awkward, hoping she would break it. She didn't. I noticed the church bells were scratchy, coming over a P.A. system.

"Listen, Lee, did Frank tell you about those checks?"

"The ones Bucky passed?"

"You know which ones. The ones Frank gave *me* to pass."

"News to me."

"Then you two aren't— It's just *his* idea, then?"

"*What's* his idea? He must have scared the living fire out of you last night. Your brains sound scrambled."

She seemed like she was playing dumb, but I couldn't snag her up on anything.

"Lee," I says, trying to throw her off balance, "let's run off together."

"Run off together? Where to? From what?"

"Your husband, your kid— Frank, for all I know."

"You'd just desert poor little Bucky?" The tone of sympathy sounded coldly fake.

"You ever do any acting in high school?"

"Not that I remember."

"You sound so vague today," I said. She seems as remote and dignified as the high oaks under which we walk. "Seems to me now like you've only been pretending to like me."

"We can't all be as sincere as *you* are."

Right in the gut. Only way I could reply to that was with lies as black as the ones *she* was dealing out. We're approaching a church, so I jump ahead to the core of my suspicions.

"What were you going to tell Frank last night?"

"Wanna come in and sing and pray and squirm?"

"Why don't we go to Asheville and look for my copy of *The Razor's Edge* in the pillar under Thomas Wolfe's house?"

In front of the church, people are waving to Lee, she stops, waves to a few, then looks down into my "beautiful blue eyes" and says, "Course, I don't know what Frank said to you last night, but my advice to you is to take his advice."

"What're you all going to do with the money?"

"I'm in the choir, I gotta go."

The bells stop, but the P.A. system sputters as the needle sticks at the end of the record.

I look down at her belly, and just as I'm about to blurt out, "Are you pregnant?" she turns on those high spike heels and clicks up the stone steps through the open red doors of the church.

With the record scratching in my ears, I walk back to the jail.

That afternoon I put through some phone calls to Bucky's victims, hoping I could persuade them to agree to accept restitution in installments from my seaman's wages and advances on the novel I hadn't really started to write yet. I had given them all the impression they would get the full amount tomorrow.

Mr. Overby said he was going to have Bucky's ass in a sling, Mr. Crigger said he had hospital bills to pay, and Pap declared that suffering was good for the soul—look at what it did for Job—and he wished it on all his friends, including me. And the Western Auto man said the company expected him to make an example of Bucky. Since I'm no good on the telephone, where I can't fix a person with my glittering eye, I didn't try any kind of plea.

When I got back at about twilight, Bucky was lying on his cot, gazing glassy-eyed at Tom as he chased Billy with an RC bottle, and Pete's bare feet showed below the toilet partition, and from downstairs the stale afterodors of Sunday dinner seeped up—turnip greens, roast pork, and blackberry pie.

"I just been laying here worrying about Momma," said Bucky.

"Well, that's fine. She's probably awake worrying about you. And Earl's probably lying awake trying to figure a way to con somebody out of his life's savings, and that'll be something else to keep Momma awake. String all the nights like this together and what do you get, Bucky?"

"What the hell you mean by *that?*"

"Nothing. And don't give me that hurt look. Good night."

"Well, by God, you can go off and let them throw me on the chain gang, if *that's* the way you feel about it! Hell, I ain't begging *no* damn body!"

"Shut up and go to sleep," I said, and stormed out of the cell in a huff.

I walked awhile, then I drove around town awhile, and then I parked outside the jail and walked some more up and down the streets of the town. As the moonlight and the crickets soothed my nerves, I began to think over Frank's proposal.

Frightened more by movies than by actual visits to Earl and Bucky, I had always feared going to the reform school or to prison—certain that someday I would.

But who said I would inevitably get caught? I had no police record. By the time the FBI traced the checks to me—even if Frank had a double cross worked out in advance—I could be in India, writing *Children of a Cold Sun* in exile.

I could *see* it, and I liked the sound of it, and I climbed the highest hill in Greenbrier so I could look down on the courthouse roof while I figured out how to *do* it.

Tipton, the next town south of Greenbrier— I could start at Tipton, where I had seen *The Spirit of St. Louis,* and hit one or two towns going into Chattanooga, then pass a couple *in* Chattanooga, and ease on down to Alabama, and by the time I hit New Orleans, I'd have enough to pay Frank's "court costs" and cover the checks Bucky passed—with enough left over for my ticket to India on a tramp steamer. Having gotten no further than Chile on the *Polestar,* I still feel cheated out of India.

But right now I had to be practical, figure out exactly how I'd do it—the story I would tell each one, the act I would pull. No, it would go better if I improvised, responding to each situation as unique. I wondered whether I had Earl's and Bucky's talents for controlling situations, at least for the duration of a con. I felt the power to *write* it. It was a challenge to risk trying to *live* it. I'd aim that Buick Streamliner for New Orleans, and I'd reach for— I settled on a target of five thousand dollars, more than Earl and Bucky had ever taken in. Not only that, I was going to get away with it.

Either way I'd win—because simultaneous with the fear of prison, I'd always wondered what it would be like to have unlimited time to write. From where I stood on the hill, I felt the mountains rising all around me. Soaring above my own triumph, I would save my brother, who, it was dead certain, would go berserk, plunge into a deep depression that could get him killed on the chain gang, full of so many hair-trigger possibilities. Sucking in the pure air, I ran back down into Greenbrier.

On the corner by the courthouse, the front of my baby blue Buick Streamliner was jacked up over a U.S. mailbox, one light smashed, the other glaring at the moon, the four doors slung wide open, a rear tire flat.

When I got up to the cell, Sheriff Thompson was squatting between the cots, petting Tom with one hand and Billy with the other, the two kids lying on their stomachs, the rough blankets over their heads, crying worse than I had yet heard them—and in the past week they had hurt each other at least three times a day.

Bucky leaned against the wall, squatting too, trying to tease Tom, in a sweet way, out of crying.

Under the weak electric light, Pete stood, one hand clapped over his mouth. I went up to him and asked him what was going on, and just then somebody kicks me in the tail. The first time in my life anybody *ever* kicked me in the tail. As I turned, thinking it was Bucky, Pete let his hand fall from his mouth, and it and his hand were bloody.

Pointing his finger at me, the sheriff says, "And *you* left the damned *door* open."

"I was mad at Bucky, I guess I forgot—"

"And *that* big hog," he says, pointing at Pete, "got mad at the youn'uns and blabbed what I told him. Does it hurt much?"

"Yeah," whines Pete.

"Good."

"What happened, Sheriff?" I ask him, but he turns his back on me and tries to console the kids.

Bucky came over to me and told me that the sheriff had heard from the hospital that the boys' foster mother had died of the gunshot wound, and then Pete, out of spite, told the kids, and said he heard that Judge Stumbo was going to send Tom to prison and Billy to another foster home, so the kids tried to run away in my Buick Streamliner.

The racket eased off a little, and I said I'd go sleep in the car, feeling unwelcome in the jail anymore.

"No, by God!" says the sheriff. "You're serving a night in jail for helping in a jailbreak."

So now I also had the sheriff against me—and that meant against Bucky, too.

After everybody was settled and it got dead quiet, I said, "Bucky . . . Bucky . . . Bucky . . ."

"Yeah, what?"

"I called up all those people a while ago and tried to get them to agree to let me pay them a little each month, but they said they had to have the cold cash tomorrow." He didn't say anything. "Bucky . . . Bucky . . . Bucky . . ."

I felt guilty now, as I had the many times I locked Bucky out of my childhood, enraged at being forced by Momma to be his keeper, just as I locked him in here each time I went out.

I wanted to lull him to sleep with a solution, as, in

our childhood, I often lulled him to sleep with a story. But I couldn't tell him my solution because I couldn't depend on him to keep his mouth shut—and he was beyond the consolation of a story.

As I fell asleep, the names of Cervantes, Milton, Dostoievski, Genet, and other great prison writers tolled in my mind.

# 14 

# *Another Educated Fool*

But when I woke the next morning, my mind was on the judge—a direct appeal.

The sheriff let me out before the others were awake, and I went up and backed my car off the mailbox. Then I went into the courthouse to work on Judge Stumbo.

The judge's secretary had long blond hair, with a pompadour, and a high school cuteness that was aging on her.

"I'm Lucius Hutchfield," I said, with the confidence of a person who knows the password. It didn't pass with *her*. "Bucky's brother."

"Who's Bucky?" She lay outside the charmed circle.

"He's going before the judge this morning, and I'd appreciate a chance to talk to him."

"The mood *he's* in, you'll wish you hadn't." Putting it as a challenge that way makes me eager to get to him. But her brassy manner and loud voice make me nervous.

"Is he in there now?" I ask her, looking at the closed door.

"Yes. And be glad *you're* out *here*. Now get out,

and I mean that in a nice way, because I'm doing you a favor, Mr. . . .''

''Hutchfield. Listen—''

That's just what the judge was doing—listening to her big mouth. Because the door cracks a foot and he's standing in it, five feet high, with an expression long ago set in concrete, just starting to crack.

''Did you say he was Bucky Hutchfield's brother?'' he asks, without, looked like to me, opening his mouth.

''Yes, sir.''

''Get out of here,'' he says to me.

''That's what *I* told him, sir,'' she says, ripping a sheet from her typewriter.

''But sir, I must talk to you before two o'clock.'' Desperate, I blurted out the theme: ''The chain gang will kill my brother!''

Judge Stumbo nods from the waist up, his eyelids slam shut three times like a gavel.

''But the prison psychiatrist said—''

''Never *believed* in psychiatrists.''

''Please, sir, I'm just trying to be my brother's keeper—''

''You're a fool.''

''Well, sir, the nation needs teachers, doesn't it? And I'm trying to become a teacher—''

''We don't need another educated fool.''

''Sir, please, sir, just let me tell you the story of Bucky's childhood, and I think you can see—''

''I've heard too *many* stories. Besides, I lack imagination.''

''Sir, at least think of my mother—''

''I have no desire to think of your mother.''

''Sir, what can I say, what can I do, what can Bucky do, to convince you—?''

"He has only to be born again and live his life over in a different way. As it *is*, he goes on the chain gang." The crack closed before I could open my mouth. But then I got to laughing. It was a great line.

"Hey, he's really a very funny judge, isn't he?"

"I thought it was funny, too," she says, throwing her carriage, "first time I heard it."

But when the morning sun hit me in the face on the courthouse steps, I wasn't laughing. I had only five hours to work a miracle.

Although I'd just experienced a failure to the contrary, I realized that my last thin chance was to approach the victims *personally* again and beg them to accept monthly payments. An even thinner chance on the other side of that was that the judge would accept their decisions. But could I achieve enough control to bluff Frank, whose checkbook was in my hip pocket—an emergency kit?

So I hopped into my Buick, started off and swerved, wobbling, into a service station. I forgot the flat.

They patched up the radiator, too, and pounded the hell out of a few other places, as if beating a donkey that won't move, and I set out for Boone's Gap. I headed for the other end of the line so I could gauge my time as I worked back toward the deadline at the courthouse.

As I drove along, I decided that if I had no luck by the time I got to Bucky's third victim, I'd start cashing those checks in the next town. Time passed quickly as I imagined the effect of such a move on my life. At least I could finish the novel about me and Anna Livia.

# 15
# *To Play the Con*

Mr. Overby squints, puzzled, against the sunburst where I'm standing in the doorway of his store. "He just left," he says.

"*Who* just left?"

"Your lawyer— Bucky's lawyer. Mr. French."

"Listen, I just came by to talk to you about the money Bucky owes you and try—"

"He just paid it off. You s'pose to meet each other here?"

"Hold it, Mr. Overby. What's going on?"

"Mr. French just paid me. See?" he says, pulling a check out of his big wallet, thonged to his hip pocket. "And I signed his paper."

"What paper?"

"The affidavit saying I don't want to see Bucky prosecuted, I'm satisfied with restitution, plus the interest for three years, like it was a loan. And a big plus feature of the agreement is that I get to keep the money even if Judge Stumbo sentences Bucky anyway—which he will."

"So you get your money on the hip and Bucky's ass in a sling any way the cookie crumbles, huh?"

"Yeah." He grins, delighted with the justice of it all.

"Plus. *Plus*. I sold Mr. French three brand-new suits, one his size and two Bucky's size, and about a hundred dollars of this and that."

"What did he look like?"

Then Mr. Overby gives me the exact description McCoy of the state bureau of investigation gave me, each item in the same order, right down to the shiny briefcase. "I'm gonna get *me* a briefcase like his," says Mr. Overby.

Then Mrs. Overby comes in, wearing that same rayon polka-dot dress, and carries on about what a handsome, dashing, though oddly dressed, fellow Mr. French was, and she makes me promise to bring Bucky by to see her; and I had to swear again not to put her life story in a book.

When I walked into Mr. Crigger's Red Dot Café, he's up on that stool smoking a fat cigar with a two-inch ash.

"You just missed him," he says, and I ask who, and we go through the whole routine, the description of French and all, the gist of which is that Mr. French came in and treated them both to Crigger's best porterhouse steak (since Crigger didn't know what French meant by Chateaubriand), and over their steaks they came to an agreement, and Crigger settled for Mr. French's terms, which were the same as Overby's.

I drove up to the pumps where Pap was whitewashing the island. He looks up, doubly surprised to see me. "I know," I says, "I just missed him."

"By less than five minutes."

"Driving a 1942 white Lincoln-Mercury Zephyr in mint condition?"

"With brand-new rubber all around," he says. "I unloaded four new double-ply nylon tires on him." He gives the island a sloppy slap of whitewash.

"Did you get a cigar out of him?"

"Smoke it after lunch. Ort to last the weekend."

I scratched gravel to catch up with Mr. French, but jerked to a stop at the edge of the lot—out of gas. Out of money.

Out of the goodness of his heart, Pap exchanged a tank of gas for my spare tire, my hubcaps, and since I wouldn't need it without the spare—my jack. He said I looked faint and shouldn't go without my lunch, so he threw in a pack of stale peanut butter crackers that I almost choked on before I got to Greenbrier.

I had the feeling there wasn't much point in going back, certainly no need to check the Western Auto man. If it was humanly possible, this Mr. French would get Bucky off.

# 16
## Leaving Everybody Happy

In the No Parking zone in front of the courthouse, aligned with the walkway, was parked the white Lincoln-Mercury Zephyr. I parked behind it, confident that Mr. French would take care of any fines.

In front of the drugstore, a Greyhound bus was letting passengers off. The driver reached his hand in, and the first thing I saw was a prizewinner's red ribbon bobbing on Majel's breast as she stepped down in her white majorette boots, the pompons swinging.

She sees me getting out of my smashed-in Buick and smiles and waves. I wave back, then go on into the courthouse.

The Zephyr, though white, reminded me of the Green Hornet's car in the chapter play Earl took me to see the day Bucky was born. Momma wanted us out of the house to spare us the shock of birth. Earl held my hand, and as we went over the bridge, he told me about Fartso the Whale, who lived in Crazy Creek. If I threw him a nickel, Earl said, Fartso would tell his gremlins to bring me a Buck Rogers gun. "Give it to me," he said, "and *I'll* throw it in."

Later, watching the Green Hornet's car force the bad guy's car to swerve and smash into a gas pump that exploded, I wondered for a minute how it was that Earl hugged two bags of popcorn when he had thrown both our nickels into the water. Eighteen years later, it suddenly dawned on me.

Dawn's rosy fingers goosed me as I stepped into Judge Stumbo's outer office, where Earl was hefting a dangling lock of the secretary's long blond hair.

As if verifying the testimony of witnesses, Earl's wearing a white Panama suit and hat that bring the sunlight indoors, and green-tinted glasses, a mustache, a pink shirt with a white tie, and two-tone brown-and-white shoes, and in a chair lies a shiny briefcase with H.F. on the gold clasp.

He doesn't see me, and he's saying, "Not many girls can wear such long hair and get away with it, but if you lived in New York, you'd be setting a style, Blue Eyes."

Her misty brown eyes look up at Earl, and she's forgotten, like many other girls, what the hell color her eyes really are, and a feeble smirk is her only attempt to control the situation.

I stayed quiet, dangling in the doorway.

I'd come in at the climax, because she gets up and goes into Judge Stumbo's office, and Earl turns and glances right *at* me, as though we had been together all morning and I'd just stepped in after a brief trip to the john. So I try to match his cool.

The door opens, and the secretary steps aside to let Earl pass. She leaves the door ajar, so from where I stand, I watch Earl walk up to the desk and put out his hand at such a distance that the judge has to get up and reach across his desk to shake it.

I can't catch all the conversation, but I see the affidavits come out of the shiny briefcase and the judge take them and peruse them, shaking his head negatively.

". . . willing to pay the court costs," I hear Earl say, his voice becoming louder, stageworthy, as he builds the scene. "I realize that in a case like this the court costs are what some people might regard as exorbitant, nevertheless, we're willing to lay it on the line today, sir. Settle it out of court, if possible."

"Sir, everybody has been at me to handle this case out of court, but I don't handle, sir, and you may as well save your techniques of persuasion until court convenes—in exactly ten minutes. Now, if you'll excuse me . . ."

I stare at the back of Earl's head as he remains seated, very still, and the judge stares at Earl's face.

"Pardon me for staring, sir," says Earl, "but isn't that—?" Then I see the color photograph of a young man in a marine uniform. "I *thought* the name was familiar. Judge Stumbo. That name kept nagging at me all the way down the highway. That's Buddy, isn't it?"

"Why— yes, but— what's that got to do with Bucky Hutchfield?"

"Nothing, sir," says Earl, rising, still looking at the picture. "Nothing."

Then he jerks himself into a posture of efficiency, puts out his hand so the judge has to get up again and reach out to it, and as they shake, the judge says, "Mr. French, what were you about to say?"

"That I knew him. The machine gun—"

"Who told you about Buddy?"

"Told *me!* I was there, at Pork Chop Hill." The judge's other hand reaches out and the four hands clasp in one fingery knot. "All I got to show is one bullet wound, but poor Buddy . . ."

Then I remember the scar under Earl's shoulder blade. In Montana, a prison guard bent over a water fountain and his pistol fell out of its holster and fired.

"What are you people doing out there?" says the

judge. "Mr. Hutchfield, your lawyer will be with you in a moment." He pushed the door shut. "Now, sir . . . What did you say your first name was?"

Muffled by the door came a few phrases: ". . . died in my arms . . . I was delirious at the time . . . didn't know him well, but . . . last words were, 'Candyman, Candyman.' . . . That mean anything to you, sir?"

At the word "Candyman," the secretary frowns slightly, then slowly smiles cunningly, then shrugs, stops pretending to work, and sits with her arms folded, listening with me.

"'Candyman' Buddy's nickname for his father?" I ask.

She smirks and nods her head. "How did *you* know?"

"Imagination," I say, and nod *my* head.

Twenty minutes later the judge comes out and says, "Mrs. Harmon, would you please write out a check for a hundred dollars? Mr. French needs some expense money to get back to Florida, and I'm afraid he can't cash a check locally without a great deal of trouble, but they'll cash one with *my* signature on it. And here's his check to cover court costs. We've settled it out of court, so strike Bucky Hutchfield from the docket."

We all shake hands, and the judge hurries out to court, thirty minutes late, content with Earl's promise to return and spend a weekend with him sometime, fishing.

"Show Mr. French the jail," says Mrs. Harmon to me, smirking.

"If there's a florist in this town," says Earl, posing in the doorway, "expect a dozen roses within an hour."

"I won't hold my breath."

As we're going down the steps toward his car, Earl says, "See you in jail, kid," and I see there's a ticket on my windshield, none on his.

Earl had improved his sudden-and-glorious-appearance-out-of-nowhere routine since the time in 1948 when he escaped from the reform school and I saw him for the first time in three years when he stepped onto the stage of the Bijou, competing for the twenty-five-dollar prize for the best imitation of Al Jolson, a promotional stunt for *The Jolson Story*. When he walked off with the prize into the rainy night, I knew that I was seeing an image of control: Earl in action.

I follow in my car, which I want *near* me up to the last minute. In the short drive around the square to the jail, I notice the new tires on Earl's car, the suits hanging neatly in the back, the boxes of other stuff stacked on the seat, and I think of all the checks he passed this morning, and hope each of the receivers got a cigar, at least. And then I think, 'Yeah, everybody but me.'

By the time I climb out of my wreck of a car and reach the screened-in porch, Bucky is already out there, his buck-toothed grin stretching from one of those big ears to the other, and Sheriff Thompson is folding a piece of paper, probably a note from the judge.

And right quick, there's Majel, draped in the doorway, decked out in her costume, the prizewinner's red ribbon still dangling, and I see in her eyes, even in the shade of the porch, that when she looks at Earl, she sees Miami in full splendor.

I stay outside in the broiling sun while Bucky hugs the sheriff's wife and shakes hands with Thompson. Earl gives the sheriff a big cigar, then loads his own pearl-handled cigarette holder and feels for matches until the sheriff lights it for him, then lights his own cigar.

They all step out into the sunlight, shaking hands, and Earl even reaches for Majel's, and when her shoulders twitch as if by a slight electric shock, I figure he's tickled her palm.

I follow the parade toward the cars, Majel cavorts and tosses her baton into the sun and it spins and sparkles, and Bucky runs ahead and jumps behind the wheel of that white Lincoln-Mercury Zephyr like it's Santa's sleigh.

"Follow *me*," Earl says, as he gets in beside Bucky.

They take off as though they have a motorcycle escort. As, in every sense that matters, they have.

Just before I pull away from the curb, I look up at the window where I first saw Bucky a week ago. Behind the silver iron slats stood Tom, his arm around Billy. They didn't wave. They didn't move.

At the intersection where the caution light blinked in the sun's glare, I took the highway least traveled by, the one that offered a shortcut over a curving route to the state line. Earl and his chauffeur, Bucky, were borne along in their dreamboat down the super highway toward the horizon.

# 17 

# *Zara Jane Ransom and the Blue Goose Hotel*

I did make it over the state line okay, and I'm far into and high up in the mountains when that old baby blue Buick Streamliner throws a rod and I had to sell her for scrap.

I felt like I ought to lay low awhile before hitting the dusty trail again, so the greasy old man who bought it let me sleep on the back seat of the Streamliner in the middle of his auto graveyard.

The next morning was Sunday, but the truck stop café a mile down the steep highway was open. I noticed an Asheville newspaper on the cigar case. Sitting at the counter, I leafed through it, hoping I wouldn't get the latest word on Bucky and Earl, nor mention of their inept brother. The news of the day was silent about all three of us, but in the Sunday feature section, space devoted to human interest stories offers a piece headlined: DID JESSE JAMES PASS THROUGH SWEETWATER: FACT OR FICTION? I tore out the article and slipped it into my pocket.

None of the truckers in the café were headed my way, so I start walking—up and down the steep curving highway, so few cars and trucks passing, the silence and the smell of the forest stimulate my imagination, and I've answered the newspaper story's question five or six different ways by the time I reach this intersection that's down in a valley.

One sign points toward Boone, which, a mountain boy told me, is near Sweetwater high in the mountains, and the other points toward Cherokee. Sweetwater's a hundred miles out of the way. "But out of the way of what?" I ask, out loud.

Four rides later, I'm dozing deeply in a rattletrap truck, an old piano tuner at the wheel.

"All out for the middle of nowheres."

Before I opened my eyes, I heard the piano tuner spit out the window.

"You mean I've slept across the Blue Ridge?" I looked out. I'd wanted to carry into Sweetwater a sense of the country surrounding it. Rain drips from the trees along the Blue Ridge Parkway. In a slight breeze, the undersides of the leaves turn up, almost white.

Just as the moronic dribble of sleep began to seep out the corner of my mouth, I glimpse a wooded niche beside the road. The low-hanging limbs of a cherry tree screen a boy standing tiptoe on the saddle of a black motorcycle. His legs are bare, and between the seat and the raised arch of one foot, silver flashes of water shoot out of the shaded place. His upraised arm hides his face, the fingers stretching, reaching for what looks like a cluster of cherries that shine with rain in the faint light of the alcove. Suddenly, the wind stirred gently in the leaves, and the image trembled out of sight. I wondered whether it was real or an image in a dream I would have that night.

My stinging eyes searched the lush mountainsides for a sign of Sweetwater. "Can't see a thing."

"Nothing *to* see—even when you get there. But you

can't miss it. Looks like God just took and threw a handful of houses and stuff up 'gin the hillside.''

I backed out of the car, rocked on my quivering ankles, and shook my head like an underwater swimmer, trying to focus my eyes, sore from grit and wind strain. The old man had stopped along the edge of the steep road, where the sky seemed to look up.

"See that fresh muddied road behind you that drops off into nowheres?''

"Yeah.''

"Just follow your nose.'' The piano tuner's nose, blue-veined, looked like a relief map of the mountains.

"'Preciate the lift.''

"Never said what you was going to Sweetwater *for*.''

"Look up a friend of my childhood.''

"Wouldn't be surprised if I knew him.''

"Me neither. Name's Jesse James.''

The piano tuner's laughter echoed through the trees, but he didn't settle for a gag. "Anybody in particular you want to see in Sweetwater?''

"Woman who owns the Blue Goose Hotel.''

"I *heard* the old lady's dead . . . Claim that newspaper story killed her—like a shot in the back.''

The old man pulls onto the highway again, headed for Roan Mountain, where tomorrow morning he intended to tune an old lady's piano in which the last chord had died about thirty years ago. Something like that was what *I* had in mind. And the melody I hoped to play would give some impression of what it was like to give one's virginity to Jesse James.

As the piano tuner's car curved down the mountain slope, his lights show a billboard painting of Dan'l Boone, one hand sighting into, seeming to salute, the West, the other holding a long rifle. YOU HAVE JUST

PASSED THROUGH BOONE WHERE THE WORLD'S
GREATEST OUTDOOR DRAMA IS PERFORMED NIGHTLY.

Standing in the middle of the parkway, listening to rain drip from the leaves, I felt like a hick in Times Square. Here, too, the only direction to look, if you want to see anything, is up.

From the muddy road, I looked down, too. The sky was clear, evening stars, full moon overhead, but on the mountain ranges below, thick clouds and films of blue mist moved. The muddy road disappeared around a bend, into dark green trees and thick bushes. I followed it, even though it would lead me now only to the grave of the woman whose story I'd come to hear.

On the bend, above shadows on the road, the foliage broke, and far ahead I saw the Blue Goose Hotel. I felt cheated. I'd gone a hundred miles out of my way home to be told that she was dead. With a few enticing facts and a few misleading rumors to start, I'd have to conjure up what she'd left untold. Perched in the moonlight, the Blue Goose Hotel was huge, pines and maples, birch and dead trees framing it solidly, miles of mountains surrounding. On a tower at each end of the Blue Goose Hotel, weather vanes and lightning rods caught and shot light into the trees. Like a fire tower, it looked down on everything. I couldn't see the roofs of whatever houses there might be near the hotel. I felt like the disembodied voice in the opening of *Rebecca* that I saw at the Bijou: "Last night I dreamt I went to Manderley again . . . but the way was barred to me. . . ."

Around the bend, a cornfield looked deliberately flooded with moonlight, a scarecrow standing among the dry husks and the crooked, kneeling stalks.

Walking under the low-hanging leaves of an oak, I saw a red brick silo, silicon-speckled rocks piled high against one side. As I passed its doorway, shafts of moonlight falling through the broken roof showed it was empty.

Coming around the next curve, I caught my breath, a rasp that echoed through the trees. In a hollow depression in the side of the mountain that'd once been cleared but'd grown over again this summer, thick as the jungles along the Panama Canal, I saw why the road was new, the mud gummy. A giant orange machine with a long arched backbone, tires taller than I am, and a scooper that carried the dirt raked up by the little bulldozers surrounding it, blocks the road. Tall new grass bearded the blades of some of the smaller machines and moonlight honed the bright steel of the others. My leg brushes a dead plant, whose hard seeds rattle.

Going around a tool shed, I stepped onto a path and climbed until I came out on a gravel road and saw a sign nailed to a wooden rail fence:

SWEETWATER

Population

1850: 102        1930: 73

Jesse and Frank rein their horses, lean, bones aching, in their saddles, and look at the sign and then at each other, and Frank says, "May as well."

The town was just as the piano tuner had said—flung out with a flick of God's wrist onto the side of the mountain, tipped like a water-pump spout, so that in the road, a man would always be either trudging up, or trying to keep from running down, slipping on ice or mud, or stirring up dust. The dozen or so houses leaned as though rolling with the earth on the 23° inclination on its axis. There in the moonlight, nothing kept it from being an evening in 1880 at about eight o'clock, until I saw the first building on the edge of town.

In the days before cinder block, it would have been

a shack. Huge windows, and the walls on three sides no higher than my waist. A faded sign insisted: FROZEN CUSTARD. A cracked oilcloth banner hung from the front of the roof: GROWING WITH THE TOWN: TOURISTS WELCOME. Rain had washed the three gigantic windows. They gleamed.

Just as I felt myself being looked at, some elderly voices on a porch high above the road hushed. Ivy entwined on wires, strung from the floor to the ceiling all along the front to the steep steps like the strings of a harp, screened the porch. Maybe they sat talking the night the two horsemen entered town. Maybe Jesse, a little dizzy from the dribbling wound, hears a swing creak, too, hears it stop, suddenly, and the wood crackle as a fat old lady in a sundress (I saw her as I came nearer) leans and looks down into the road.

And if somebody didn't snap off a light or a gray-fringed head didn't appear ghostly behind a pane, I might as well forget the whole thing. But as I pass the eighth house, one *does*. I have the feeling that I am giving the cues, until I realize that the books I have read, the movies I've seen, not to mention the life I've lived, have called them before. But the light didn't snap, it *faded*, on the window, to black.

Along the steep road, the glass insulators on the stiff, outspread arms of the telephone poles gleam in the moonlight, wireless.

In front of the Sweetwater Trading Post, two old men sit on a bench. Hoping they'll be partly satisfied I'm not some prying stranger, I go on past the Blue Goose Hotel without a glance.

A chimney and the charred foundations of a house that once faced the hotel rose out of the rubble where I sat on a rusty barrel under a young, shivering walnut tree and gazed at the Blue Goose Hotel, hoping the old lady's ghost would turn on a light so I could focus my nerve.

The Blue Goose Hotel seemed the sole reason—and enough—for the stars' and the moon's glow. The clouds and mist below were a stream that smaller hills like green boulders broke. In those milky depths, a legend had hooked me and fished me out.

Beginning at the towers in front, sagging verandas run around each of the two stories. Cracked stone steps lead up to the hotel. A wide, glassed-in porch and two large glass doors front the middle section— hundreds of small panes. I imagined the way it would look at sundown certain evenings in October and how the color would turn at twilight tomorrow. Now, it was cool blue. The view below and above was steep. In the milky stream that was rising now from the valleys be- low, the hotel seemed anchored. 'It seemed to rock gently like a clipper in a bay,' I wrote, in my head.

Sitting on the barrel, rust scaling off when I moved, I knew I could imagine the whole story, and it would not be much different from the way it would be if she were alive to tell it. If she *would* have told it. But un- derneath my desire to hear it, I felt an itch to know the truth, even as, knowing a scrap of it, I was already turning it into fiction. I'd felt certain that even though she had refused to give the story to a local newspaperman—who went ahead and printed the rumors alone—she would have looked into my "glit- tering" blue eyes and told it to me. She would have recognized me as one of her own kind, she would have known that at last someone had come who understood, and she would not have been able to keep silent.

Affecting what I hope resembles a saunter to the eyes that watch me as they must have watched Jesse, I move on into the young trees. Before I can drop the

affectation, I trip over a rock. Groping around on the
ground in the dark, I felt a slight gully, then my fingertips stroke like Braille the chiseled marks on an upright
stone slab. I remembered the grave in Kearney,
Missouri, and Jesse's marker, like a curbstone in the
weeds.

# 18

# The Rising of the Stage

As I vaulted over the balustrade, it swayed like the limb of a tree. The porch receives me without a mutter. I walk along the side to the rear, glancing into the small rooms through lace-curtained windows. In one of them, Jesse keeps in touch with the Bible by the moonlight through the window, and in another, Frank reads Shakespeare. People accuse me of making that up, but quoting Shakespeare nearly got Frank captured one time, and the Bible was a throwback to the days when Jesse vowed to become a preacher.

At the back door, I knock lightly, pause a few minutes, then turn the porcelain knob. The hinge whines like a cat. Entering a creaky hotel, booked solid with ghosts on the roof of the world, I am in my natural element, as when I broke into Thomas Wolfe's house in Asheville the first time I ran away from home. The scene was different, but the element, created at will, is always the same.

Moving from room to room, I tapped lightly at each door before opening it. In the lobby, where the register book was open and moonlight puddled the chairs and sofas, I stopped. And I paused a moment in the middle of the ballroom, as though the waltz had just come to a stop in me. But the creaking did not stop. Trapped in a pitch-black theater, moments after the last door is locked, you hear wood crack, like ice on a pond—it's "the rising of the stage," someone once told me.

It was all right if she was following me, because *I* was following *her*. Did she think I was someone she'd been expecting all her life—someone who, now that she was dead, had finally come?

In one of the bathrooms, I took a leak. On a Sunday morning, the sun on his belt buckle, Jesse reads the Saint Louis paper—a letter he wrote to the editor, castigating him for defamation of character, signing off: Yours respectfully, Jesse James. I let down the seat, the wood felt warm.

I pulled the chain. A bird flies out of the water tank over my head and thrusts itself repeatedly against a high window. I open it and watch the bird fly straight into the moon, now ringed with clabbered cloud in a reddish glow, and vanish in light.

On the second floor, in the west wing, I open the door on a room like all the others, except that she sits there, in full moonlight, in a wicker rocker, lowering a Coca-Cola bottle from her lips. She holds the bottle, half-filled, poised in front of her, and says, "Jesse?"

"No, ma'am," I said, finally, a painful ache in my chest, holding hard to the knob, believing and disbelieving in apparitions.

"Who are you?"

"Lucius Hutchfield, from over in Cherokee."

"That means nothing to me."

"I hope I didn't scare you."

She sets the bottle on the sill. Her gray hair hangs long and thick behind her head, thin around her face. The hair, and the eyes, were the only things I hadn't already imagined. The dated shoes, the dated dress, but not the hair and the eyes. I'd expected her to be able to see the outside world only dimly, but her gaze, as I stood in the door, seemed to scrutinize me in microscopic detail.

She folds her hands and looks out the window. When I see that her hands tremble and the veins are swelling, I realize in panic that she's terrified, apt to scream on the instant.

"Please . . . I'm harmless."

"You have no right."

"I'll go, if I'm intruding." I turned as though I was leaving. "Don't you want to know why I've come?"

"I care neither where you've come from nor where you're going."

"That leaves me dangling. For a moment, anyway, long enough to tell you *why* I've come. Will you listen and stop trembling like that?"

"You have no right."

"It'll take less time than for you to finish that Coca-Cola."

She looked into my eyes, flint blue like Jesse's, though not, like his, slightly crossed.

"I got hold of a story about you. Some hack reporter in Boone claims you knew Jesse James." As Eve *knew* Adam.

She walked past me out of the room. She had looked into my "glittering" blue eyes and it had made no difference.

I followed her into the hall. She moved, very strong, very slowly, like a figure on an urn.

"No, look, Miss Ransom. I want to do it right. I just want to sit in the lobby with you and let you tell it. You don't have to— tell— I don't expect you to tell about— I mean, just tell *any*thing about him that comes to you."

We were on the stairs, dark, windowless, although the lobby below is white. I take her elbow to help her down. But when I felt the bone tremble, I jerked my hand away as though a moment's more pressure will snap it.

"I'm not a newspaperman. I hate that stuff. I understand how you feel about it. Look, I used to tell stories about Jesse James to the kids at the orphanage, and I was still playing Jesse James after I was too old to play legends, and it's like I was raised with him, but I want to lay my hand on a part of the legend where I can feel the blood still beat. I understand how you feel. It's personal. Well, that's how *I* take it, too. It's something I have a need of, that I can't explain, but that you, you surely, can understand. It takes two to resurrect—one to call forth, and one to witness."

Zara Ransom opens the glass door on the left of the glassed-in porch, and when she turns on me, the look in her eyes makes me step aside. If she had lived ninety percent of her life in the past, the other ten percent was, for me at that moment, unbearably immediate. She's not afraid of me now—it's rage that makes her tremble.

"I've come a long way, Miss Ransom"—feeble persuasion.

"So have I. And a long way to go. You in that direction, if you please, and me in my own."

"Think about it, please. Good night."

I step out onto sandstone, and at my back, I hear the click of the lock, like a pistol cocking.

# 19

# *Hart Woodring Rides*

I crossed the road, stumbled through the ruins opposite the hotel, climbed down a hill to the creek, and followed it to the highway. The first car that comes by picks me up, and lets me off in Blowing Rock in front of the Dixie Supermarket where the manager stood at the door, fumbling for his keys. I persuaded him to let me in, so I could get some saltines, cheese, and a box of dried apricots.

At the edge of Blowing Rock, I decided to stroll to the other end and look for surprises, expecting none. I've seen such self-conscious towns all over the country. Churches like doll's houses, modern or rustic, a neat post office with a crisp flag, a smart Chamber of Commerce office and a polished fire hall, a small library, a modest art gallery that the summer citizens are proud of, a movie theater where the movies are better than ever, they say, but the popcorn is warmed over, several drugstores, handicraft shops, souvenir shops, antique shops and restaurants in old houses, auction "art" galleries, a park with rides and picnic pavilions, an exhibition of quaint thises and quaint thats.

I reached the other end of Blowing Rock without

being surprised, except that *Gone with the Wind* at the movie theater was a stroke that set the town off a little and me off stride. A large banner proclaimed that it was bigger than ever on the new wide screen. I begged to differ. It couldn't be bigger than it was when I saw it three times from the front row of the Hiawassee Theater in 1939 and again at the Bijou when it was re-released in 1946.

As I approached the amusement grounds, the roar of a motorcycle broke from the rim of a merry-go-round and the sonority of a calliope boomed from its hub. I caught the multiplied image of black-jacketed-rider-black-motorcycle in the many-faceted mirror around the hub before I caught *him,* going around and around in the soft dirt.

The yellow lights hanging through the trees like fireflies strung on a string glare off the polished wooden horses. Children hug the poles that pierce the necks of the rearing and plunging and snarling horses and scream at the antics of the motorcyclist who races the horses and whose motor seems to harmonize with the calliope music. The rider didn't rev the motor, he played it like an iron cello.

His silicone windshield and his masklike goggles caught and thrust the overhanging colored lights off into the awed faces of the crowd.

The children's bodies, like Tintoretto cherubs, twisted around, following the black rider.

The crowd parted and the manager, a wizened little man in a gray cotton-candy-streaked smock, took a look at the situation. He had the face and stance, there on the sawdust, of a man who has just called the "authorities." A siren in the distance testifies that he has. He stands in front of the crowd, crosses his arms, and, sneering, nods to the cyclist as he cyclones past.

The wheels wore a circular ditch in the dirt which would remain even after the cyclist is gone. Around the children, too, he wove a magic circle, for they had never seen anything like it in the flesh.

Standing on an iron bench behind the crowd, I hear a siren die at my back and, turning, see a finned, black-and-white car bounce up the sawdust drive. I pitch my last dime in front of it.

The sheriff, a burly man in a Western hat, khaki shirt and pants, rust-tinged corduroy jacket, and engineer boots, pops out and cuts sharply around in front of the car and looks up at me. "What was that you throwed in front of that car?"

"Dime to stop on. Don't think you did."

"*Don't you move*," he says, pointing a loaded finger at me.

Like breaking open a half-split melon, he parts the crowd. When the manager sees the sheriff, his hands on his hips, one palm riding his gun butt, he signals to the operator of the merry-go-round to stop. It takes a few moments for the operator to put a halt to what enthralls him. The music and the dish of the merry-go-round groan as it slows, and by the time it stops, the motorcyclist slowing with it, the children are screaming a different tune.

The parents rush forward to catch the drunken children, a few of whom dismount and, bellering, tip forward off the slanted dish like June bugs off a screen, and roll in the dirt, raging, indignant, a little sick.

When the rider swung off, the cycle leaned on its stand. He picks up a little blond boy in a red sunsuit, turns him right side up, and gives him a little push toward the woman whose open arms move in on him. When the rider turns, the sheriff puts his arm around his neck as if to kiss him, but the face beneath the goggles and cap show the fierceness of the sheriff's grip.

The boy's gloved hands claw at the sheriff's corduroy arm, but his body, though turned unnaturally, moves gracefully with the force that pulls him away from the merry-go-round.

A deputy kicks up the stand and pushes the motorcycle along behind the sheriff and the outlaw.

I'm standing on the bench, watching the sheriff escort the boy across the street to a filling station, as if to gas up his cycle. The deputy leans the cycle against the front of the dark station and flashes a light through the window of a wheelless 1949 green Hudson Hornet that dangles from a block and tackle attached to a crosstree.

Someone left the window above the station, and behind a door at the side on the ground floor, a light comes on. A woman opened the door, the light glaring behind her. She pulls the boy away from the sheriff, shoves him against the doorjamb, and I heard the slap she lashed at him. The light went out, and the sheriff starts slowly back across the street, the deputy skipping ahead for the car.

In what seemed to be a neglected, older part of the park hung some old swings with wooden seats. A single naked bulb hung off to one side like a light in a one-streetlight town. I sat on one of the swings and ate the crackers and cheese and started on the apricots. Then, bracing my toes in the soft dirt, I twist the swing, lift my toes, and let it spin me.

I twisted and spun until the merry-go-round over there stopped, the lights blinked off in the trees and over my swing. Then I crossed the street, my pockets filled with the rest of the apricots, and glanced up at the window over the filling station. It was dark. The motorcycle was leashed like a panther to the water hydrant that stuck out of the wall beside the air pump.

The flinty, nostril-pricking smell of oil, grease, gas, and tools put me back in the *Polestar* engine room, and on back in the Dixie Vim filling station where I used to work in Cherokee, daydreaming of going to sea.

Someone sat behind the wheel of the raised Hudson. Numb from need of sleep, I stepped over to the window.

"Friends of mine sent me for something they left in the glove compart—"

"Shhhhhhssssss," said the boy, rolling the window down. "My mother . . ." He jabs his finger up and down under the car roof.

I looked on top of the car, then stuck my head in. "She ain't there."

The boy laughed, soundlessly, snorting and hissing into his hands, cupped over his mouth and nose, his elbows clapped against his ribs. Unmasked, he wears a fresh white T-shirt and tight jeans. Quickly he rolls up the window on his side, and I go around, ducking under the front of the raised, wheelless car, and get in beside him.

I rolled up the window on my side. I rubbed the dust off the nameplate on the dash over the disgorged radio: Hudson Hornet.

"Only made three hundred that year," the boy says. "Some guy passing through sold it to Momma for the parts in it. Only thing is, not many of those other two hundred and ninety-nine Hudson Hornets buzz through Blowing Rock hurtin' for parts."

Bucky had written to me about his Hudson Hornet. I felt certain this was it, abandoned in Blowing Rock.

I looked in the glove compartment. No gloves. There never are. I find a book of matches from a joint

in Laredo, which I give to the boy, a beer opener,
which I give to the boy, a map of Florida, a box of
No-Doz, a comb, some hairpins, a deck of cards, and
four rubbers sealed in gold foil. No blank checks in
evidence.

"Let's go a few hands of blackjack," says the boy.

"I'm busted before I start."

"Owe me."

"Okay."

We played.

"My name's Lucius Hutchfield. What's yours?"

"Hart Woodring, and I ain't ashamed to admit it."

"Who says you should be?"

"A few who don't know no better. And the next
day, they get fitted for dentures."

"I'm a stranger here myself."

"I know. Noticed you . . . Somebody'll blab it, so
I'll tell you myself, so you'll get the facts. My daddy
robbed a filling station when I was little and got the
road gang for it. A big coal truck hit him when he was
standing beside the highway honing a sickle 'tween
here and Boone. They can all kiss my royal butt.
Blackjack!"

Hart liked to slap his cards. Now and then as he
talked, he shifts his cods to show he has a cool attitude
toward the whole subject.

"You handle that motorsickle like a pro, Hart."

"Now, don't I?"

"Kids ate it up, anyway."

"Nobody but kids enjoy a damned thing. She didn't
have to slap me. I don't act ashamed of *her*. Your
mother ever hop tables in a tourist resort?"

"No. She's cashier in a restaurant in Cherokee,
Tennessee."

"Did you ever go 'round Cherokee feeling like
scum?"

"More than once."

"That's how this damned town makes me feel. 'And what does your father do, Hart?' 'He died in the war,' she makes me say. Well, by God, he *was* a hero in the blamed war. 'And what does your mother do, Hart?' 'Oh, she's a hostess at Mayview Manor.' Damned table hop!"

"Money's not everything, Hart," I say, for no good reason.

"Huh! Ever ride up to Mayview and watch them people?"

"No."

"Look, this girl that stays at Mayview, if I had me the right kind of car and clothes and a mother that didn't serve her three meals a day, I could drive up to that swimming pool, order me a highball, and meet her like a goddamn gentleman."

"You hurting for girls?"

"I'm hurting for this one. Sabra Van Ness. Can you beat that? Sits beside that pool in a bird's-egg blue skin-tight bathing suit . . ."

"Bikini?"

"Bikini? Hell, no, she don't want to kill you—just drive you *in*sane. And long blond hair, natural blond, and green eyes and legs God didn't want to chance twice, and— Well, the rest of her's my business . . . Two summers! And I ain't even said three words to her. What if I did? And her find out my old lady waits her family's table. *Her* old man's in oil. Just like being made of gold."

"Well, your mother's pretty good to buy you that Harley Davidson."

"Hell, I robbed trains all summer to get that little honey. And then I had to rescue it from the junkyard."

"Did what all summer?"

"They hire me to rob Tweetsie—this old-timey train

that lures the tourists—three times a day. Proceeds go to the community chest.''

''Like Jesse James?''

Hart sneered. ''Used to see him in chapter plays on Saturday. Big gyp.''

''I ever tell you about the time Jesse came through Louisville, Kentucky? There was this famous detective named Bligh, see, that wanted to hunt Jesse down. One day he met a very good natured traveler at the Baltimore and Ohio Railroad station and they got to talking and Bligh set him up to a cup of coffee and in the course of the conversation, Bligh declared that as he neared retirement age, his one wish was that before he died he could at least *meet* Jesse James.

''The next day he tells several friends about the fine gentleman he chanced to meet. Few days later, he gets a postcard from Baltimore. Says, 'Dear Mr. Bligh, You have been quoted as saying on more than one occasion that if you could only meet Jesse James, you'd be content to lie down and die. Well, Mr. Bligh, you can now stretch out, lie down, and die. The gentleman you met the other day in the railroad depot at Louisville was yours sincerely, Jesse Woodson James.'''

''Don't sound like the Jesse James *I* saw.''

''Blackjack,'' I said, and sighed.

''Well, I better get back up there. She'll raise holy hell if she wakes up and catches me gone. Never saw such a bright moon.''

''Yeah,'' I says, ''and raised up like we are, that hood pointed at the man in the moon . . .''

''Well, see you around, Lucius.'' Hart opens the door and drops down to the concrete. ''You staying in town awhile?''

''Just passing through.'' I wondered how Hart would react to the silo. ''Sleeping in that old silo outside Sweetwater.''

"*Silo? Silo?*"

"You don't go for *si*los?"

"That kills me, boy."

After he went in, I sat awhile in the Hudson Hornet, on the driver's side, staring at the moon's sheen on the windshield.

In the headlights that struck my shirt on the highway, I didn't look, at midnight, like a good risk to the cars that passed me up. I walked the highway, up and down hills, to the muddy road that led into the woods.

In the silo, I lay on corn shucks and looked up through cracks in the roof at the moon. Listening for snakes and running my hands over my body, imagining black widows, kept me awake until I was too weary to sleep. Hearing dogs bark up one of the hollows, I remembered sitting in the quiet of my sanctuary one night, listening to the wild dogs barking, running along the river, shattering the black stillness, and I knew I wanted to be a writer because I wanted to tell about the dogs and the river and the way they made me feel. Then I listened to Sweetwater Creek flow by the silo at the end of the path, and when the frogs got quiet, I even heard sand in the foundations of the silo trickle down the bank into the creek. The blasting and the rumble of the machines had loosened the weak foundations, so that though the machines had been quiet for weeks, the earth still moved.

I don't tell Bucky and Earl nor anybody else stories about Straight-Hair and Fatsy, or Buck Jones, or Jesse James, or Huck and Jim anymore. The storytelling ritual I continue, in the absence of a community of warm-bodied, hot-eyed listeners, in the solitude of writing. The two-part nightly ritual no longer delays sleep: I don't review, serial-fashion, the events of my life anymore. If I'd had no thoughts back then of passing the images of my life on to posterity, I had sober intentions of preserving them for myself. Nor the second part of the ritual that ended in sleep: the conversations with God. I long ago realized that my conversations with God were monologues, and as I wander over America, the beautiful greed for adventure so exhausts me each night that the ritual of remembrance has disintegrated.

I wondered whether the Blue Goose Hotel was real or an image in a dream I would have after I fell asleep. Drowsing, I tried to distinguish between things I'd dreamed and the things I'd actually done. Hunger and sleeplessness blurred the distinction. But it had never mattered before. It wasn't liable to now.

Shining through the breaks in the roof of the silo, the moon, I thought, fell on one of the few remaining romantics. I've always seen everything in my life by the light of a full moon. "The unmoonlit life is not worth living." The only gospel I ever took to my heart is the gospel of dreams. More an addiction than a habit, and I'd long been hooked. Escape—it's called escape if carried too far, if you don't snap out of it. My family and Cherokee offered plenty to escape from. But, no, I reject the word "escape." The word is "surrender."

# 20

# *Sweetwater*

During the night, the caterpillars and bulldozers didn't move. They waited. The weeds and the wild flowers didn't soften their arrogance, their aura of purpose. They would do their job quickly, efficiently. As soon as a way was found to dissolve the human element. I sneered and shook my head and spat on a blade as I passed.

Four old men sat on the bench in front of the Sweetwater Trading Post. Dressed up. Maybe she had died in the night, or killed herself, walking in the dark. Pale-faced, they turned on me looks of suspicion.

Staying on the side opposite the hotel, I walked on up the hill. At one house, an old lady in a black-and-white polka-dot rayon dress moved slowly down the steps, sideways, carrying a covered plate. On the porch stands another woman, shading her eyes against the sun, trying to see something over at the Trading Post. Both stopped and watched me pass. Suspicious and resentful, they looked straight across the road at me.

The church doors open, and the bell begins to toll. In Kearney, Missouri, Jesse James stands up and asks the congregation to pray for his wayward brother Frank, called Buck.

At the edge of the woods, I searched for the gravestone that had tripped me the night before. Giving up, I headed deeper into the woods until a blaze of roses five times my height stopped me.

The rosebush had entwined itself around a pine tree. They must have started together from sprigs. The roses grew profusely and the weight of the bush had deformed the pine as it reached for more sunlight. But its needles were dark green and the sap smelled strong and pure. Younger vines grew from the ground at the outer rim of the tree where the branches had sagged under snow in winter and now roses. The new vines had pulled the branches even lower.

Through a narrow gap, I eased in under the tree. I put a petal in my mouth and enjoyed its velvet on my tongue. Morning sun sifted through the thickly woven dome, and hues of brown, green, and red pulsed in the light.

"I knew," I said, aloud, "as I stood there in the morning sun under the coolness of the trees that this freak of nature was the most beautiful thing I had ever seen. And here, so the story goes, stood Jesse James in the moonlight one September night in about the year 1880, winding his gold watch, taken, it was later learned, from the wife of a judge who had unfortunately bought passage on the Mammoth stage."

The roses and their thorns were so tangled up in the tree that climbing the pine, I felt as though I was also climbing the bush. When I finally looked down through whorls of petals, tiny green leaves, needles, thorns, and crusty bark from a limb near the top, my cowboy shirt was frayed, and the backs of my hands stung.

God's spy, I looked down on ten or eleven roofs of the town. A group of people crossed the street at a long angle from the Trading Post toward the Blue

Goose Hotel, where the sun on the windows glared at them. In the vanguard, a few women wore old-fashioned bonnets. Some of the men hung back.

I was certain, as I watched them mount the broken steps and stand outside the glassed-in porch, that they were paying their first visit as a group to Miss Ransom—ever. But they seemed charged with a mission, and they came, no doubt, to the walls of the fort armed with the best of intentions, all of which I, the stranger, knew would fire blanks. They stood there, awash in heat waves from the boiling sun, until one man opened the front door and shut it again four times before he went on in. They turned their backs a few moments, then shifted sideways, glancing through the windows like passengers on a train.

She appeared at the tall front window of the west tower, visible from the waist down. The townspeople didn't see her. The green shade wavered once at the side and I saw half of her face. I hoped she hadn't seen the tree quaver when I climbed and that the roses hid me now.

When the missionaries went in, twenty minutes later by my radium-handed, gold-plated Elgin wristwatch, I started down the tree. Looking up, I see that a wasp's nest, like a faded Japanese lantern, hangs within inches of where my head, dome of many-splendored glass, had spun images. That sent hot chills through me as I climbed down. Standing on the ground in the enclosure of curving limbs, needles, and roses, my feet humming from the strain, I sucked my wounds. On my empty stomach, the blood was sickening.

I come out of the woods just as the missionaries emerge from the wall of panes, heads bowed low. They cross the road at an angle and enter the church. As I pass, the choir is singing ''Power in the Blood.''

The good, duped, disappointed, doomed old folks of Sweetwater were all in church, marking time with toe taps and fan beats. One day soon, they would make way for the course of empire, and join the fourteen thousand Indians of the Cherokee nation who had made way for *them*. Under the eyes of Zara Jane Ransom, I would take a last loving look at the town Jesse James passed through. I would leave Miss Ransom's privacy enshrined.

Between the Trading Post, the first building on the precipice side above the creek, and the Blue Goose Hotel, the last building on the side where the mountain continues to rise, I stood in the road. Dappled by the shade of a maple, looking up the long steep block, I see what Jesse saw. Nothing seems to have changed. Along the sides of the road, wooden walkways had probably raised the stroller above the dust, mud, and ice. Now, cracked, tipped, jutting slabs of concrete showed where a sidewalk had been attempted on a more metropolitan model. No other attempt at change had left a trace. Taking a last look, I try to see Jesse and Frank, dressed like cattle buyers or railroad agents delayed in a little mountain town, walk down the boardwalk. But in the absence of moonlight, all I see is the empty town of eleven buildings, deflecting where it could the bright noon sun.

When I was gone, back on the *Polestar* bound for India, I'd see this place, I hoped, in the light it needed to reveal itself. Living my own pale life as a seaman, maybe I could simultaneously live the week in Jesse James's life that had transformed Zara Ransom's.

As I turned to go, I caught a glimpse of a man on the porch of a house three doors up the hill. He seemed to be shading his eyes against the sun. To see what? I turn, see an old white horse, grazing in a vacant lot beside the old store, and when I look again toward the porch, I realize the man is beckoning to *me*. He backs toward the front door, waving me on. I walk toward the steps that lead up to the yard.

When I reach the sunken flagstone walk, the man is standing on the threshold, the screen pushed out, the door open behind him. "You— looked like— you was— about to— leave— town," he says, in a strangely jerky, taut voice, as though he's on the verge of gagging. "Come on in."

I step inside. At the end of a cool hallway, the back door stands open. A few feet from the edge of the back porch, the mountain continues to rise, large-leaved vines sprawled over it. The wide door to the living room is open. Then I sense that the man is gone. He seems to be stomping around on the porch. A shattering fit of coughing convulses him. I walk on into the living room. The shades are drawn against the sun, the room is cool, but in a space between shade and sill, I see the man's legs as he dances in front of the window. I stand in the middle of the Thirties and wait. The man comes in, stuffing a handkerchief into his back pocket.

"They come *on* me like that sometimes. Sit down, boy."

I sat in a chair beside a small round table where a pitcher of lemonade sweats on a carved, brass tray. There's only one glass. The man pours and hands it to me. As I take the glass, he catches me looking at his missing thumb. Jesse lost the tip of one in a raid with Quantrill.

"In those days, boy, railroadin' was rough." He sits across the room. "I ain't the only one noticed you walking around. Reckon you been reading that article." I nodded, sipping the lemonade. "Well, you're looking at the man that helped get it wrote. That young reporter come up from Boone to write about *me* — offered me twenty dollars just to talk about the old railroad before it was Tweetsie — and ended *up* writing about *her*. He said something about Jesse James being an old railroad man, too — something smart aleck like that, and I let it drop about Miss Ransom, and he took hold like a starving dog on a bone. So if you come to get what he couldn't, you may as well as to stayed home. I *told* what little *I* know."

Noticing that the room appeals to me, the man says, "Joists in this house is all hand-planed and fitted. Hardly no nails atall. Wooden pegs, hand-turned. My people built nearly ever' house in Sweetwater and the ones they didn't build did a swan dive right off the mountain into the creek. One snowflake too many, they say. And when they sic those wrecking machines on the whole town, I'm gonna open me up a tourist court in Florida. Ain't *no*body staying close't by to Sweetwater."

"What's gonna happen?" I step onto a back porch in the back of my mind, feel the rumble of machines in the loose boards underfoot.

"Ever see a picture of that Jap town they bombed?"

I look through a bombsight at the negative of an aerial photograph. "What I remember is the newsreels."

"Like *it* was — except with a frosting of concrete over it. You come just in time. Take a good look."

I saw the flash, then the colossal puff. I saw the shadow of the man about to flog his horse that the blast cast like dye onto the pavement in Hiroshima.

"Damn three-lane highway, the way I hear it," he says, "— right where you're sitting."

"Why?"

"Boone is a farm town that wants to be metrop'lized and pull in all the parkway tourist trash. They got a outdoor drammer that gyps part of 'em. 'Fore you get to Blowing Rock, they's a little toy train called Tweetsie that some days a thousand city folks pays to ride. And Blowing Rock ain't nothing *but* a tourist town— I mean it got borned in the cracked head of some butthole sitting in a office in New York. They got three auction houses full of junk imported from all the points of the compass. Some way they're all in on that nightmare, like a half dozen people on a party line, so they figure, wouldn't it be the berries if we could just hook all our wagons to the same star and ride it to the moon? Way to do *that* is to build a highway over the mountains between Boone and Blowing Rock."

"But I came *up* on one."

"Oh, but the new one'll get you there three minutes quicker—and no curves! So what they're gonna do is shove us all down the mountain and burn the houses where they land—wood better than what you'd find in any new house today. Time. They say they ain't got time, because they lost the summer, and winter comes sudden and takes a hard hold up here. When *she* goes, it *all* goes. Wasn't for her, I reckon most of us would of been long gone. We woulda gone *out* on the highway you come *in* on. Lots of 'em *has*. Claimed she give 'em the creeps, and moved on out. How far *you* come?"

"New York."

"And you going back empty-handed?"

"Empty-headed, you say?"

"Handed!"

"Yes!"

"Then you come to the right man. I'm moving out soon. Few days from now. My wife promised that if they couldn't get Miss Ransom to see the truth, she'd go. We got all that money the state give us for the house, but she won't go, long as Miss Ransom's on her throne up yonder.''

"The truth? You mean about the wrecking crew?''

"Not just that— she don't know about *that* or won't believe the sound of it. But the taxes. They got till next week to persuade her to go to the poor farm or the wreckers'll come in and tear it down around her. They've done alerted Sheriff Odom. I figure Odom's trying to do the right thing by her, trying hard as a man can, but they got that law waiting for him to carry it out. And if he has to, my wife says, as sure as they's a sun in the sky, we'll bury the lady next day. And some claim they'll bury a few machine jockeys before sundown the same day. For my part, they ought to be able to see she's as old and worn out as that mare down by the store that's headed for the glue factory soon's we all pull out.''

"Does she know about the back taxes on the hotel?''

"—And her living off what folks send over and leave on the back porch. What? Yeah, she *knows* about that. But nobody can make it sink *in*. They hoped she'd sell when she saw that, and go to the poorhouse, and not know that they'd tore down the hotel.''

"What about her relatives?'' I asked, glad to have found someone who was willing to talk. Trying to shove away, for the moment, the question, why?

"Not a living soul. But that ain't what I started to show you.'' He took a small black box from the fringed piano stool and crossed the room and bent over and opened the box. "Know whose watch that is?''

"Yours?''

"What do you mean, mine? Does that look like *my* watch? I got on a *wrist* watch. Only *chain* watch I ever owned got smashed in that wreck on the mountain just before they stopped the run. If ever a son-of-a-bitch ort to been shot— Anyway, damnit, this here's the one Jesse James dropped on the road as he was leaving town.''

I remembered mention of it in the newspaper article. ''That's very nice.''

''Nice? Nice? Goddamn it, that's Jesse James's own watch. Dropped it in front of that old brick silo down yonder and I found it when I was just a kid. Listen. Hear it tick? It's still ticking. Now listen here.'' He points with the thumbless hand at his chest. ''Go ahead, I don't mind, hell, I don't mind. It ain't in the catching stage, either, so don't rare back like that. Nice? Hell, mister, how much you give me for that damn thing? I ain't got all night. You want me to die standing right here talking to you? You think I want to die in this town, right in the middle of all this dying? Ain't I got a right to die in some place where they's young boys chasing bare-assed girls and the heat's dry and the ocean's cool?''

''I've never been to Florida myself.''

''Don't tell *me* it's nice. How much you give me for it?''

I stood up. ''I'm sorry, mister. I'm just passing through.''

''Give me what you can. The wife's afraid to go just with what we've *got*. She thinks you have to be rich to cross the state line.''

''I hope you make it, mister.''

''All right, you young bastard.''

''Mister, you want to sell that watch or eat it?''

''Well, you forced me into it. I'll *tell* you!''

''Tell me what?''

''About the time Billy the Kid robbed the train I was—''

"That's the best lemonade I ever tasted, mister. Thanks."

The sun was so bright when I reached the steps, I threw up my arm before my face. The watch hit me on the shoulder and skidded down the steps.

"You young tramps don't believe in nothing!"

# 21

# *Jesse James Under the Rose-Pine Tree*

I searched the hotel for an hour, listening to the rising of the stage. When I came down the steps, she's standing by the front door, her hand on the knob. She opens it as I walk toward her on the carpet, and the moonlight pouring onto the glassed-in porch bursts into the lobby as through a sluice in a dam, lapping at my feet.

"Yes, ma'am, I see it. The door to the Blue Goose Hotel, where you met Jesse James about seventy years ago. He's waiting for you now up there in one of those rooms—and I bet you don't know which. You never found out. That's why you go from one to another, more a transient in each than any of the guests *ever* were.

"I almost left town at noon today. I don't want to hurt you, this is not just a story, I could tell you why I— But I can see you won't listen. And you'll never tell me, will you? You put *me* right with all the others . . . I see the door okay.

"I also see you going *out* that door one day soon because you can't pay your taxes, and I see tourists flooding in here to see where Jesse slept with— Maybe the same joker who thought he hit on a good thing with that frozen custard shack down the road. You ever see it? I bet all the shades are drawn on the town side, so you won't have to be reminded. But if *you* can't find Jesse's room, that joker *can*. Any one of them will do. And the card on the door facing will tell all about it—*his* version.

"One time I was hitchhiking across country—now this will take just a second to tell—and I dropped down a hundred miles out of my way just to hit Saint Joseph, because I wanted to see where Jesse James lived out his last days. They'd moved the House on the Hill down to Highway 71. It's surrounded by a Jesse James tourist court, a service station, a dance hall, a souvenir stand. You can buy hot dogs, beer, soft drinks, and an assortment of plastic mementos. Nearby is a bronze monument of a rider for the pony express, opening the West at forty miles an hour. But what *they* want to see is the place where a bullet opened up Jesse James.

"'STOP!' the neon sign blazes. 'SEE THE BULLET HOLE!' I saw it. Made by a cannon—a cannon out of which tourists have been shot, barbed with their ball-point pens, their stubby pencils, their penknives, so that *their* names will be immortal—the lucky ones around the hole, the hordes of others all over the wall and the floor. Do you want that desecration for the Blue Goose Hotel?

"All *I* want is for you to *tell* me, any way you want to tell it, and I'll be true to your words in the magazine that publishes it, and it'll be a memorial to him that nobody can ravage. *Harper's Bazaar* has already told me they'll buy it. I don't even want the money. I'm saying it's yours for telling me, yours to pay those taxes so you can spend your last days in the Blue Goose Hotel, instead of in the poorhouse."

The old man with the fake watch had slipped me an ace, and she'd forced me to play it. But I was concealing the killing fact that, paid taxes or not, the hotel would come down, within a few weeks.

Miss Ransom let her hand fall from the knob. I closed the door as we stepped down to the porch into the wavering flood of light, the pattern of frames across the floor.

"Come after dark, the way you came tonight."

"So you were watching me."

"No. I heard you in the trees. I heard every step in the hotel."

"Whatever you say, Miss Ransom. Believe me, I—"

"I want cash."

"Ma'am?"

"I'll tell it every night for three nights."

"Fine."

"But I want cash."

"Well . . . Well, I'll call my editor, and when I come tomorrow night, I'll give it to you."

"I must have three hundred dollars. Not all at once."

"May as well."

"I am eighty-eight years old. I may be dead when you come some night. I refuse to accept money for something I have not given."

"Well . . ."

"And do not hand it to me. Hide it—one hundred dollars at a time—in the hotel."

"Sure. Where?"

"Anywhere. And don't tell me."

"How will you—?"

"I'll find it."

"But—"

"I know the Blue Goose Hotel better than you know your own body."

"I don't doubt that."

Her look says good night. Or *go*. "I've forgotten your name. Please do not remind me. It will be easier to forget you." She opened the door. "Pass through the reading room and leave by the side."

Walking among the bulldozers toward the silo, I doubted that my agent would advance me a penny. "Truth is beauty." "Beauty is difficult." With such talismanic phrases I tried to ward off the evil of my conning Miss Ransom's story out of her. In the name of art for art's sake, I justified the con.

In the morning, I thumbed a ride into Blowing Rock, where I called Mendell Sarett, my agent, who informed me that the air-conditioning unit had broken down and that everyone was "*pos*itively *roast*ing, Lucius, darling." I outlined the story and quoted the old lady's price. Mendell Sarett couldn't *pos*-sibly advance me three hundred dollars on a story of that description. If I wanted to take the risks, I could write the story on speculation, and if it was at all salable, she would place it quickly. Okay?

Meanwhile, I strolled into the Blowing Rock branch of the Watauga National Bank, exchanged a dollar bill for dimes, then strolled out, feeling like neither Bucky nor Earl, but somebody in between, a book of blank checks concealed in my pocket.

All day I walked the mountain paths around Sweetwater, weary with déjà vu, trying to forget my check-passing plan to risk prison to get Bucky off the chain gang, trying to decide whether the romance of Jesse James was worth risking the reality of the penal system. But just before the old man closed the trading store, I bought pencils and Blue Horse tablets. After the sun went down and the moon came up, I sneaked through the woods into the Blue Goose Hotel.

After a rarefied game of hide-and-seek, I found her

sitting in the lobby, where she told the first part of her story. Her voice drew me into a zone of being where the facts and illusions of everyday life and the problem of making distinctions between them were irrelevant. That I was totally and perfectly in that zone was as much a fact as an illusion—if that mattered—and it didn't. While I was there, I was not aware of being in the zone. Later, I realized that I had been there before, with Mammy when she told stories, with Earl as Mr. French in Greenbrier. *With* them? No, *because* of them. I was in it alone.

Finished, Zara Ransom mounts the steps, stiff as a poker.

In one of the letter slots behind the desk in the lobby, I stick a check for one hundred dollars, wondering how she will react when she discovers that I've gone back on my promise to pay cold cash through the nose.

At the population sign nailed to the fence, I cross out 73 with a pencil and write 78, including Charlta Ransom, Zara's mother, Davis Woodring, Jesse and Frank James, and Lucius Hutchfield.

Day breaking in the silo woke me.

Writing in the ruined silo reminded me of "Glory in a Sanctuary," a story I wrote when I was ushering at the Bijou—about a famous bandit in France who escapes his obsessed pursuer by taking sanctuary in a cathedral, and while he's imprisoned there, he begins to write great music, and plays it on the church organ, having taught himself about music from scratch, and his fame spreads throughout the Western world. And I was aware now as I wrote in the silo of the many sanctuaries of my own where I had written very different things— Mammy's circus wagon turned into a coal house, before the Bijou time, and the old chicken

house when we moved, and that back porch converted
into a little room in the house on the bluffs above the
river, the caves under the Bijou, the tower by the
river, feeling then the presence of Yeats's and James
Joyce's towers in Ireland, and the hallway at the head
of the stairs at Pearl's, one of our landladies that I
wrote a story about, and the basement room on
Sequoyah that Daddy took over when I left for New
York, and the bare, iron cabin on the *Polestar*.

Miss Ransom's Bostonian manner of speaking,
picked up and preserved unaltered from her affected
mother, drew from me a Jamesian response. A legend
of Jesse James rendered in the style of Henry James,
transcribed on Blue Horse tablets with a number-two
pencil bearing the legend "Ride Tweetsie" and honed
to a point on sandstone blasted out of the side of the
mountain—thus I preen my bizarre appetite for irony
and paradox.

*I do not know who my father was, but my mother assured
me again and again that the blood of Boston gentility
flowed through my veins. That may well be, but because of
that Boston gentility, which somehow found its elegant way
to the servants' quarters of that house which I have always
imagined was on Beacon Hill, I wore on my body from
infancy until my fifteenth year a faint film of dust from
roads that led always away from Boston. We had always
enough money to live well; and as a servant, my mother,
blooming out of the Glasgow slums, learned not only how to
arrange a rendezvous with the son, but also how to behave
like the mistress, and how to behave among men such as the
master.*

*No one we encountered betrayed the slightest doubt but
that she was what she pretended to be: a widowed
gentlelady with sufficient income to live in the manner and*

*in the towns in which she pleased, and she was pleased, it must have seemed to those looking forward to seeing her again — although she was arrogant, stingy, and snobbish — never to visit the same town twice.*

*My dear mother was convinced that her reputation, although both created and exposed solely within the walls of that house on Beacon Hill, would some day confront her across the lobby desk of some resort hotel, as if her reputation were a physical thing, capable of following her and provided by the devil with funds equal to her own. This strange routine, somehow, over the years, became known, and the story of the widow and her child, now a lovely girl of fourteen, unmistakably genteel, who moved from one resort to another, did indeed one day await her in a little town on the Carolina coast.*

*There was no mistaking, not even by the girl at her side, the smile and the way the clerk pointed the handle of the pen toward her as she stepped forward to sign the register. With that gloved hand still raised, Charlta Ransom, as my mother called herself, turned and touched my cheek with the tips of her fingers and whispered, "They know." Without a word, I followed her out of the hotel, but what she said to me in the lobby became, as soon as I felt upon me the eyes of those seated on the porch, the two most horrible words in the world.*

*We crossed the Piedmont and rose into the mountains. In Winston-Salem my mother had learned of a town in the mountains, one of the highest in America, and one morning when I opened my eyes, I looked down at a sea of clouds and what appeared to be the very spine of the world.*

*I have never known what reason Sweetwater ever had for being. Either something extraordinary or nothing at all could cause men to build a town so high, so perched on the edge. I like to think nothing at all, that it is its own reason for being. It was here when we arrived, it is here now, and in every sense that matters, it will always, like the mountains, be here.*

*BLUE GOOSE HOTEL. When my mother saw that sign, she turned one of her rare smiles upon the town and the mountains. Perhaps her reputation — she said it as one would say "my lover" — would stand in the road, the devil's money jingling in his pockets, and smile, too, and turn and go away, never imagining that it was here that Charlta Ransom had decided to spend the rest of her life.*

*No summer people sat on the porch. A few people sat in the lobby, but when they stared, they stared frankly and honestly. And one man, I remember, stood up, as though that enabled him to see better, while the newspaper he had been holding floated to the floor, carpeted, I saw, as I crossed the lobby a step behind my mother, with a rug that bespoke the future of the hotel — it would have to last until the hotel nailed up its windows.*

*The room to which we were shown had its secrets perhaps, but with secrets of our own, we never sought out others. My mother sat on a hard chair by the window and gazed out at the wisps of mist that moved through the tops of the pines. Suddenly, she rose and left the room. That was probably the second and final impulsive act of her life.*

*When she returned near midnight, she stood at the window, her hand resting on the curved back of the chair, and, aware that I had sat up in bed, she said, "You are never to leave this room except with me, after all the lights in Sweetwater are out."*

*I did not learn until 1928, forty-eight years after our arrival in Sweetwater, that sometime before midnight my mother had bought the Blue Goose Hotel. Although she behaved as though she owned it — I often heard her voice in the hall, never stern but always clear — it never occurred to me that she might.*

*From my window, I saw nothing of the town, only the pine forest, the birches, the sycamore, the buckeye, the oak,* the cedar, the ferns, the mountains and the clouds below, the clouds, oh, my God, the everlasting clouds, and fields of wild flowers blazing in the distance, snow so prevalent that I knew what the North Pole must be like, and a forest fire smoking all the month of March.

But my mother, I sensed by echoes of one kind and another, arrogantly kept at a distance from the townspeople. They were tolerant, but they came to resent her. The tone of voices in the hall changed over the winter, while my mother's remained the same.

In April, a chopping sound woke me one bright morning. An old man going into the woods was all I had seen of a human being out that window, so I stood there in my dressing gown with the sunlight burning through the pane, seeing nothing, the bright sun was so direct. But when I stepped aside, I saw a young man with an ax raised over his shoulder, the sun flashing on the blade, wet with the juices of the pine, his head back, his bare chest heaving. He could not see me now, I realized, because the sun glanced back at him off the window. If I stepped back into the full flash of the sun, I would not be able to see him, either. I moved as though responding to the sun, until the window and the lace curtains framed me again. I knew that for him the sun burned my thin nightgown as if it were mist.

He seemed so alone under the pines, but I sensed that his, unlike my own, was a sweet solitude that was born with the first stroke of the ax and would linger in his body after the last.

I sat by the window all day long and watched the pines fall around him. A little boy brought him water; an old man sat on a trunk and talked to him and after a few hours got up and walked away, leaning on the cane he had whittled while sitting there; but I knew that the young man was conscious every moment of the face in the window overlooking the pines.

He worked a week, chopping and hauling the pines

*away. I had a mortal fear of my mother, who taught me, since I was old enough to understand the human voice, that men were evil and cruel. In our wanderings, she made use of every opportunity to point that out. If a man gripped his wife's arm in suppressed anger, Mother nudged me and pointed with a glance of her cold gray eyes. The female tutors who came stiffly to my rooms in the various hotels all seemed to have had previous training from Charlta Ransom. I was an impressionable student, and my mother impressed me with everything she said or did. I feared her, although she never struck me.*

*I was afraid of the boy who cut the pines, but the fear he inspired was so different from what I felt in my mother's presence that my confusion and fascination made me impulsive and reckless in my daydreams. But my body felt drugged and cumbersome as I moved about the room.*

*One night he threw a note tied to a pine chip through my open window. He could not spell, his grammar was poor. What he said terrified me, but after a while I realized that what I felt was also elation. I answered his note, intentionally misspelling, using poor grammar, but I couldn't resist signing my name with a Spencerian flourish: Zara Jane Ransom.*

*By July, we had managed to meet on the back porch of the hotel. As I felt the hard thumping of my heart, I knew how a frightened bird must feel. I was startled when the boy emerged from the shadows and crossed the porch in the moonlight and spoke my name. "Z-Z-Z-Za-ah-ara — Zara," he said. All he managed to stutter that night was my first name and his own full name — Davis Woodring.*

*Before the first week in September, he had told me that he loved me and I let him hold my hand, which prevented him from speaking at all. My mother, of course, never knew. Perhaps she drank, and passed her nights in a deep sleep.*

*Ritualistically, she came to my room every night some-*

time before or after midnight and took my hand, and I went with her down the deserted halls, down the narrow back stairway, rank with an animal odor, and out onto the porch at the rear of the hotel. We always wore simple but elegant dresses, especially if there was a moon, and often she let me get a few steps ahead of her on the path along the mountainside and I felt her eyes on me. In her own way, she was proud of me. Of the figure I presented to the moon.

On one of the walks in the moonlight in early September, she came up behind me and took my hand and turned me gently around and kissed the corners of my mouth. That brief moment of bliss, the only one we ever shared, ended abruptly with the sharp little shriek that came from my mouth. It was the first time I ever knew that I was capable of hurting my mother, but I had not intended to. And I could not explain that it was not her kiss that startled me — although there is nothing more startling than impulsive expressions of affection from cold people — but the sight of a man, leaning against a tree a hundred yards away, winding, I learned later, a gold watch, at midnight in the middle of the forest. At his back was a deformed pine tree to which clung profusely a mammoth rosebush whose briars twisted and looped among the branches and whose erratic blooms now seemed to open in the moonlight.

## 22

# Pleasure-Dome

At noon, the tale transcribed, my finger aching, I stepped out of the silo. Not the trigger finger, like Jesse's—the third finger, which bore a writer's callus by the time I was thirteen.

A crust of grasshoppers clung to the bricks of the silo. "Worst this year," I'd heard somebody say, "than ever I remember seein' 'em." Whatever juice had once flowed here, the grasshoppers had gotten years ago.

From the creek bank, the Blue Goose Hotel, visibly balanced on the hill, looked like a decrepit Xanadu. I hadn't forgotten the lines I'd memorized to defeat boredom, painting the engine room of the *Polestar:*

> In Xanadu did Kubla Khan
> A stately pleasure-dome decree:
> Where Alph, the sacred river, ran
> Through caverns measureless to man
>     Down to a sunless sea.
> So twice five miles of fertile ground
> With walls and towers were girdled round:
> And there were gardens bright with sinuous rills,
> Where blossomed many an incense-bearing tree;
> And here were forests ancient as the hills,
> Enfolding sunny spots of greenery.

> But oh! that deep romantic chasm which slanted
> Down the green hill athwart a cedarn cover!
> A savage place! as holy and enchanted
> As e'er beneath a waning moon was haunted
> By woman wailing for her demon-lover!

I washed my hands and face in the creek and went on upstream to the woods above the town.

From the top of the rose-pine tree, I hoped to discover a shortcut over the mountain to Blowing Rock. I climbed very slowly to avoid disturbing the wasp's nest and sat very still, fresh thorn wounds stinging. I saw a trail that appeared to go to Blowing Rock, but I was reluctant to leave this dome of roses and needles. I turned my gaze downward at the girl who stares over her mother's shoulder at the man directly beneath me. Hart Woodring's possible blood relation to Davis Woodring interested me less, at the moment, than his nascent relation in spirit to Jesse James, who gazes at the girl in the long dress, her mouth open, her eyes open, startled and surprised.

I looked out at the Blue Goose Hotel, that "miracle of rare device," but as a physical image of what I had been feeling since Zara Ransom stopped talking, it was deficient. So was the tree. Both were pleasure-domes, like the Bijou, like the *Polestar,* like Bucky's cell in Greenbrier. But the shadow that lay across my imagination came from a different "dome of pleasure." To help focus my thoughts, I said the rest of the poem aloud:

> A damsel with a dulcimer
> In a vision once I saw:
> It was an Abyssinian maid,
> And on her dulcimer she played,
> Singing of Mount Abora.
> Could I revive within me

> Her symphony and song,
> To such a deep delight 'twould win me,
> That with music loud and long,
> I would build that dome in air,
> That sunny dome! those caves of ice!

Zara Ransom's voice had sent me into the Pleasure-Dome, where I felt pure pleasure. Everyday life is an effort to disentangle facts and illusions. Those are rare moments in our lives when we transcend captivity in fact-and-illusion through pure imagination and dwell in the Pleasure-Dome, a luminous limbo between everyday experience and a work of art. There is only one Pleasure-Dome, but when we enter it, we feel it is ours alone. This morning I'd tried to capture what I saw and felt in the Pleasure-Dome and preserve it in a work of art.

> And all who heard should see them there,
> And all should cry, Beware! Beware!
> His flashing eyes, his floating hair!
> Weave a circle round him thrice,
> And close your eyes with holy dread,
> For he on honey-dew hath fed,
> And drunk the milk of Paradise.

As I approached the filling station, I heard a woman's strident voice coming through the window on the second floor. I got into the back of the Hudson.

A three-seater station wagon, Mayview Manor painted on the side, swoops into the drive and stops in front of the pumps, the motor idling voluptuously.

A tall woman in a white uniform comes down the steps and walks toward the car, glancing at me. She came to a full stop, her long, thick chestnut hair bouncing on her shoulders, and took a quick straight look at me. She was pretty, as only certain very hard-working, self-sacrificing southern mountain women can be. She opens the door, gets in, slams the door, and flaps her hair with her wrists until it drapes over the back seat. Without looking at her, the Negro driver drove away.

Something hit the trunk of the Hudson behind my head. I look up through the windshield and there's Hart, sitting in the window in jockshorts, a grin on his face, an apple core in his hand, cocked back to throw.

"Looks like you got up on the right side of the moon this morning," I said, sticking my head out the back window, Frank talking to younger brother Jesse.

"Come on up. Have a bowl of corn flakes."

The stairway was dark and cool. Halfway up, I turned and watched a beat-up wrecker stop in front and a short, fat man in a soldier's cap, a changemaker flopping on his belly, walk toward the front door. Knocking on the door where the stairs end, I hear the man downstairs unlock the station door.

"Come on in." Hart thrusts his legs into some blue jeans.

Two bowls of corn flakes covered with fresh peach slices faced each other on a table in the middle of the kitchen. On a cot against the wall lay the black leather jacket. Under the cot, one boot leans against the other.

Hart pours milk on the cereal. "How's life in the silo?"

"All the comforts of a silo."

"That silo kills me. Say, you mind if I ask you a question? I been worrying it around in my mind what you doin' here. What I mean, I never seen anybody look so much like he's really doing something important—like tracking down a Russian spy or something. It ain't none of my business, but . . . ."

"First, *I* want to know something."

"Shoot."

"You any kin to Davis Woodring?"

"Who's he? I know all the *Wood*rings in through here. My daddy's name was Jody."

"What about Miss Zara Jane Ransom over in Sweetwater? Know *her?*"

"Yeah, I read about that in the paper. I used to hang around Sweetwater when I lived in Boone. Used to run errands for that old lady. Blue Goose Hotel?"

"Yeah. Well, I'm here about *her*. I'm writing a story about Miss Ransom's love affair with Jesse James back in about 1880."

He liked that so much, he tried not to show it. "Well, she never admitted *any*thing 'bout Jesse James. Just some damned rumor got started when some old man that's moving out blabbed. My momma swears it's a packa lies and somebody ort to take a horsewhip to that old man. But she made me stay out of Sweetwater when she found out I's doing Miss Ransom favors."

"You don't believe it about Jesse James?"

"No proof."

"Proof? What if it *were* true?"

Hart studies a minute, rolling a slice of peach around in his mouth, then he spits it out into his hand. "Excuse *me*. Got a rotten spot . . . I don't know. Never thought. Sure would be interesting, wouldn't it?"

"And what would you say if I said you remind me of Jesse James? Would you laugh at me?"

Hart grinned. "Why? *Do* I?"

"Enough for me to notice it."

"All right, men. Tonight it's the Sante Fe stage . . . Oh, you kidding me, boy . . . ."

On a brown paper sack that's lying on the table, I start to sketch Hart. "You got blue eyes."

"So have you."

"You know, they say all the outlaws of Jesse's time had steel blue eyes, like Jesse's. But yours don't blink all the time like his did. You know, he wasn't just a legend, he was a very interesting everyday person when he wanted to be. One of the things that set him apart from other outlaws, including his brother Frank, who almost never smiled, was his sense of humor. He was always cheerful, always joking. One time, he robbed the bank at Liberty near his home grounds, and he knew the banker's name was Bird, so he says, 'All birds should be caged—into the vault.' But at Northfield, the banker shoved ol' Jesse into the vault. Another joke on Jesse out of Northfield was that after he and Frank split up from the Younger boys, they stole two horses in the dark, and they stumbled all night long, and at dawn the horses turned out to be blind."

Well, actually one was blind in only one eye, but I thought Hart would like it better the way I told it.

"And he got a kick out of taking unnecessary risks. During the time he was laying low, after the Northfield disaster, he entered a horse race in Nashville right in front of the police and Pinkerton detectives, and—won."

Knew he *could* have won, but held back in a last-minute seizure of caution.

"And after they robbed the bank at Corydon, Iowa, while everybody was gathered to hear a political speech, Jesse rode up and got the speaker's attention as if he wanted to debate the issues (which he could do and often did in other situations). 'Mr. Dean, I rise to a point of order, sir.' 'What is it, friend and fellow citizen?' the orator asked. 'If anything of paramount importance, I yield to the gentleman on horseback.' 'Well, sir,' says Jesse, 'I reckon it's important enough.

The fact is, Mr. Dean, some fellows have been over to the bank and tied up the cashier, and if you-all ain't too busy, you might ride over and untie him. I've got to be going.'"

"I don't believe it," says Hart. But his face shows how much he likes it.

And my hand, drawing his picture, helps to focus his attention.

"You know, it's not certain Jesse's dead. Most of the people who identified his body had good reason to contribute to a hoax, to allow him to retire in peace. And seven or eight men since then have stepped into the spotlight to announce they are the real Jesse James coming out of hiding. One of them in 1948, and when he died in 1951, only two years ago, almost as many attended his funeral as they did the man Robert Ford shot. I'm not saying he *is* alive, but I'm not saying he's dead, either." Like Mammy believing that Uncle Luke, reported missing in the invasion of Italy, would finally show up at the screen door, someday. "But he was probably most alive when he made love to a girl he saw one moonlit night in Sweetwater."

"More power to him, by God," said Hart, thinking bitterly of his own failure to act. I see him standing in white noon sunlight among gleaming Thunderbirds, Buicks, Cadillacs, Pontiacs, MGs, Volkswagens, Jaguars, Mercedes, gazing upon the suntanned dove in the bird's-egg blue swimsuit.

"That's one of the main things that reminds me, Hart. Jesse was shy, too, and he ate his heart out over Zara Jane Ransom with an appetite as ferocious as yours for Sabra Van Ness. And if they had had motorcycles in his day, Jesse would have picked a Harley Davidson."

"Think so?"

"*Know* so."

"Did she tell you herself?"

"Last night. The first part."

Hart gets up and laughs and slaps things in the room, thrilled by what I told him. As he puts on his boots and stands at the table and drinks three-quarters of a quart of milk, I bask in the heat and light of the flame that ignited Hart.

"See?" I show him the drawing, and when he sits down to look at his resemblance to Jesse James, I begin to tell him the story. Giving the Jamesian manner a rest, I reach for the voice of Mark Twain, the one I always used on Bucky when we were little. Feeling the old compulsion to tell a story, I see that, without knowing it, Hart is in the vicinity of the Pleasure-Dome.

". . . So one day Jesse and Frank James come to Sweetwater, looking for a place to hide out until Jesse's wound heals. He'd never entirely recovered from the wounds he got in the Civil War riding with Quantrill, either. Jesse was an impetuous fellow who did exactly what he wanted to do. So they took one look at the Blue Goose Hotel and knew they'd found a place to rest, recuperate.

"They'd sit in the lobby and smoke, looking like traveling salesmen behind their newspapers, shoes shined to a luster there in the light of the kerosene chandeliers. They were polite to the guests, they played a little poker with the men, they loved to talk about politics and the state of the nation—about crops and cattle. And they seemed reasonably well informed on the subject of railroads, too.

"But Jesse was restless. One night, he takes a walk in the woods. The moon was bright. It came through small openings between the trees. He stops under a pine that has roses growing on it to wind his watch. Glancing back down the path, he sees a lovely girl of about fifteen in a long white dress, her black hair like velvet in the moonlight. Humming to herself, she holds a sprig of honeysuckle in her slender hands. The sound of Jesse winding his watch turns her where she's stopped on the path—and then she sees him."

"Great spoons alive!" says Hart. "Okay. Then what?"

"That's where she left off—till I see her tonight."

"Well, foot-fire, Lucifer! That's a dirty damned trick— get a body up in the air like that and say—"

"See you later and tell you more."

"Well, I got to rob a train anyhow," he said, and reached for his garish cowboy shirt.

Walking between a Jaguar and a Mercedes with the intention of looking over the hedge for a glimpse of Sabra Van Ness, I see her immediately. It took no effort at all to see her through Hart's eyes, because I'd seen her before through my own—on the stage of the Bijou, singing "Heartaches," and in the Garden of Eden in the Market House, sacking Concord grapes.

The wide ledge on which she lay, on top of a narrow yellow towel, seemed made to complement her long blond hair, her pale blue swimsuit. Sunglasses coated with an opaque, silver substance hid the eyes Hart, no doubt, waited hours in the sun to see. The legs God had been afraid to chance twice lay ankle-touching-ankle, the legs tan but the soles pink as a baby's butt.

No, she didn't need a bikini to drive men "*in*sane." All she had to do was strum the insides of her thighs with her fingertips, with the unconsciousness of one who is bemused by the sun.

A middle-aged man and woman walk toward Sabra as if they own her but are afraid to touch her.

The man, tall, bronze, hairy, wearing zebra trunks, sandals, and a straw cap with a long bill, stops half a step beyond the girl's head, looks over his shoulder down into the silver oblongs that flash his own distorted image back up at him.

The woman, shapely, but made flabby by repeated crash diets, wore a black bathing suit, a wide-brimmed straw hat with a green silk band, and Greek sandals. She stops a few feet from father and daughter, walks on, stops again, and glances back disdainfully.

The father doesn't have to pick his nose to convince me he hasn't been in oil all his life, nor does the mother have to turn suddenly away with the rhythm of habit to convince me that she could prove her ancestors came over on the *Mayflower*. Getting no response, no human response, from the child on the lip of the pool, the father moves on.

I didn't want to leave without seeing Hart's mother in action, "hopping" tables. But I lacked the brass to barge in, wearing soggy clothes. Just as I started back down the long, winding, narrow drive, a truck pulled up to the service entrance, loaded with potatoes. "I been a-lookin' fer you," I said, reaching for the wire handle on the bushel basket.

"You have? What fer?"

"To help you carry in these 'taters."

Having set the basket down, I glanced through the window in the service door. Hart's mother, her hair up in a net, but still voluptuous, stands at a table at the end of the dining room, stands on one foot, the toe of the other foot raised slightly off the floor as she reared back to see what an old lady with a crimped smile was pointing at on the large, half-closed maroon menu. One hand on her hip, Hart's mother holds a pencil in the other, jabbing the air as if prodding it to yield the thing she has forgotten—whether they are or are not offering lamb chops tonight, maybe—her face turned up to the ceiling where the answer might be written. (Leering at Sabra Van Ness, you experience one kind of lunacy. Contemplating Hart Woodring's mother, a mature, seasoned, mountain woman, as she physically dredges up something momentarily forgotten, you experience *in*sanity even more benign.) Puncturing the air with a thrust of recognition and in the same instant putting her foot down, she smiles, with a charm that makes the old lady blush, and heads straight for the kitchen with a lope that makes me turn away, as I often do from something so beautiful it hurts.

In downtown Blowing Rock, I picked up the pay phone on impulse to put in a call to the Garden of Eden. I hadn't spoken in person to Anna Livia since the day we broke up in the Shanghai Gardens Restaurant, when she finally made the decision that a life of quiet desperation was to be preferred over a life of spectacular disintegration. Now she'd made a further decision, concerning a husband, children, a car, a mortgage on a ranch house (the ranch itself consisting of other ranch houses), instead of the old streetcars we'd dreamed of converting, and a church of *his* choice, no doubt, a convenient shopping center, and ultimately, the secretaryship of the Dogwood Festival.

I picked up the phone in a flush of sentiment, but when I told the operator it was a collect call, I knew she would hang up. I hoped my voice would have such an impact that she'd respond.

"Garden of Eden, can I help you?" Anna Livia's voice.

"Collect call for Cathleen Blackburn from Lucius Hutchfield, will you accept the charges?"

Long silence over the Sahara Desert.

She says, "I can't, Lucius," a catch in her throat, and hangs up.

I wished her well, and hiked back to Sweetwater as the sun sank and the mist in the valleys rose.

Had I really failed her? Having taken her to the Bijou to see a re-release of *Waterloo Bridge,* with Vivien Leigh as a ballet dancer, and later *The Red Shoes, The Tales of Hoffmann, An American in Paris,* and *The Spectre of the Rose,* that inspired her to dream of glory as a dancer, how can she ever say to her grandchildren, "Lucius Hutchfield failed me"? But she might with good reason have asked the question earlier, had I taken her with me when I saw Leslie Howard and Wendy Hiller in *Pygmalion,* a movie that aggravated the attitude I had already been showing toward her for three years. Then I remembered the last letter she wrote to me. The note she closes on goes through me like a cold needle: "You always told me you thought I could become a great dancer, but that night you got mad at me last spring, you said, 'I was lying,' and I always knew you were." I have an awful feeling that that will haunt me the rest of my life. I'm a fool. I deserve the pain of losing her, and I'll never lose the pain.

# 23

# Jesse James and Hart Woodring

From twilight to deep dark, listening to the rising of the stage, I searched for Zara Ransom. Finally, from one of the rooms, her voice came through the walls, telling me to leave the hotel and never come back. I had deceived her. Cash. She'd insisted on cash, and I'd left a check in a mail slot behind the lobby desk.

I thought and spoke fast and regretted it immediately. I'd heard, I told her, that some tough characters were convinced she had a cashbox full of money hidden in the hotel. If she was robbed, checks could be canceled; cash could not.

When she unlocked the door and let me in, she didn't appear frightened by images I'd put in her head. Simply convinced of the soberness of my argument.

I am in the Pleasure-Dome and Zara Ransom is in the middle of Part Two of her story when she stops talking, lays her hand on the windowsill, quickly but softly, as she might have laid it on my knee to quiet me. I listened with her, and heard nothing. She didn't seem certain. "What is that sound? It stays in the distance. Before, it was always in the daytime." She puts her hand back in her lap, among the folds of her dress, and continues.

After she finished the telling, I said, "It's probably

170

just a rumor—about that guy who thinks you've got money hidden in the hotel."

Tomorrow night, after the end, I'd tell her it was only a joke. Nobody, I'd say, has the heart to rob the sweetheart of Jesse James.

Wanting to know just how much better she knew the Blue Goose Hotel than I knew my own body, I slipped exhibit B in the case of Watauga Bank vs. Lucius Hutchfield under the carpet on the stairs.

When I left the Blue Goose Hotel, I didn't go to the silo. I had time, I hoped, to see the last showing of Marlon Brando in *Viva Zapata*. The path that led to the rose-pine tree and to the ledge with the view seemed to continue down the mountains and come out on the highway near Blowing Rock. But it ended half-way down in briars, large-leaved plants, ferns, and mud. The moon in the clouds shed little light.

The ticket booth was dark. A boy on a stepladder hands down huge letters to the manager, who stands under the unlit marquee. Ten-thirty by the clock in the booth. The marquee says: GENE AUTRY IN *VIVA ZAPATA*.

"What's this Mickey Mouse about Gene Autry?" I ask, standing on the curb, picking beggar's-lice from my pants, leaves from my hair.

A stack of letters in his arms, the manager turns, frowning. "We ain't took him down yet. That's where Marlon Brando goes. Didn't come in time. We keep an old Gene Autry movie and a Three Stooges comedy for emergencies."

"Hey, this the one where ol' Gene sings 'Back in the Saddle Again'?"

"Never paid it no mind."

"Mind if I catch the end of it?"

"Help yourself."

On the screen, Gene Autry is shooting cowboys off their horses. What had once seemed to me the most serious endeavor in the world now seemed strangely serious in a different way. Coming down the mountain, ripping through briars and weeds, I had gotten into the mood to watch Brando bring a legend alive. And here I stood, transfixed in the aisle, viewing once more the world I had known before I realized other worlds mattered at all—in which a desert strewn with dead bodies was followed by a mellow song around a campfire. I was aware that what I felt, as Gene Autry mounted his already moving horse, Champion, and rode after the leader of the outlaws, was not much different from the feeling I would have had watching Brando do Zapata. And I never even cared that much *for* Gene Autry.

The audience of summer residents and tourists and year-round townspeople seemed restless. They fidgeted and groaned. The dirty floor, gritty underfoot, and the smell of the air makes me feel I'm back with the Bijou boys in the Smoky Theater, full of country Hoosiers from Market Square.

Just as I settle into a seat, a fat woman in shorts, her hair in curlers, jabs me in the ribs. "Didn't Gene Autry die a few months ago?"

"No, ma'am," I said, annoyed. "That was Machine Gun Kelly."

"Oh. Must've been."

Gene Autry lassoed a villain and pulled him off his horse. "That's a buncha bull!" a drunk near the front row yelled. "That's not how Jesse James would have did it!" I peered between the heads of two lovers in front of me, who pull apart to see who yelled, and we see Hart Woodring sitting in the second row from the screen, his boots crossed at the ankles, resting on the top of the seat in the front row. "This stuff ain't real!" Hart yells, waving his arms in front of him like brushing cobwebs aside in a dark basement.

"Hey, cut your motor off down there. Some of us *like* Gene Autry," yells a deep masculine voice.

"You think it's really happening, don't you, boy?" says Hart, conversationally, not looking around, staring at the screen.

"You tell 'em, kid!" yells a husky female voice cured in whiskey.

The villain, who has a Derringer up his cuff, shoots Gene Autry and rides away into the hills.

"See that? See that?" says Hart, not yelling, trying to reason with the faceless unenlightened. He turns and looks at them. "Did you all see that? You'd never catch Jesse James pulling a dirty trick like that."

The manager comes loping down the aisle, arms swinging, hands flapping. I barely heard what the man says to Hart. "Listen, Hart, you gonna shut up or get out?"

Tilting his head back so the sun over the California landscape that twinkles on Champion's bridle and silver saddle lights Hart's face, Hart shuts one eye and aims the other at the manager, says, "Fuck *you*, Smiling Jack," not loud, but clear.

"Want me to throw you out of here?"

"Where's your army?"

"Okay. Okay! That done it." The manager strode back up the aisle.

"He's gone for a posse, folks!" says Hart.

Just as Gene Autry nods, sways, and smiles into the first line of "I'm Back in the Saddle Again," Sheriff Odom appears in the aisle opening, the manager at his side, pointing to the front row.

"Hey, Jesse James!" yells an old woman sitting on the aisle, one strap of her sundress drooping. "Here comes the law!"

As though sucked down a drain, Hart slides down in his seat. When the sheriff reaches the second row, he looks at the manager. I don't blame Hart for being scared of Sheriff Odom, but it still made me a little sick to see him cringe out of sight. Then Hart pops up on the other side of the theater, Gene Autry's campfire blazing over his shoulder.

"Hey, Dick Tracy! Over here!" He holds his hands up and, in silhouette against the screen, wiggles his thumbs at the sheriff.

Sheriff Odom moves along the aisle toward the other side, stumbling over the feet of spectators who pretend to be engrossed in Gene Autry. A blossom of popcorn bounces off the sheriff's cheek four or five seats from where Hart stands wiggling his thumbs. "Who threw that?" he yells, clapping his hands to his hips.

When the sheriff turns to leap across the seats at Hart, the boy has already ducked under again. I watch his progress across the theater floor by the way the bodies of the spectators move as they lift their feet for him to crawl through.

"Stop that boy!" the sheriff commands the audience. Popcorn rises and rains on Sheriff Odom. "I'm the law here! You people stop that little hellion!" He runs up and down the aisle and back and forth across the rows, looking for Hart. The manager shines his flashlight frantically over the faces of the audience, who protest.

"Over here, over here! Hey, Dick Tracy, here I am!" Hart is a few rows in front of me.

The sheriff plows down one row and grabs at Hart across two rows. Hart dives under the waves of moving heads.

"Light! Light! Give me some light in here!" yells the sheriff.

"The play's the thing" —I yell, unable to resist getting into the act—"wherein I'll get the goat of the sheriff!"

"Who said that?" yelled Sheriff Odom.

"Shakespeare!"

The audience got tickled, and popcorn shoots up and pours down on the sheriff as the house lights come on, bleaching Gene Autry, who is shooting it out for the last time. Then the screen goes white and the only sounds are the feet of the spectators and derisive shouts and cheers as Hart suddenly appears on the stage. One concerted moan of outrage, horror, and astonishment rises from the audience. I looked. The sheriff had drawn his pistol. He surprises himself so shockingly, he holsters it immediately, muttering, "I'm the goddamned law in this theater!"

Jesse hears the click, turns to receive the bullets from his own gun and to catch a glimpse of his friend, Bob Ford, behind the thickening veil of smoke.

"Hey, Dick Tracy, I'm up here!" yells Hart, arms up, thumbs wiggling, sticking his head out of his black leather jacket and tightly shutting one eye. Striding up and down in front of the screen, he tripped on a cable and fell off the stage. The manager rushes forward and grabs hold of the sleeve of his jacket. Hart drags him across the front of the theater to the exit door where Sheriff Odom catches him in his arms and gives him a bear hug that makes the audience groan. Then he releases him and catches him by the hair at the back of his head and hits him in the face with his fist.

I was in the lobby when the sheriff dragged Hart out of the auditorium, where the booing grew louder. Both the manager and Sheriff Odom look huge and red, sweat dripping profusely. The sheriff curses Hart rapidly, stridently, incoherently. In the black outfit, twisted on his body in the struggle, Hart looks very small. As people burst hostilely into the lobby, I went over to the sheriff.

I says, "Sir, I'm a friend of this boy's and I'd appreciate it if you'd let me take him home and keep him out of trouble.''

''What's your name?''

''James Austin Frank. I promise to keep him out of trouble.''

''You stay around him and *you* be in trouble before you know it.''

''Somebody sold this child beer. He's a minor. I think I know who, and I reckon those citizens coming up the aisle are like me, they wonder why you haven't closed that place up. I don't mean to be rude, sir, but you've already been stampeded with horse-laughs. Best thing be to let it ride.''

The sheriff pauses, and I catch my breath. ''Hart Woodring, if I see you on the streets after sundown in the next six months, I'll send you to the reform school and you won't see daylight for weeks. Get him out of my sight!''

''But, sheriff, what about—?'' asked the manager.

''Kester, do I tell you what movies to show?'' he asks, and his hip strikes mine as he passes. The tires squeal as he drives away from the curb.

Hart doesn't speak until we reach the motorcycle, parked between two late model cars. ''Let's ride, Lucius. Sober me up.''

I see that Hart is crying, licking blood from under his nose.

I thought I'd ridden a motorcycle before, until I rode on the buddy-seat behind Hart Woodring. At every curve on the winding mountain highway, I saw signs of the future: SUICIDE CURVE. Bright ribbons of water flowed below the cliff on the left, jagged rocks ripped past on the right, and the yellow line curves like a whip directly beneath the machine. A few cars pull over onto the shoulder and watch the motorcycle pass. A diesel truck shrieks and swerves.

A sign said SLIPPERY WHEN WET, and the dew is on the pavement. Another says WATCH FOR FALLING ROCK, and I imagine boulders bouncing out of the steep cuts in the mountainside.

We pass Tweetsie, where the toy-looking train is dark on the hillside, but a bright red light shines on a billboard: DON'T PASS TWEETSIE BY—FIGHT OFF THE REDSKINS WITH YOUR CAMERA. SEE BANDITS ROB TWEETSIE!

Four miles further on, we pass the gates of Mountain State College and enter Boone.

At the sign that points to the Daniel Boone Outdoor Theater, he turns left, and we come out into the open theater and stop under the rain shelter. We dismount and walk down the steep steps toward the dark panoramic stage, divided into three parts, each as large as a Broadway stage: a cabin set; a large open space with real trees, bushes, false rocks and a fake steeple behind the real fort logs; and an Indian country with teepees. Hart is drawn to the teepee and I follow.

"You was supposed to talk with Miss Ransom tonight, weren't you?" he asks, after we settle inside the teepee.

"You mean *listen*."

"Well, did you?" I nod, and he says, "Then tell it, Lucifer, tell it."

I fixed him with my glittering blue eyes and told it, watching him enter the Pleasure-Dome, his eyes still full of it after he came out.

"So next time, we find out whether the hero got the girl—or ran off with her."

"He did."

"How do *you* know?"

"He did. I bet you good money."

# 24
# Jesse James and
# Zara Ransom

Hart let me off at the road to the silo.

"Hidi, neighbor," I said to the skeleton of the scarecrow as I passed. Because it just occurred to me how the bad-check cycle worked. Even if the tax clerk took her money and erased her debt without pointing out that she had in no way saved her hotel, or even won a reprieve for it, the checks would go through Watauga National Bank and be returned to the tax clerk.

But maybe the tax clerk, like so many others, will know about Miss Ransom and want to spare her feelings. He'll shut up. And she didn't even know about the grand sum the state had paid for the hotel and put in trust for her.

Approaching the silo, I felt relieved. But what if she cashed the checks first at the bank? Then the bank would go to her for the money. How many understanding hearts could I depend on? One for certain was out of the reckoning. My own.

When I stepped over the sill, somebody inside the silo slaps my face. Unable to see, I throw up my arms. Whoever hit me is part of the dark.

Somebody slapped at me and kicked at me rapidly as

I backed away from the door. I stumbled over a rock and fell backward.

A body fell on top of me, kneeing me in the groin.

Reaching up to catch hold of my attacker, my hand catches hold of a breast. Even through the dress, my thumb feels the nipple vividly.

"You get out of this town, you hear me, you get *out* of this town, and you *stay* out!" she screams, slapping at me. I catch her around the waist and pull her down to me, and slide my arms up her back until I can hug her tightly. Her hair hangs about my cheeks and I can hardly catch my breath, the scent of cheap jasmine perfume is so profuse.

"Who are you?" I ask, a stupid, pointless question.

"You better leave or the next time I'll use something more than my fists!" she yells into my ear, breaking out of my arms.

She rises, kicks me in the ribs, and runs off down the road.

Lying in the silo on the straw, I felt thankful to the phantom woman. She'd introduced an element of risk. Physical risk. It went well with the risk I had introduced myself: the checks. I slept the sleep of the absolved.

The next morning, having told it to Hart, I wrote Part Two of the Legend of Jesse James and Zara Ransom.

*Again, the following night, he was there, but hidden by a limb of the pine tree that touched the ground, laden with roses. Walking behind my mother, I looked for him. One can always see well enough in the dark when there is something to see. His solitude seemed like mine, as though it needed another solitude to make it bearable. I thought I heard him breathing at the same moment in which I was most conscious of the scent of the roses, but I heard something behind me and turned with my mother to watch a deer leap out of some ferns across the road.*

*I never thought for a moment that he had come there to wait for me, yet I was certain that he would be there the following night.*

*Although there was a fine drizzle and water dropped from the leaves and clouds hovered around the moon like a hand, he was there, the toes of his shoes protruding from the roses and needles. His coattail, flung back where he had his hand in his pocket, showed through an opening in the leaves.*

*The following night was very hot. A rose lay on a stump beside the path; my mother stared straight ahead. I caught it in my hand as I passed, and when I lay on the bed an hour later and opened my hot fingers, the rose was bruised. I pinned it to my nightgown, and the mingled smells of the rose and my own body kept me awake until dawn.*

*The next night, he was not there. I hung back, trying to see through the moonless darkness and the foliage, but my mother called to me to hurry before the rain caught us, and I stumbled up the path to the summit.*

*From a ledge, we had a view of the mountain ranges that was said to overreach three states or more. We often drank from the spring that fell into a natural fountain shoulder high before turning left across the path and stepping onto the ledge. That night, my mother drank first, and as I bent close to the sound of falling water, I sensed, even before she grasped my wrist, that she had stopped abruptly. As she turned, I turned, my mouth wet, and saw him. He stood on the ledge, facing us, the sky violet and endless behind him, the mountains like furrows below him. The clouds having passed, the light from the quarter-moon shone on his face. He bowed solemnly, and said, "Good evening, ladies. Please forgive me if I startled you. My name is John Howard."*

"*Mr. Howard,*" *my mother said, "this is a private walk. If you must walk at night, be good enough in the future to take the paths on the other side of town.*"

"*But am I likely on the other paths to encounter ladies so charming as yourselves?*" *He did not bow again, but tilted his head slightly, and new shadows enhanced the glow on his face.*

*When he smiled, my mother put her handkerchief to her mouth, took my hand, and walked swiftly down the path.*

*Knowing our walks would end until Mr. Howard should leave Sweetwater, I wept that night.*

*The next day was incredibly hot. I walked about the room in my undergarments with a damp cloth in my hand and the dead rose in my hair. At noon a pebble struck my windowpane. Davis Woodring stood below with a note in his hand. I pretended not to see him.*

*That night, the air was cool as I sat in my dark room by the open window, looking down into the clearing Davis had made with his ax. Two men, one taller than the other, stepped off the porch below and walked among the stumps. I heard the murmur of their voices. The short man sat on a stump and drew on a cigar, revealing Mr. Howard's face.*

*Suddenly he rose, stood before the tall man, spoke quickly and sharply, and then strode off toward the forest, flinging his cigar, in a shower of sparks, high into the air. I felt much nearer him when I saw that he limped.*

*The tall man shook his head, turned slowly, and returned to the porch. I heard the swing creak as he sat down and swung.*

*I was still at the window when Mr. Howard emerged from the trees, far to the right of the path. He passed directly below me, and just as he disappeared, I coughed. Stepping backward, he came into view again, his head back, his face dark. "Zara?" he said. I said, "Yes," before I realized with surprise that he had spoken my name. With those two words our solitudes touched, as though our hands, not our whispering voices, had touched. I closed my eyes for a moment, trying to stop trembling. When I looked again, he was gone.*

*An hour later, I heard a soft knock at the door. I was too terrified to open it. He knocked only once more. Then I heard his footsteps on the carpet in the hall and listened for a door to open. But the sound of his footsteps faded.*

*The next day, I stayed by the window, but he did not come. When Davis Woodring came, I leaned back and hid behind the curtains. I felt guilty and ashamed. I knew what he felt, and I knew that my mother was wrong: cruelty was not a special quality of men, and perhaps even in men it was sometimes regretful.*

*When midnight came and Mr. Howard still did not come, I knew that he was torturing me, and I suffered all the more intensely. My mother came to say good night. I stayed out of the light because I knew that I looked sick and that she — she, certainly — would know immediately what ailed me.*

*That night, when he knocked, I felt the vibrations against my bosom and stomach, and even in my knees. "Zara?" he said, and I said, "Yes," and opened the door.*

*He walked past me across the room, very slowly, and sat where I had sat all day. Standing against the closed door in the dark, I knew that he felt the warmth of my body on the red velvet seat of the chair.*

*"Please sit with me," he said, rising and putting out his hand. I took his hand and sat where he had sat. Still holding my hand, he reached for the hard chair and pulled it over and sat on the other side of the window.*

*"We can't talk," I said.*

*"We don't have to."*

*We held hands for a long time, and then he got up and held both my hands and kissed my mouth as my mother had done on the path that first night. He pressed my palms against his cheeks and left the room.*

*The next night, he slipped a note under my door, and at two A.M. I slipped out and met him in the springhouse.*

*"It's chilly in here," I told him.*

*There was no moon. The woods were dark. We moved among the trees and vines very slowly to the ledge, aware of miles of mountains below us in the absolute dark. We sat and talked for a long time, until one faint spot of red, like a blemish, appeared on the sky.*

*The following night, I lay with him in the enclosure of the rose-pine tree. The first and last time in my eighty-some years that I ever felt blissful pain and ecstasy.*

*The following night, he began to teach me courage. I had told him how frightened I had been of him, how terrified I was of people, of my mother above all. He laughed gently and said, "Every man in this world lives in mortal fear. Some men avoid it, some men embrace it. Let's say only that I've never avoided it, and that the minute — no, the instant — I do, I'll be dead the next."*

*When I told him that I had never been out of my room in the daytime, had never seen Sweetwater by daylight, and at night only through the trees as my mother and I climbed the hill behind the Blue Goose Hotel, he became so angry that he stuttered and slammed his fist against the trunk of the rose-pine tree. I told him that one ride in a buggy through the town would satisfy me, that it would be almost like Paris.*

*He put his arms around me and said, "At noon tomorrow I will be waiting in front of the hotel with the reins in my hands and if you don't come out on the porch sharp at noon, I'm driving on, and not coming back."*

*He didn't say another word to me that night. I lay awake until dawn, quivering, because I knew I could never open that door, much less ride with Mr. Howard through town.*

*At eleven-thirty, a knock startled me. I had spent the morning praying he would come, and I would be able to persuade him to forget his reckless notions. But a stranger stood in the hall.*

*"Are you Miss Zara Ransom?" he asked.*

*I told him I was, and he asked permission to come in and talk to me. "I'm Mr. Howard's brother."*

*I let him in and stood by the door. "If my mother should — "*

*"I know. I'll be as brief as possible. It may hurt you, but it will hurt less than the future will if you go on seeing my brother. What would you say if I told you he is married and has children?"*

*"I've never thought about it."*

*"Think about it now."*

*I had never really lived in a society, and did not have the thoughts, the fears, most young girls probably had.*

*"I can see by your eyes that it means close to nothing to you. Perhaps you're too young to understand what that can mean. Except for his wife Zee, you're the first woman ever to really interest my brother. Well, I packed our bags in case I'd have to tell you and then tell him that I had to tell you, so — "*

*"Tell me what, Mr. Howard?"*

*"That our name isn't Howard. It's James. We're from Kearney, Missouri. My name's Frank."*

*I couldn't speak for a few moments. I saw a man's eyes between the brim of a hat and a red kerchief.*

*"Where is Mr. Howard —  Mr. James now?"*

*"Like a plucked goose, he's sitting in front of the hotel that's named after him."*

*"Thank you for coming to see me, Mr. James."*

*"It's your own business what you do about it — yours and Jesse's. My horse is saddled. I've got a wife and children, too. The difference is, I ain't forgot. Good day," he said, and I opened the door for him. He was a real gentleman.*

*I put on the dress I was wearing the night Jesse first saw* me and opened the door and went into the hall. I was not afraid. I was going for a buggy ride with Jesse James.

For the first time since the night my mother and I came to the Blue Goose Hotel, I descended the stairs into the lobby. It was full of people, waiting for dinner. As they all watched me cross the lobby and glide toward the door, I held my head high, imitating my mother's carriage, thinking, 'They all know Jesse James is waiting for me on the porch.'

I glimpsed my mother's back where she stood just inside the dining room. A waitress saw me and dropped a handful of forks, because although she had never seen me, my resemblance to Charlta Ransom struck her.

Jesse must have seen me even where he sat in the sun as I walked across the cool, dim lobby. He was at the door when I reached it. He lifted me into the buggy, and as I waited for him to climb in on the other side, Frank James sat smoking a cigar in a rocking chair, his feet on the rail, his saddlebags leaning against the rungs, and my mother came out onto the porch. But we were down the drive and almost on the main road before she called to me.

We rode up and down the main street four times. Jesse bought me a transparent apple from a farmer whose wagon was full under a tree. When we entered the drive to the hotel an hour later, I was even less afraid than before, because I realized something about fear. I had ridden brazenly with my lover up and down the single street of Sweetwater, unafraid of these strangers, or of my mother, because I knew that Jesse James, the most famous and daring outlaw in all the world, was at my side. But not until we entered the drive did I remember that no one but I knew who he was.

Frank James was not on the porch.

As Jesse held the door open for me, tipping his hat to the ladies in the rockers, I glanced back at Sweetwater and saw Davis Woodring, walking uncertainly up the drive.

*In the lobby, Jesse bowed to me and strolled into the dining room as I ascended the stairs.*

*When I opened the door, my mother laid her hands on me and beat me until, tasting blood in my mouth, I sank to the floor.*

# 25
## Jesse James and Davis Woodring

I finished at noon. Still in a fever of vicariousness, I hung around the silo, listless, like Zara Ransom confined to her room, until time to sneak into the hotel to listen to the final episode.

Again, she made me search for her in the dark, listening to the rising of the stage. I was "it." So dark in the hotel, the moon in the clouds, I had to *feel* for her. Finally, I stumble over her feet where she sits on the ottoman in the lobby.

Telling her story, she mentioned the silo, and when I say, "Ah," so faintly I didn't realize it was audible, she says, "I suppose you have been to the rose-pine tree too."

"Yes, ma'am."

"Do you promise on your sacred honor to leave town—" She stops and sits very still, rigid, her head tilted, her eyes flicking from side to side.

"What's—"

"Sssssh," she says, "listen. Do you hear it?"

"Hear what?"

"That strange noise again?"

"It's only me, breathing."

"I heard it only in the daytime at the end of spring,

day after day, and then it stopped, and some nights in April and May, I have awakened with that strange rumble in my head. And you don't hear it?''

I listened with her. I heard only the crickets, but I realized what she meant. The resentful silence of the bulldozers found expression in their dreams under the moon and echoes of their roar reached her ears.

''No, I can't hear a thing, Miss Ransom.''

''Why do you lie to me? I can see in your eyes that you hear something.''

''Probably the cars on the highway. Please continue your story. Jesse James and Davis Woodring are about to draw on each other.''

''Do you promise?''

''Yes, on my sacred honor—to leave town when you've told your story.''

''Forever.''

''Forever.''

''No, that's all I'm going to tell you.''

With Jesse James and Davis Woodring facing each other, she stops.

''But Miss Ransom, did you or did you not run away with Jesse James?''

''You do not have to give me another check. I didn't realize until I saw them standing in the road just now, again, after all these years, so vividly, what a sacrilege I have committed in telling you *any*thing.''

''But Miss Ransom, isn't there some kind of a sin against telling a story to its climax, then getting up and walking away?''

''I realized something else in the same moment. I'm finally beginning to understand why you're here. So when I say I am not going to tell you any more, I'm not being mean-hearted, for in stopping here, I surrender everything to your imagination.''

In the silence, I tried to understand. Then I did. Finally, she had recognized me as a fellow human being. Perhaps she'd recognized me as being someone like herself, an adept at living in three realms at once: the realm of fact, the realm of illusion, the realm of imagination.

Elated, I said, "Thank you, Miss Ransom. I understand. You are a very kind and wise lady. You know, I was telling a friend of mine just yesterday that I had not done, seen, experienced everything, but that I *felt* as though I had. That having felt *every*thing, I now felt nothing. I'm glad you believe in my capacity to feel again so strongly that you—"

"No. No, you don't understand. You are cursed with consciousness, young man. Perhaps that saves you from lunacy. But, no, you see, I don't think you've felt anything yet."

I heard her dress as she stood up in the dark. I didn't move as she climbed up the stairs.

After a while, I had control over myself again. Then I realized that having control didn't speak well for me either.

I went to the top of the stairway and counted the steps, down to the thirteenth. I felt under the carpet for the check I'd left the night before. It's gone.

"I'm leaving the third check anyway, Miss Ransom," I say, in an even voice, knowing she hears me. But I put nothing there. My legs are weak as I go down the stairs to the lobby.

I go to the kitchen. Her fantastic ears no doubt caught me there. I take off my shoes and go into the dining room where places are laid for dinner. At the place where I imagine Jesse James sat after that noon buggy ride, where he sat with fork in hand when Charlta Ransom, her hands ringing and aching from the blows she gave her daughter, entered and strode across the room to his table, I lift the plate and place the check in the white circle that I cannot see but know is there on the dust-laden tablecloth.

In Sweetwater Creek, I wash my hands and my feet. In the dark silo, I ate pork and beans from a can with the fork I took from the table where Jesse James once sat.

Then, by the light of the candle I had bought for that purpose, I wrote the incomplete final episode.

*My mother had never locked the door to my room. She trusted more in the certainty of my captivity in her own personality than she would ever have trusted the lock on a door. But she stood over me for a moment as I lay on the floor, and the realization must have come to her that now I was a woman of fifteen, and the time had come when it was necessary to shake the fist of authority in my face and to put me under lock and key. Perhaps she realized later, too, as I did soon after she left the room, that she had taught me that cruelty and destruction may be the province of the male but it was also ground upon which a woman might occasionally stand to advantage.*

*On my feet again, I went, of course, directly to the window. A man walked off the porch from below, carrying a shotgun. Through my tears I mistook him for Jesse James, but when he raised his face, I did not recognize it. There were so few faces I could have. But Davis came around through the grass at the side and stopped a few yards from the man with the shotgun, who turned to face him. Half an hour later, Davis went away.*

*During that hour, I learned later, my mother sent for "John Howard" and ordered him to leave the hotel immediately. His bags would be packed and brought to him in the street. It was not the gentleman, "John Howard," who limped and smiled politely, but Jesse James, who laughed in my mother's face. "Madam," he said, "the way you treat your daughter, you should be horsewhipped." He informed her that he had paid in advance for his lodging and he would gladly depart early the following morning.*

*But when he went through the hotel asking for his brother and was told that he had ridden out of town an hour ago, he went to his room.*

*The sheriff was on the porch when he came out. They shook hands because the sheriff liked Mr. Howard and was glad he had come out of the hotel before he could reach it to carry out Charlta Ransom's request. "I'm going to meet my brother," he told the sheriff. "We plan to rob a train tonight." The deep laughter I heard all the way up to my room where I lay crying on the bed must have been the sheriff's.*

*I did not know that Jesse James had left at all. At one-thirty A.M., a pebble struck my windowpane and I was startled out of a dream of love. The aura of the dream still hovered over my mind as I looked down into the yard and saw Jesse, wearing traveling clothes, standing astraddle the prone body of the man with the shotgun. The shotgun was broken in the middle, as the man himself seemed to be, and lay with two shells at the man's feet.*

*I opened the window, and the way Jesse opened his arms, without a word of encouragement, so confident that his open arms were enough, and because I was still in that inter-rupted dream of love, I jumped from the second-story win-dow and he caught me in his arms. And his fervent kiss ended the dream.*

*I walked blissfully at his side across the grass to the gravel drive and down to the road where the same buggy waited.*

*He took the reins in his hands and looked at me. "Is this what you want, Zara?"*

*"Yes, Jesse — you* all *my life."*

*"Who told you my name — ?"*

*"Your brother."*

*"Then it's a good thing for him he left me here alone. He told me he would leave if I took you for that drive at noon today, and I didn't believe him. I thought those saddlebags and that act of sitting on the porch, wearing a frown like Jove, was to scare me. I reckon he knew he'd better git . . . He tell you anything else?"*

*I lied.*

*"Anybody else know who I am?"*

*"No."*

*"And you would run away to one nowhere after another with a man who tempts death and the devil every day?"*

*"Yes."*

*Jesse snapped the reins and the buggy moved slowly down the hill past the dark houses in the soft dirt of the road.*

*Just out of town on the old road (that has grown over with weeds now, I suppose), there was a silo. Davis Woodring jumped out of the doorway with a pistol in his hand, and grabbed the reins and stopped the horses.*

*He stuttered the name of "Mr. Howard" and vowed he was going to kill him — a very horrible and animal sound. the spittle from his mouth spraying my cheek.*

*I begged him to put up his pistol and turn the reins loose so we could go on. I told him that Mr. Howard and I were going to be married.*

*In the moonlight, I saw that Jesse James's knuckles were white from the hard grip he had on the reins. He would reach for his gun, I thought, if I weren't beside him, and he would kill poor Davis Woodring for my sake. I did not want anyone hurt.*

*"Let us pass, mister," said Jesse. His lips did not seem to move.*

*"Move again and I'll shoot you where you sit," Davis stuttered.*

"You don't hold that pistol like a man that's ever used one. You might hit Zara. Now be so kind as to let us go on our way."

"I ain't done much shootin', Mister fancy Howard, you're right, so get down from that buggy and step in that silo so she won't see me do it."

"What claim you got to such anger, sir? Do you know this lady?"

"I do. She's my sweetheart. You shut up."

Jesse looked at me very slowly. "Has this man known you as I have known you?"

The click of the pistol as he cocked it made us both turn toward Davis.

"No. No, I swear."

"Get down or I'll fire."

Jesse gave me the reins and got down, and Davis was over on his side when he stood in the road. Davis led Jesse around the back of the buggy and I pleaded with him to put his pistol away, and swore to Davis that I never loved him.

"But let him go, and I'll go with you, Davis," I said.

They were at the side of the road and the black doorway of the silo was just behind Jesse and he was in black, so all I saw was his pale face under the hat.

"I'm set on killing him and I'm going to kill him. Get in that silo."

"If you're trying to show her you're a man, mister, this is a certain way to show her the opposite. Uncock that gun and give me a chance to reach for mine and then *show* yourself a man."

Davis looked at him a long time. Then he slowly released the hammer.

"Just allow me my coat unbuttoned," Jesse said, "and I'll call you, even despite your having the ups with the gun in your hand."

Davis nodded, and then he glanced at me. It did no

*good to beg them both to stop. Jesse unbuttoned his vest and the watch chain winked in the light from the creek.*

*"You ready?" asked Jesse. I realized for the first time that there was a tremor in his voice — the sweetest, kindest voice I have ever heard.*

*"If you are," Davis stuttered.*

As I lay on the loud corn shucks, I did not worry about snakes and black widows. I worried about the effect on Hart Woodring of the ending—whatever it turned out to be, for she had left it up to my imagination. I decided to sleep on it, dream through it.

# 26

# *Zara Ransom
# in Sunlight*

I awoke before daybreak. The candle was a puddle of wax. I waited for light. When it came, dimly, I began to write, my own imagined ending, out of neither fact nor illusion—out of my Pleasure-Dome experience. But after a few hours, I set fire to what I had written and warmed my hands—the first time I ever burned anything I wrote.

I'm sitting on a bench in front of the Sweetwater Trading Post when the old man comes down the road and opens the unlocked door.

"What fer *you* this bright and early morning?"

"Bottle of milk and a poke full of oranges."

"What's the matter, bowels stopped up?"

"One way to put it."

"Stick around a few more days and them bull-dozers'll clean you out, plumb through."

"You all ever persuade her to move to the poorhouse?"

"Never could. Give up tryin', I reckon. Few of 'em gonna try again tonight, though. Behind them drawn shades, we're *all* packed. Ever'body's got 'em a truck hired and ready to go, a few steps ahead of the trac-tors. Guess no harm in telling you, a stranger, all this, since you seem to take a liking to this town."

Looking around at the items in the place, I couldn't believe that in several days the old store would "disappear from the face of the earth." That expression didn't seem too strong for what would happen to a little country store, to a small town like Sweetwater that no one ever heard of. Nothing to compare, though, with Hiroshima or Taltal. *People* had died there. Perhaps that was the difference. But I imagine this old man in Arizona, and the old man with the fake Jesse James watch in Florida, and others living with children they haven't seen in years and mercifully forgotten, and others sitting against the walls of public buildings in strange metropolises. And I wondered if those who perished in Taltal, Chile, hadn't the better deal.

The old man talked without a tremor of the impending shove over the precipice, but between that evening a week ago when I first saw him and this bright September morning, a ghostly pallor has risen to his skin, such as you might acquire after recurrent journeys across the landscapes of nightmares.

I took the cardboard cap from the top of the bottle and drank long. "Who you selling your merchandise to?"

"What you offering me?"

"Me? Nothing, I—"

"Just as likely you as anybody else. This is all old country store merchandise. Nobody I know would want stuff on his shelves that come from a store that took a swan dive off a mountainside, anyway. Spooky feeling. I used to worry bout that adam bomb, but I don't no more. What's it gonna bust up that I give ary damn for, after this?"

"So you're gonna leave it all and—"

"And one of these first days, I'll just walk out, get in the car, and let my son take me *on* som'mers. I ain't the only one's leaving stuff behind. But I reckon we all got things we can't part with for the world. You cut me off from my old coffee grinder and see if I don't cut out your blamed heart fer it.'' The old man hugs the big old machine, a murderous glint in his eyes that made me feel as though *I* had threatened his coffee grinder.

I walked toward the Blue Goose Hotel, intending to eat my oranges under the rose-pine tree. Then I would climb it for one last look.

Somebody raised a shade and looked up and across the road at the Blue Goose Hotel. The woman turned quickly to somebody in the room. A man wearing suspenders comes to her side. I followed their gaze.

In the bright morning sun, Zara Ransom stands on the steps, the multipaned glass façade blazing behind her back. I didn't recognize her by what I'd seen before. Now, she's dressed in white organdy, a blue sash, and a blue ribbon trimming a wide straw hat. I wasn't looking at that old woman who had sent me into the Pleasure-Dome with the story of a young girl's romance with Jesse James. I'm looking at the girl herself, pausing before the glass façade as if waiting for a gentleman in a buggy to come up the gravel drive. Not until she moves, going down the broken walk to the steep stone steps, is it apparent that she is a very old, decrepit woman whom the sun might kill at any moment.

A cluster of flies sip at my orange-scented hands and a sweat bee bit the corner of my mouth.

I ran to the store, but the old man was already out front, looking up the road, shielding his eyes against the sun like an Indian scout. I stand at his side and see that the glare of the morning sun has turned the white goddess into a shimmering moth.

"Somebody's got to stop her," I said.

"Where's it any of *your* concern?" asks the old man.

The old people appear on their steps, the men in good coats, the women wearing hats.

Another grandfather appears in front of the store.

"She looks like a woman," says the storekeeper, "that's finally got holt of the means to get what she wants."

"But where would she get three hundred dollars for them taxes? Rob a bank while we're all asleep?"

"No use to go near her. The way she come out of that hotel and stood on the steps, I vowed to myself wouldn't nothing do no good."

"Yes, sir," said the old man, "I may as well finish my packing and send word to my son that it's finally time."

When Miss Ransom, walking down the middle of the road, gets within a hundred feet of the store, I step back behind the two men, and, unnoticed, reach behind me, open the screen door, and back into the cavelike gloom of the store. Between the heads of the men, I watch her pass, the hat and parasol masking her face.

"Well, I didn't get a good look at her face," the storekeeper said. "Did you?"

"Who needs to!"

"Sure as the world she's headed for the courthouse in Boone, a-walkin' it!"

"Can't you stop her?" I ask.

They just look at me through the dusty screen, until who saw me the clearest was *me*.

Those million readers of *Harper's Bazaar,* sitting under hair dryers, like seduced Martians, were waiting for Lucius Hutchfield to provide them with an hour's diversion. With that sense of mission, I left the two natives of Sweetwater and turned back onto the old road that would soon be the newest thing in time-savers and time killers.

The caterpillars and bulldozers squatted like ruins capable of coming instantly alive and devouring everything in sight. I picked up a rock, spit on it, and threw it through the windshield of a bulldozer. It made no response, and did me no good.

With the Blue Horse tablet on my knee, I wrote almost compulsively, improvising upon endings to the legend, settling for this one:

*They were just about to draw their guns, when Jesse James said, "Just one thing you may like to know before I kill you, mister. And that is that you have the immortal honor of dying at the hands of Jesse James. Reach!"*

*I screamed, "Jesse!"*

*Davis dropped his pistol as though it hurt his hand and then threw his arms into the air, shouting, "I'm unarmed!" without a stutter.*

*Jesse James laughed at him, a Colt revolver in his hand. The tone of that laugh froze me to the marrow.*

*I jumped down and flung my arms around Davis's waist and pleaded with Jesse not to kill him.*

*"Don't see any reason why I shouldn't."*

*I told Jesse I wanted to marry Davis Woodring. I told Jesse that I knew he had a wife and children, and that I couldn't live with guns and killing.*

*Davis told me that he couldn't live with me, reminding him daily that he was a coward. I could feel his stomach tremble against the inside of my arm.*

*"You're no coward, Davis," I said. "You're his equal."*

*"He's Jesse James."*

*"No. He's Mr. Howard. When he had to tell you his real name, he became Mr. Howard forever. He told you that to frighten you, because he was afraid himself."*

*Jesse James laughed. "Go with her, mister. My brother*

*was right. I'd probably leave her somewhere, someday, and ride fast as I could to see my wife. I don't admit to being scared, but I'd hate to die knowing I had broken the commandment against adultery. My momma raised me right. She's just got one arm now, but she'd tear me apart. Get in that buggy before I take a notion to walk over your dead body."*

*We got in, and Jesse pulled out a money sack and pitched it into Davis's lap. He just looked at it.*

*"There's enough change to set you up in business in Ohio or someplace. If there's any love between you, you'll have to make that yourselves."*

*He took my hand and kissed it, and stepped back and slapped the rump of one of the horses.*

*When I looked back, he was standing on the road in the moonlight, putting his pistol back into the holster, buttoning his vest, blotting out the wink of light on the chain. The same pistol Bob Ford used to shoot him in the back in the spring of the following year.*

Exhausted, I lay back on the corn husks and thought of myself as a monk in his cell. Voluntary imprisonment, for the purpose of meditation and transcription, and, if possible, atonement. That was how I would look at it when they drove me through the gates of the penitentiary. In the absence of monasteries for agnostics, the penitentiary seemed appropriate. It's one thing to arrange your own punishment, but how do you go about arranging to feel the one thing necessary if the punishment is to be meaningful? Shame. I did not yet feel shame. Only self-loathing.

At seven o'clock the sun began to go behind the mountain. A mellow yellow glow moved down the curved brick wall of the silo through the rents in the roof. Where there had been only a thin gauze of green moss the day before, I saw testimony to the fact that I and the snakes and black widows I imagined were not the only transients in the silo. White chalk proclaimed: RUFUS GOT GLORIA JONES CHERRY JUNE 14, 1953. Was that worth recording? I looked at it as I'd once looked at a crude cave drawing. I start to rub it out with the sleeve of my shirt, but it occurs to me that the world is a museum without walls, and I felt like a vandal who had refrained.

When the silo got dark, I went out and sat in a clearing on the bank of the creek and watched the darkness thicken on the water under low limbs. To cool my feet, I took off my shoes, and, pulling off a sock, snagged it on the dead toenail of my left foot, one result of an operation to transplant some bones to arrest an incipient clawfoot deformity. Somewhere, packed down in one of Momma's storage barrels in Mammy's circus-wagon coal house is a picture of me in a wheelchair, my legs in casts, barechested in the hot August air of a hospital ward, Anna Livia standing behind me, her hand on my shoulder.

I took off my clothes and waded into the creek. The water's ice cold. When I come to a place that slopes, I duck under and rub my body vigorously with my hands. I crawl out and put on my clothes, but I still feel unclean.

Suddenly, the mountains seemed to groan. I ran up the path to Sweetwater, a siren growing louder. On the road, a red-and-white ambulance, with a red swirling light on top, races past me, leaving a film of dust over my face and hands, and I brush it off my clothes as I walk swiftly up into town.

People are in the road going up to the Blue Goose Hotel where the ambulance has parked in front of the main entrance. They give me hostile glances as though

I, being a stranger, am an accomplice to whatever has happened in Boone. An old man shoves past me, the legs of his overalls rasping together.

When I reach the steps, the ambulance is already edging through the old people, back down the drive. I knew that all the houses were empty, that here in front of the Blue Goose Hotel the entire population of Sweetwater was gathered. I thought of the villagers of Taltal. I counted them at a glance: twenty-five, one of whom was a spastic child. A woman seemed to guard the door. From her comments to the people, who appeared to take turns speaking to her, I learned what had happened.

Miss Ransom had appeared at the tax clerk's desk with three checks for one hundred dollars each choked in her hand, and they'd decided to tell her for good and all that no amount of paid taxes would save the hotel, that a four-lane highway was coming through, and that she should enter a rest home or stay with relatives, if she had any.

She had tried to walk back in the sun, but she'd fainted in the middle of town, and somebody had carried her into the supermarket, where it was cool, until the ambulance arrived. They realized that if they did not want her to die, they'd better take her back to the Blue Goose Hotel.

I broke through to the woman on the steps. "May I see Miss Ransom?"

"*I* been seeing *you* roaming the town for a week. In *my* day, somebody would have shot you by now. We don't appreciate newspapermen—"

"I swear, I—"

"Even her own townfolk can't get in to see her. Ain't *no*body gonna disturb her privacy."

I wondered whether, if I got close enough, I'd smell

jasmine perfume on her. I looked at her breasts. She was younger than the others, not over fifty, and looked willful enough, strong enough to jump a man in a dark silo.

I start to ask if any of them know of anybody who's kin to Miss Ransom, but I remembered something the old man with the fake Jesse James watch said: "She's the last of her tribe, 'less that little bastard of hers, if she had one, is still roaming around."

I started walking out of town. Looking back at the Blue Goose Hotel, I remembered, "If the hoar frost grip thy tent, thou wilt give thanks when night is spent."

At least, I could honor my promise, and leave. But I'd made promises to Hart Woodring, too. I wanted to leave him something to remember me and Jesse by.

# 27 Hart in the Silo

Hart's motorcycle wasn't parked at the filling station in Blowing Rock, but a warm light shines through the window upstairs and Goldie Hill singing ''Don't Let the Stars Get in Your Eyes'' on the radio seems to invite me up.

Hallie Woodring answers my timid knock, dressed in a green rayon dress with yellow roses across her breasts. She steps back, slightly, as if startled. Not knowing, on the instant, what to make of her response to the sight of me, I made nothing at all of it.

''Uh— Is Hart home?''

''No. He's not.''

''Know when he might be home?''

''No. I don't. You mind telling me—?''

''It's okay. Just a friend. Thanks.''

She stands in the doorway till I'm downstairs and outside again, and then I hear her slam the door as if she's recovered herself.

''No corn flakes about her,'' I said to the Ethyl pumps.

Failing to find Hart anywhere, I headed back to pick up my notebooks. Approaching the silo in Sweetwater, I see the black motorcycle parked in the middle of the rutted road. ''I might've known it,'' I said.

Sounds, like fish flopping in the water, come from the creek.

"That you, Jesse?" I said.

I heard Hart coming up the slope toward the road. Didn't see him in the black clothes till I could almost touch him. The white bill of his cap made him look like a wild black swan.

"Hello, Lucius." He's still holding some rocks, and as a reflex, I almost dodge. "Look, I come to hear how it all turned out."

"Thought you didn't like Jesse James chapter plays?"

"Don't kid around. This is serious."

"I been looking for you."

"To tell it to me?"

"To tell you good-bye. I'm going home."

"She won't die."

"You heard about it?"

"Sure. But she won't die. I thought you'd come to Blowing Rock last night and tell me the end."

"Imagine the rest of it for yourself, Hart."

"I want to know what *really* happened, boy."

"I got to leave, Hart."

"How?"

"Thumbing."

"I'll give you the Hornet if you'll tell the ending."

"Don't put it on that basis!"

"What I mean is, I'd give it to you anyhow, even if you told it to me just because you wanted to."

"It's got no wheels. Where can I go without wheels?"

"Where can a story go without an ending?"

"I'll tell you, damn it, I'll tell you."

"Then, you just come on by the station early in the morning and the ol' Hornet'll be setting there, rubber on it, and gassed up."

"Let's go in the silo."

I felt around in the corn shucks and was certain Hart hadn't found the Blue Horse tablets. Maybe he'd stood there in the dark and chalked on the walls what the morning light would reveal: HART WOODRING GOT SABRA VAN NESS CHERRY SEPTEMBER 9, 1953. No, Hart would show her off to the world if he could, but in his heart she'd always be a virgin.

"Well," I says—and I tell the boy in the dark that Jesse James ran away to Montana with Zara Ransom and that he returned to his family for a brief time a year later and was standing on a cane-bottom chair in the House on the Hill one April morning, using a feather duster on a picture of a racehorse named Skyrocket his wife had asked him to dust, when Robert Ford picked Jesse's Colt revolver up from the bed and shot him in the back.

# 28

# *Cherokee*

At dawn, I stepped between the pumps and opened the door to the Hudson Hornet. The Harley Davidson motorcycle was chained to the wall, and Hart Woodring was probably hard and fast asleep.

On the edge of Blowing Rock, Sheriff Odom's patrol car is parked behind a car in front of the Covered Wagon Motel. The sheriff himself squats beside the rear axle of a car from which all the wheels have been slipped.

At noon, as a gesture to Thomas Wolfe, I pulled off the Blue Ridge Parkway and stopped at the post office. I'd found some string and some heavy brown sacks in a trash can in an alley. With the manuscript, I included a note to my agent, promising to pay her to get it typed.

"This wrapped okay?"

"Well, I wouldn't put it up as a model. What's in it?"

"Dust blown off the moon," I said, matter-of-factly.

The clerk sizes me up. "Okay, neighbor, dust blown off the moon. First class?" He seems to enjoy playing along.

"Vintage 1880."

"Fifty cents parcel post."

"Well, the fact is— it's a— manuscript."

"A who?" he asks, as I knew he would.

"A— Educational material, okay?"

"Sure. Twelve cents."

Now that I'd entrusted to the mails the story of Jesse and Zara, with my own fanciful, unhappy ending, I broke out in a cold sweat.

Running away from Cherokee and Raine's scorn, I'd passed through Asheville on my way to India seven years before, and broken into Thomas Wolfe's childhood home to commune with the hero through his artifacts. As I'd told Lee that night in her car on the traffic island at the intersection in Greenbrier, wondering whether my first typed-up story, "Helena Street"—the Tennessee Kid meets Billy the Kid—and my stolen copy of *The Razor's Edge* are still stowed in that niche in the brick pillar that holds up the back end of Wolfe's house had haunted me sometimes, had given me an aching desire to return and look for them.

That urge made me drive over to Spruce Street and pause in front of *The Old Kentucky Home*. The possibilities of finding them still there after seven years, or of finding them gone, or of sticking my hand into a nest of black widows, made a prickle crawl over my scalp. And that surprised me. Without looking, I headed on toward Cherokee.

The next morning, I woke up in my basement sanctuary on Sequoyah Street, miles outside the magic circle Zara Ransom had woven around me and I had woven around Hart. In my mouth, the sour taste of the milk of paradise that fear of jail had curdled in my dreams. My daddy stood in the doorway, drunk.

Handing me my draft board notice to report for a physical, he reminisced about Eddie Slovak, "the only

American soldier executed for desertion in World War II," the order given by General Dwight David Eisenhower, to set an example.

Then he surprises the hell out of me by going to his room by the furnace and coming back with a fifteen-page manuscript, written in pencil on the backs of pink format paper from WLUX, where I wrote commercial copy for several weeks last summer. Wrote it, he said, sitting right there in my sanctuary. All about the time he got lost in some caves during the siege of Metz in 1944. Pretty weird, since he also got lost one night in the caves I discovered under the Bijou—he was drunk, running from this man who'd broken out of Petros penitentiary and wanted to kill him for messing with his wife, and I never have been able to make him remember it. And now this. I guess writing it made him sentimental and sad, because his handwriting got wavier and wavier, like mine, at first, when I tried to write on rough seas, till finally I couldn't figure it out at all—incoherent gibberish. Daddy says, "You can do anything you want to to change it and make it what you call a best seller, and we can cut it two ways on the profits, because look at *The Naked and the Dead, The Young Lions,* and *From Here to Eternity,* which is all dreamed-up bullshit, but *this* is *real.*" I told him I'd work on it, and gave him fifty cents to get himself a shot, then tried to drift back to sleep.

I went over to Mammy's at about dinner time, eager to see her and the Chief and Momma, of course, but full of a general need to look inside the old pine quilt chest I used to sleep in the times we stayed overnight. When Mammy married the Chief, he brought a beautiful mahogany chest into the house and she moved the pine box out to the shed that used to be a circus wagon. And she let me stash my movie stills and books and writings there when I went to sea. Whenever I opened the lid, I felt again a little of the fear I had when I slept in it as a child—that in Mammy's pitch-dark bedroom, the lid would fall and I would suffocate. If I needed an excuse to get back in touch with the things that were in the clothes box (and many that weren't), I did want to look at the still of Tyrone Power as Jesse James wearing a wet black raincoat and black hat, his back toward us, embracing Nancy Kelly as his wife Zee in a doorway, her eyes startled by his sudden appearance out of the night.

So when I go in, we all hug and kiss and talk sixty miles an hour, but I feel a kind of phantom circuit of electricity jumping through us, and not until they settle a little, enough for me to feel right about going down to the shed to root in the pine box, do I see where the current comes from.

Out in the backyard, full of flowers, lolling in the hammock under the mimosa trees, is Earl, smoking this fat-assed cigar and wearing the uniform of a Texaco filling station attendant. Just when I had gotten used to the picture of him on the lam in the best Bogart tradition, there he is swinging in Mammy's hammock, raising a cloud of Dutch Master, grinning at me.

"Didn't think I'd be seeing you again," he says, "except on visiting day."

"On which side of the bars? You're the one they're looking for."

"Not if I've been pumping gas for the past month at Shorty's Texaco in South Cherokee. Shorty runs a professional alibi service."

"Why didn't you just keep going— to Mexico or Canada?"

"I'm dying to hear what they got to say about Mr. French and how he fooled every damned one of them."

''Where's Bucky?''

''Kept running. I couldn't do anything with him. He'll be eating jailhouse gravy in less than a week.''

''If you don't care any more than you seem to, why'd you ride to the rescue?''

Earl gives me a look like he thinks I'm stupid. ''Why else—for the fun of it. Just to show I could do it. I hope they come for me today. I hope they walk right out here while we're talking. Then I'll show you how a master controls the situation, kid.''

This was the first time I'd seen him in our native environment in four or five years, so I sat on this white kitchen chair Mammy'd propped up the curtain stretchers with and tried to help him get back in touch with Cherokee and to feel as if he were a part of my own life, because despite his brazen self-confidence, he seemed to be one of the loneliest men I'd ever met.

When I told him I was studying to become a teacher, he says, ''Listen, kid,'' in this Yankee accent he picked up and stuck to since his first trip to New York, ''what you wasting your time teaching English for? Why don't you become a doctor or a lawyer where the *big* money is?'' That tipped me off balance, and I made some lame excuses, and he says, ''What's this they tell me about you got a book going to be published?''

''Well . . .'' I didn't tell him it was still in the notes stage. I didn't think he could picture that, and I was afraid he'd make fun of the whole idea of *Children of a Cold Sun,* so I just broke out in a face-aching grin.

And he says, ''Listen, kid, you better watch out for these editors. They'll try to cheat you out of what you got coming to you. I *know.* What *you* need is an agent.''

Well, I was still feeling the reunion scene, so none of this soaked in. I was thinking, 'Here's where I'll make him feel he's a part of my life, and not just a three- or four-time loser con man fresh out of the pen.' He was still kind of thin and hollow-eyed. And here I was, the first of the family on both sides to graduate from high school and even go on to college, and about to become a respectable teacher, and trying to become a novelist, and a clean record in the local police and FBI files, and— I didn't want to show off and make him feel bad, I wanted to make him feel part *of* it. We were two brothers having a reunion at Mammy's house—the home place.

But then he says, "What's it about?"

And I say, "'Bout when I was in the merchant marines," surprising myself. It was news to me, but it sounded like a good idea. It made him give the hammock a good swing with his dangling foot and look at me squint-eyed through the cigar smoke. "Kid, when were *you* ever in the merchant marines?"

"I been shipping out for almost a year." Hurt my feelings that he didn't remember all the money orders I sent him from Panama and Chile and New York for tobacco and stamps. But I didn't say anything.

"Whatever made you go into the merchant marines, kid?"

I got choked up a little because I was about to grab him with it. "Well, Earl, remember the time . . . ?" Then I filled him in on our childhood and the time he came back in the merchant seaman's outfit. "And you told me and Bucky all about New York and shipping out of New Orleans to Rio de Janeiro and New Zealand. Remember, Earl? It got Bucky to running off from school and taking little trips that finally landed him in the detention home.

"It stirred up the wanderlust in me, too, but good, little ol' Lucius, you know, stayed home, and dreamed about it, and saw movies about it, and wrote novel scenarios projecting himself into it, and read Conrad, and finished high school first. You know, sitting in the union hall waiting for India to show up on the call board, I started reading *Lord Jim*. Conrad's character Marlow says something I've been feeling for many years, something I felt long before you and Bucky started to illustrate it in your own wanderings: 'There was such magnificent vagueness in the expectations that had driven each of us to sea, such a glorious indefiniteness, such a beautiful greed of adventures that are their own and only reward! . . . In no other kind of life is the illusion more wide of reality—the disenchantment more swift—the subjugation more complete.'"

"That the kind of crap they make you memorize in college?"

To keep from breaking the mood, I took up the thread of my story again as if I hadn't even heard him. "Then I went to New York last summer, worked at the White Tower hamburger joint by night, sat in the union hall in Brooklyn by day, till I finally got sent out on a ship to Chile Christmas Eve."

Earl braked the hammock with his foot, and kept it still, one eye squeezed shut against the smoke from the Dutch Master hanging in the corner of his mouth. Then he gives the hammock a little push, takes a long draw, spews out the smoke, dusts the cigar, and says with a smirk, "Why, kid, I ain't never been in no merchant marines."

I heard a mimosa blossom drop. "But—"

"But, hell," Earl said. "I just wore that outfit so I could hitchhike across country easier."

Fading away from that green thought in the green shade, I walked down past the pine box in the circus-wagon coal house, thinking maybe I'd look for the

Jesse James still later, went down the alley, and wandered.

Passing Bonny Kate Junior High, I almost inhaled the odorless but deadly vapors that seemed to poison me when I sat in the principal's office, like the time I got expelled for sassing the teacher who started to tear up my Billy the Kid meets the Tennessee Kid story, confiscated in her American History class.

I began walking my old paper route, almost as if it were a refuge from the rest of Cherokee. But when I saw that one of the houses of our childhood was now only charred debris and red clay under a mat of dewberry vines, I felt sick. A locked basement garage door under the white house across the street made me try to remember whether it really happened or I dreamed that the handsome man who lived there, until he was killed in the war, had worked many years to build a monoplane in his basement. Looking at the closed doors, I imagined his widow finally opening them to let it out, as a tribute to his memory, or to be rid of it, discovering that the wings spread too wide to go through the doors.

That paper route ended a few blocks from the corner where my second paper route began, so I walked it too, where I used to daydream of going to fight with the Jews in Palestine and I'd miss at least two houses every day, till Dusty Harper had to fire me. Later, I wrote "The Palestine Story," a saga of the Jewish struggle for independence.

Following my paper route up Clayboe Ridge, I passed the house where Raine used to live with her bootlegger daddy. The house looked very different, but under the gigantic oaks, I remembered our last argument as sweethearts, the day I ran away to India and got bogged down in Asheville.

In broad daylight, I walked through the hollow where one night, after an earlier breakup with Raine, I had vowed under the stars to "make my mark on the world."

In the Clinch View neighborhood, where we'd lived in five different houses, I walked slowly past the one where we lived during the Bijou time. I rested in the shade of the tree where I sat the first day we moved in, writing "Glory in the Sanctuary," interrupted by the steel taps on Duke's shoes, ignorant of the fact that before the year was up, the boy I was meeting would shoot his mother and father and end up in the insane asylum. His swagger seemed now a grotesque exaggeration of Hart Woodring's.

A bus came by, where streetcars used to run, and I caught it, on impulse, and transferred uptown to another bus and got off a few blocks from Victor Savage's mansion that sits on a cliff above the river. Maybe Gaile would be there too, home from New York acting school on a visit. The Savages were my second family. Gaile was the greatest female friend I ever had. The first time I ever saw her, I was up in the tower gazing at the moonlight on the river and heard her walking below in a clearing among some chunks of marble the quarry had junked, and I watched her lie back on a marble slab and offer her naked body to the moon. And then she turned up with her mother at a symphony concert her daddy conducted at the Bijou, where I was ushering. And then, there she was at the first meeting of the Cherokee players, trying out for the part of Laura in *The Glass Menagerie*. After she went away to study acting in New York, I often baby-sat with her little brother while her mother went to rehearsals with Victor Savage. He contributed part of my tuition for Cherokee College last year. Like Cornel

Wilde as Chopin in *A Song to Remember,* Victor Savage inspired me to merge the glamor of movies and writers with the romance of classical music and composers.

Walking from the bus stop down the highway to the Savages, I passed a house some eccentric had named Wuthering Heights. The house was high on a hill, but he'd built a tower on it, as if to view the moors of England, when the light was right. I'd been in the tower, for the house was a museum of the Civil War. As I walked past slowly, on the dangerous highway — there were no sidewalks to encourage outsiders to stroll through this exclusive neighborhood — I felt upon me the eyes of that solitary Union soldier who had made a sniper's nest in the tower, drawing pictures of himself and his sweetheart on the walls, waiting for the day General Saunders would ride by on a white horse on the road below.

I didn't turn down the drive to the Savage mansion because I knew I wouldn't be able to restrain myself from telling them in a mimicking, entertaining way, the whole story of Zara Ransom.

I was in bed before it was fully dark, hoping Anna Livia was lying awake in the dark too, listening to the "Nightwatchman" program on WLUX where I was an announcer for a while in high school, maybe remembering the time I dedicated Tchaikovsky's "Romeo and Juliet Overture" to her and got fired because it was strictly a popular music show. But then I remembered she wouldn't be lying awake alone. I slept until mid-morning, arising from dreams of Anna Livia.

I risked a visit to the Market House, where at a little lunch counter that offered a clear view of the Garden of Eden, I gagged down rancid banana pudding, waiting for a glimpse of Anna Livia. But she wasn't work-

ing. When I noticed that her daddy looked much older,
I concluded that her break with the past was total now.
Married, she was beginning a new life, cut to an ancient pattern.

Leaving Market Square, I passed, with a shiver, the
alley behind the bank, where Duke and I did a dry run
of our scheme to rob the manager of the Bijou, Mr.
Hood.

Suddenly, fear that the Bijou had been subjected
in my absence to the Hiroshima effect, I broke into
a run.

On the *Polestar*, I read John Hersey's *Hiroshima*. A
fan-shaped city, Hiroshima is spread out over six islands formed by the seven estuariles that branch out
from the Ota River. Cherokee is spread out over six or
seven hills, and many creeks flow into the river. Driving and walking around Cherokee, looking for houses
where we used to live and for other places that evoked
a sense of my life, I had found that many of them had
been demolished. Some of my favorite places were Saharas of concrete. What happened in Hiroshima
seemed to be happening in different ways all around
me, everywhere I traveled. The Hiroshima effect.
Early in the evening of the day the bomb hit, a
Japanese naval launch moved slowly up and down the
seven rivers of Hiroshima, a neatly dressed young
officer shouting at survivors from a megaphone:
"Don't worry. A hospital ship is on the way." It never
came. Some called it a *genshi bakudan* — "original
child bomb." Others called it a "Molotov flower basket." It stripped the dome of the Museum of Science
and Industry to its steel frame, and reduced everything
else around to ground zero. Near the museum a man
on the bridge was about to beat his horse when the
"original child bomb" struck, reducing him to a

shadow on the pavement. A man painting the façade of the bank was dipping his brush into his paint can. His shadow is now like a monument on the stone façade of the bank building. Living victims were so shocked and awed by what they saw that they died mute, no screams of pain or outrage. A woman office worker in a tin factory was crushed by a shelf of books.

The Bijou marquee was lit up in the noon sun: THE MOON IS BLUE, banned in Boston and its spiritual suburbs as obscene because one of the two characters, I forget which, speaks the word "virgin."

Where the hotel across the street next to the theater had burned, there was still only a parking lot. And directly across the street where the old Pioneer Theater had stood, another parking lot did good business. Since my ushering days, I'd learned that on the lot where the Bijou stood, there had once been a store, and before that the jail. The store had burned, and out of its ashes, flapping its wings, had risen the Bijou. While I was at sea that summer, the Hiawassee Theater in North Cherokee had burned, and nothing had risen from its ruins.

I paid fifty cents to enter the Bijou, not to see *The Moon Is Blue,* but to hook up again to images of the past that were electrically charged with feeling and meaning—fused.

The absence of ushers attested to the fact that the Bijou was going down. I stood at my old post, On the Spot, my back to the screen. Gale, looking like Errol Flynn, glides toward me, slender in his tight uniform, perfect fit, like a figure on an urn, across the lobby, slow-motion, to spark my cheek with electricity he scuffs off the carpet, like Michelangelo's God touching Adam's finger across the cosmos—similar action, less voltage—and Alan Ladd says to Veronica Lake in *The Blue Dahlia,* "Every guy dreams of meeting a girl like you. The trick is to find you,'' while in the dome of my skull Hart Woodring's shadow falls across Sabra Van Ness, who rises from the ledge by the pool and removes her silver-coated sunglasses.

I dreamed of returning to the Bijou someday, after television had forced it to close and it had been left abandoned. Rich and famous, I'd restore it and bring back all the old movies and live in the tropical heat of the projection booth, writing my stories and changing reels, living in mortal fear of the smell of smoke.

Out of the ashes of the Bijou, what phoenix might rise? What bird might fire make of the Blue Goose Hotel?

In my basement sanctuary, I tried to make a few notes on *Children of a Cold Sun,* but gibberish is all that came out. I had brought the scenario up to the suicidal sojourn in Maine, but not feeling the compulsion to tell a story, I couldn't focus on that time when I first dreamed up *The Idealists.* Just as I reached the threshold of concentration, Zara Ransom's voice interrupted: ''The music in my heart I bore, long after it was heard no more.'' I began to resent, not her voice, but the way lines from poems I had memorized on the *Polestar* usurped my own thoughts about my experiences in the Pleasure-Dome in Sweetwater. ''And singing still dost soar, and soaring ever singest''—like that, they kept ringing in, upstaging my own consciousness. Trying to conjure up an image of Zara Ransom, I saw nothing, but heard clearly: ''The splendors of the firmament of Time may be eclipsed, but are extinguished not . . .'' Ringing phrases gave me comfort, but what I craved, reluctantly, was understanding, insight.

To clear my head, I left my basement room and took a bus across town to Mammy's house. When I walked away from her house Sunday, I'd left my car behind, too. But when I turned down Holston Street, the car wasn't parked out front. Mammy told me Earl had hot-wired it, borrowed it to look for a job. To hold down, or to pull?

It was a time of evening when I knew Mammy would be alone. She sat in her chair by the door. I sat in the Chief's chair near the TV. "Tell me a story, Mammy," I said, "like you used to."

Without embarrassed hesitation, she intoned, "Well . . ." and told about the time the wildcat tried to climb down Gran'maw's chimney, driven mad by hunger in the worst winter ever to hit the mountains of Tennessee. And Gran'maw, all alone in the cabin, stokes up the fire, heats a black iron pot full of scalding water. When Mammy raised her eyebrows as if to let the implications of that sink in, I felt very old, because when I was little, she always told the ending literally, graphically, leaving nothing to understatement. "And then what, Mammy?" I begged, but she'd dropped her storytelling voice, and let it trail away.

At one time, her voice, sending me into the Pleasure-Dome, had been more than enough, but that night, I recalled Great-gran'maw's past, how she came to Cherokee, and saw that it was similar to Charlta Ransom's flight from Boston, and I nagged Mammy for details about the early life of her dead husband's mother.

I got more than I asked for, and this is the story I got: Mammy had always told us that a young man in a little mountain town had gotten my great-gran'maw pregnant, and that the boy's family had given her a thousand dollars to leave town. But the fact is, Mammy told me now, "and you're the first, not even your mother knows, and you must swear never to tell her, for it'll worry her to death," her own family gave her the money, because her father caught her in bed with her own half-brother. "So she drifted down to Cherokee and with part of that thousand dollars built, with her own hands and sweat—and her pregnant—a one-room shack."

"Where?" I asked, knowing, but too steeped in the new fact to remember.

"Why, honey, right where we're sitting. And before your gran'paw brought me, pregnant with your mother, into this house, he built on the kitchen and the room at the back. Now," she said, nodding her head, looking me in the eye, as if to say, "Swallow that."

It went down hard, because the "truth" conjured up other possible facts. My great-gran'maw died of cancer of the rectum, raving with pain, Mammy nursing her. That could happen to anybody. But, as Mammy had finally revealed when I was thirteen, my gran'paw, a high-strung man all his life, had shot himself. And was there some connection between the love-making of the half-brother and the half-sister and the incipient claw-foot deformity that turned up in the great-grandson, Lucius Hutchfield?

Like that jar I'd tossed on impulse over the fantail of the *Polestar* into the Gulf of Mexico, the tides of the past had finally left this little message on the most familiar coast of my life. The truth, the facts, at last.

Earl pulling up in my Hudson Hornet outside the shaggy hedge rescued me from further discoveries. But as I drove back to my room, what I already knew began to be too much. Perhaps it wasn't Great-gran'maw's half-brother at all, but some boy entirely unrelated whose blood thrummed through my trembling body. But that meant that I carried the uncertainty of physical deformity, madness and suicide, around with me now like a time bomb, a latent inner Hiroshima.

I rushed to my room, turned desperately to the consolation of Pater's words at the end of *The Renais-sance*, the text for the life I must live with this new knowledge ticking inside me. "A counted number of pulses only is given us of a variegated, dramatic life. How may we see in them all that is to be seen in them by the finest senses? How shall we pass most swiftly from point to point, and be present always at the focus where the greatest number of vital forces unite in their purest energy? To burn always with this hard, gemlike flame, to maintain this ecstasy, is success in life. Victor Hugo says, 'We are all under sentence of death but with a sort of indefinite reprieve. . . .' Our one chance lies in expanding that interval, in getting as many pulsations as possible into the given time. Of such wisdom, the poetic passion, the desire of beauty, the love of art for its own sake has most. For art comes to you proposing frankly to give nothing but the highest quality to your moments as they pass, and simply for those moments' sake."

In fear and awe, I lay down to sleep. I cranked up the old night ritual again, trying to dredge up images of Jesse James as he affected me when I was little. Comes this image of me playing Jesse James—I'm about six—and I sneeze into my red bandanna, and in that instant of blackout, I see Jesse reach up to dust a picture on the wall, and that was the moment when I knew, for the first time, I, too, would die.

In my sleep, a voice saying, "And the world's one breathing may at first attain true time," woke me, before daylight. Words I could trace back to no book I had ever read.

When the sun rose, on that fourth morning home, it showed the green Hudson Hornet on the Asheville highway.

# 29 

# *The Phantom Circuit*

I had to go back. Not to get the truth so I could transform it into fiction. I intended to make no substantial changes in the story submitted to *Harper's Bazaar*. The only changes, if any got made, would be in me. Something that would, I hoped, mix well with despair.

No, I was going in search of the facts, thus declaring a break in the phantom circuit of the imagination. "To make fiction agile," I'd written in my notebook the night of my twentieth birthday a few months before, "one must cripple fact."

I took it as one of life's ironic acts of complicity that the green Hudson Hornet had a blowout just ten miles south of Cherokee.

Not lust for the truth compelled me to return, because fiction, when its images are charged to the highest degree with feeling and meaning, *is* truth. Beauty. What I wanted were the facts. Did Zara Ransom actually lose her virginity to Jesse James, or did she not? Answer yes or no. Answer in the broad light of day, not in the moon-flooded lobby of the Blue Goose Hotel. Did Jesse James show a sharp, thin streak of cowardice, as I had imagined, or did he not? Did Zara Ransom run away with Jesse or Davis? Is Zara

Ransom living now in the Blue Goose Hotel for its associations with Jesse James or with Davis Woodring?

Now I knew, from the lady's own mouth, how it felt to lose one's maidenhead to Jesse James. I knew how other people *still* felt about it. One woman so strongly, she'd attacked a strange man in a dark silo. But I wanted now to know if the romance really happened. The facts, I knew, would change nothing. After all these years, there's no point in believing in them. But I expected the facts to give me—especially if they contradicted the illusions—a certain feeling I knew I needed, although I didn't like knowing what it was: superiority, and a sense of control. The thought that each of these people had come out of the Pleasure-Dome captives of a myth made me feel sad, but it also made me sneer, reflexively.

I'd promised Hart I'd return someday. That was one promise I didn't have to break after all. But in keeping that one, I was breaking the one I'd made to Zara Ransom. The promise to leave "forever," as soon as she'd told her story. But with self-loathing self-righteousness, I took solace in the possibility that she'd conned me.

As I drove through Boone and headed for Sweetwater, I realized that by now the sheriff might be looking for me. To get the raw material from which I might conjure up the fictive image, I'd been willing to risk the penitentiary. Were the mere *facts* worth that? They were not. Yet, in self-ignorance, I was taking the risk anyway.

The silo was gone. Not a trace. Not even such a shadow as the anonymous human made on the bridge in Hiroshima. More like the way Flash Gordon used to disintegrate people and objects with his ray gun.

The bulldozers, caterpillars, and tractors were gone.

The path didn't end at the trees. It went on: a wide swath of mud up to the old road into Sweetwater where the population sign was nailed to a fence. But when I reached the road, my shoes full of dirt, I saw no fence, no sign.

Glancing down the hillside, I saw the frozen custard shack, lying beside the creek, the cinder blocks strewn, except for one wall in which the large pane of glass remained, reflecting the early morning sun, winking up at me.

The trading store lay beside the creek, crumpled, a spectacular wreckage. All the houses on the same side where the store had stood, including the church, have been goosed off the edge of the cliff.

The Blue Goose Hotel and the other house remain. Clouds of dust the machines had stirred up had rained down on them.

On both sides of the sloping road the machines, yellow and orange, their windows dew-streaked, are parked.

"Silent as a tomb," I say, standing on the edge of the cliff. But that sounded weak for what I sensed. No, this town was as silent as a town with no one in it.

On the *Polestar,* I memorized only one stanza of Keats's "Ode on a Grecian Urn," the one about the empty town, the one that gave me a heart-stopping intuition of death:

> Who are these coming to the sacrifice?
>   To what green altar, O mysterious priest,
> Lead'st thou that heifer lowing at the skies,
>   And all her silken flanks with garlands drest?
> What little town by river or sea shore,
>   Or mountain-built with peaceful citadel,
>     Is emptied of this folk, this pious morn?

> And, little town, thy streets for evermore
> Will silent be; and not a soul to tell
> Why thou art desolate, can e'er return.


I hear a truck leave the smooth pavement of the highway and hit the gravel. Standing among the branches of an uprooted and fallen tree, I watch for the truck to break through the foliage below. The truck stops alongside the tree. A man in khaki gets out and takes a bright leak in the middle of the road. Now I know, as I watch a look of relief spread like a stain across the man's face, that nobody remains in the town.

But when the man, buttoning his trousers, looks up and sees me, I ask, "How much did you bring this morning?"

"How's that?"

"Progress."

"I didn't get that, buddirow. You fish?"

"I might be."

"That's a hot one," the man says, laughing, and he reaches over the side into the pickup truck bed and pulls out some fishing gear and starts toward a path that once sloped from the store down the cliffside to the creek. "Got an hour yet before we crank up. Fish ever' chance I get."

"Say, you know where they took her?"

"She's up at Fair View Rest Home," he says, disappearing over the rim of the cliff.


The gas gauge quivering on E, I pulled up alongside the pumps at the filling station where the Hudson Hornet I was driving once hung. I hoped Hart would sneak me enough gas to make it to Fair View Rest Home. The problem then was to discourage Hart from going along with me.

The black motorcycle was parked at the curb in front of the pumps under the Texaco sign, FOR SALE painted on the windshield. I climbed the stairs, wondering, what the hell!

Through the open doorway at the top of the stairs came the sound of a refrigerator in the kitchen. Standing in the doorway, I saw Hallie Woodring in a pink slip, sipping a glass of tomato juice, her head tilted at an angle, her free hand on her hip, enhancing the curves of the bone. Her eyes softly closed, her long chestnut hair hanging back. Her feet bare. When she opens her eyes and sees me, she isn't startled.

A toss of her head, and she finishes drinking. Then she sets the glass on the clean oilcloth-covered table and, without wiping the smear from her lips, walks over to the door and slaps me across the mouth. I thought she'd slapped me for the look in my eyes that she'd seen when she opened hers, but in the swing of her hand, she wafted a scent toward me that I recognized.

I wiped my mouth and looked at the blood on the back of my hand. "You've got tomato juice on your mouth, Mrs. Woodring." She brushes her lips with the tips of her fingers. "And I'd give my life to make love to you."

"That's what it'll cost you if you're standing in that doorway three seconds from now."

"Where's Hart?"

"As if you didn't know."

"There's a lot I don't know, and most of it I'm not so sure I want to know. One thing I *would* like to know, though, and that's who it was slapped me in the face in the doorway of that old silo in Sweetwater."

"Who are you? I mean, what do you want, anyway?"

She'd worked among wealthy urban people for ten

years, but she still could come up with the look and
voice of a woman raised in the mountains where a
man's business was his own. Her ominous tone stated
clearly that hers was not mine.

"I'm a—"

"Why have you plagued Miss Ransom?"

"I—"

"Why did you tell Hart about Jesse James?"

"Mrs. Woodring, I—"

"Why did you have to come here and dig up—?"

"Why did you ambush me in the silo that night?"

"I—"

"When you slapped me just now, you fanned that
same jasmine perfume in my face. Don't be ashamed
to admit it."

She almost smiles. "What good did it do? You just
went plowing right ahead and dug it all up, and—"

I didn't know specifically what she meant, but with
the force of impulse, I asked, "So it's true Jesse is
related to Miss Ransom?"

"Good God, don't Hart show it by what he done?"

"*What* did he do? I've been in Cherokee . . ." I
didn't even have time to be shocked by what I'd
stumbled into.

"Oh, God. Please, don't torment us. Listen, I don't
want no more trouble. For years I kept it hid from him
while we was living over round Boone. When my foster parents died I had to get out and work because my
husband was in the army— He was killed in the war,
you know . . ."

"Yes, ma'am," I says, remembering what Hart told
me about the truck on the highway.

"So we ended up over here in Blowing Rock. And
now if I ever get my boy out of this pack of trouble
you brought on him, we're moving away as far as we

can get—even if it's Alaska—from any breath of Jesse James. But at least Jesse went for a lady, where Hart—"

"Then she's his great-grandmother?" Now I was shocked—that my imagination coincided with the stark facts.

"You claim them that loves you. And as for what's true and what ain't, I don't know. I just heard hushed-up stories all my life, some claiming one way, some claiming another. But one thing I vowed from the start: my son ain't gonna have whatever Jesse James blood he's got in him get drained off in no ditch with no sheriff's bullets in his back."

"It was Bob Ford that did it, Mrs. Woodring."

"I know it! And I saw that wild streak in Hart when he was little, and after his father was killed, I vowed something else—and that I have been true to—that I would never let another man touch me, that the chance of Jesse James getting another start in another one of my kids wouldn't ever come up."

"Mrs. Woodring, that's a goddamn shame," I say, looking for some sign that she might be attracted to me.

"It's even more of a goddamn shame that instead of a lady like Zara Ransom, my boy had to risk the electric chair for kidnapping a little whore that's jumped in bed with every nigger in this town."

Stunned, I recovered enough to ask, "Is that true, or another rumor, or your imagination?"

"I'm not going to talk about such filth, but I know for a fact that the nigger chauffeur who brings them up from New Orleans every summer makes money off that corrupt child. And, listen, you, if you don't stop standing there looking at me in my slip and get out of my house, I got a foster brother over in Boone that if he gets wind of you, he'll pack a gun and come a-lookin' for you.''

''I just want to see Hart one more time, then I promise I'll leave him alone for good.''

''For good? He's already gone as far to the bad as a boy can without ending up like Jesse James. If you've got a life of your own and you want to live it out, you better find a place for it. It ain't worth nothing here.''

''I want to tell him something that *may* do some good yet.''

''Then go to the county jail in Boone and say it and get gone from here!''

As she reaches up to push the door, I see the soft, thin hair in her armpits. She slams it in my face. I had enough time to turn and avoid that cliché, but I took it as more than deserved.

Now I wanted to stop. Now I wanted even to forget. But I couldn't. And I felt so keenly my inability to walk away, that if I didn't feel sorry for myself, I felt sorry for no one else either.

Driving to Boone, past Sweetwater, I got a hard-on, seeing her take off that slip. To make love to Hallie was somehow to make love to them all—Zara, Jesse, Hart, and on into narcissism. Zara. What would it be like to make love to a century?

With my penchant for fitting great lines to the occasion, I sang one of Ted Daffan's old hillbilly hits:

> Are you satisfied now,
> After breaking each vow,
> Have you found all the things you desire?
> In the wreckage of dreams,
> With your plans and your schemes,
> Tell me, dear, are you satisfied now?
>
> Does your heart ever ache,

For mistakes that you make?
Do you think of the ones left behind?
Tho' you now seem so gay,
What price do you pay?
Tell me, dear, are you satisfied now?

In the cold, cold gray dawn,
Do memories linger on
Of all the harm you have done?
Do the tears slowly fall
At the things you recall?
Tell me, dear, are you satisfied now?

# 30

## Hart Woodring and Sabra Van Ness

The county jail in Boone is a reconverted brick mansion so similar to the one in Greenbrier where Bucky had awaited rescue, it spooked me. On the first floor, the house was a home, as if white trash had moved into something that once was grand and was trying to live decent. On the second floor, the windows were barred, the screens made of thick wire.

On the screened-in porch, a fat woman in a housedress and apron, her hair tied back, sits in a rusty, green-and-white glider, holding a naked baby and drinking a Pepsi Cola. Majel wasn't polishing her majorette boots, but a girl of about thirteen, wearing shorts and halter, a farmer's blue kerchief tied over her hair, sat beside the woman, shelling beans into a speckled saucepan, and another girl of about sixteen sits in a wicker rocker, her feet tucked under her luscious buttocks, reading a funny-book.

As the woman and the girls look through the screen, suspiciously, "Hi," I says.

"Hidi do. Can I help you?" the woman asks, holding the Pepsi out of range of the baby's reaching hands.

"I come to see Hart Woodring. When's visiting hours?"

"Georgia, show this boy how you get in. Sorry, I can't get up, I got this back, and with this youn'un loadin' me down, I—"

"Oh, that's okay, ma'am . . ."

Georgia got up and rolled *Daffy Duck* up and jammed it into the back pocket of her shorts, a pair of jeans cut off or chewed off above the knees. It took her a long time, while I glanced at the way her pale blue rayon blouse clings to her moist breasts.

She opens the screen that leads inside the house and as I said, "Thank you," I glanced at her face and saw she was cross-eyed, but it didn't strike me that other eyes could improve her beauty. In the cool hallway, following Georgia so far behind she glanced back several times to see if I was still with her, I smelled green beans cooking to go with the shellies. I passed the kitchen where a bushel of potatoes sat on the floor beside an old Kelvinator. On the bed in the bedroom was a green chenille spread and by the window a treadle-action sewing machine. I saw the back porch where panties and three large, stiff pairs of overalls hung.

Georgia stops at an iron door on which the silver paint is peeling. It looks like the door to the *Polestar*'s engine room. When she reaches up, straining with her fingertips along the ledge, her blue panties showing below her shorts, I'm back in Greenbrier with Majel. She unlocks the door and I help her pull it back.

I waited for her to hand me the key, as Majel had, but she clutches it, saying, "When you get done, just beller."

I started up the wooden steps. The iron door clanged shut behind me, and I wondered if this was a trick to catch the check passer.

A man in coveralls comes to the door at the head of the stairs as I climb. "Pardon me," I say. "Hart Woodring up here?"

"Get off the pot, Hart!" the man says, stepping back barefoot into a puddle of his own tobacco juice. "Got a visitor." Then to me, he says, "He's so full of it, he needs to stay *on* there. He ever pump *you* full of Jesse James?" The coveralls are too large and over-starched. Every time he moves inside them, the man seems to bruise himself. "Got a smoke, neighbor?"

"Sorry, only smoke cigars."

Hart stepped out of a wooden booth that leaned against the wired window, one of its legs lifted several inches off the concrete, as if primly trying to avoid the overflow from the tall latrine.

Hart's hair is wild, his face is red from oversleep, but his eyes, seeing me, become crystal, and he leaves one strap of his jailhouse overalls dangling, waves to me, walks down the long narrow cell to the door. "Well, by God, I did it, Lucius. It didn't last forever, but it'll never be over. Nothing'll ever be like it was."

"What happened?"

"What *hap*pened?" asked the man, backed up against the wall, wiping his foot dry on a paper sack. "This boy went off his pea-pickin' rocker. It's all over 'bout what he done. Where *you* been?"

"Okay, Chester, this is a friend of mine, you just zip it up and sit over yonder awhile, nobody's gonna miss you."

"Ain't nobody ever missed me yet," says Chester, going to the booth. From inside, he says, "Can't *ever*'body be Jesse James the second."

"You want me to tell you about it?" Hart's hands gripped the bars of the locked door between us, his teeth gritted and grinning.

"I have to *pay* most people when it comes to Jesse James."

"You don't have to pay me to hear a lot of made-up

junk. You're looking at the real McCoy, in the flesh. Just stop anybody on any street and they'll tell—"

"*You* tell me."

"You told *me,* first. Remember? Then I went out on my sickle and rode all night and thought it all out—part in my mind and part right there on the sickle—what I'd do come daylight and she stroll out to lay down on that damned flying carpet by the pool. I'd zoom up like a rocket from Mars and take her, towel and all, and even that plastic squirter of suntan lotion. But come daylight—"

"Like it always *does.*"

"Hush. And I saw how it was. That I didn't have that kind of guts—the Jesse James brand that should have got passed on if we're kin. So I chickened out, Lucius, and cut back for home in time to get my face slapped for roamin' out the night. 'If you don't take to coming home at a decent hour, I'm gonna slap the face off you,' she said, like the idea just occurred to her. Now, don't get me wrong, ain't nobody loves his momma like me, but I was getting sick of *some* things, and that was one of them.

"My momma always talks about the fine people she serves, and that morning she gets off on Sabra Van Ness. How Sabra was bored to tears with Blowing Rock and begged her daddy to pack up and take her to Monte Carlo. 'Cordin' to Momma, he wasn't about to take her. She was there during Christmas holidays and never got over it. Momma said Sabra seems to hate her own folks and the Mardi Gras society they talk about at nearly every meal. And Momma says Sabra told her father to go jump off the blowing rock, and took her Lobster Newburg and let it slide off the plate and run down the thick candle that was glowing on the table.

"I couldn't get that out of my head all morning, and

I just laid on my cot there in the kitchen till it was time to rob Tweetsie, thinking about her laying on the edge of that pool in the sun, burning up with boredom, wanting to be in Monte Carlo.

"Out at Tweetsie it was hot, too, even under the tree where I'm supposed to lay in wait for the train to come tweetin' around the bend after the Indian raid's over. I saw the Indians walk up the path behind me to the makeup shack, showing the hangovers most of them had, and I get this queer feeling. I knew we had one of the summer's biggest crowds on that train, some even standing in the aisles.

"Even jumping down on top of the train felt different. For some reason, I was scared. My hands sweated on the pearl-handled pistols as I kicked open the door.

"You can always depend on some woman to scream at the first sight of a man with a mask over his face and a pulled-down hat. The kids went ape more than usual, and I reckon the way they yelled or just stared bug-eyed, those mouths like cats' butts, I got carried away more than I already was. I think people love this part best of all, getting robbed, knowing it goes to the community chest. Well, there was one chest needed plenty of fillin'. I thought of that as I watched my hat go around and the money drop in. One kid pulls at my gun belts and whispers, 'Do me a favor, mister. Kidnap my brother. They give him half of everything I ever get.'

"When the train slows for the curve at a place where they trimmed pine trees for the right-of-way, I took the hat full of money and jumped off. Faces at the window and arms waving, as usual, but this time I wave back with my free hand.

"There's this cook in the restaurant part who always runs to the back door when he sees me coming down the path from a holdup, and he yells, 'Hey, stop that man! He's a train robber! Holdup! Help!' I hated the sight of a stupid moron that could milk a dry joke for two summers. But that morning he acts like it's something new, and it gets me. And I go ahead and do what I was already seeing in my mind.

"I run toward the parking lot where my sickle's parked by the phony white fence and I hop on, stuff the money in the saddlebags, hat and all, and just before I strike up the motor, I hear the cook laughing like he thinks I'm putting on a good show and he's calling the cues. I didn't hear what he said when he saw me rip out of that parking lot and down to the highway and off up the hill past Sweetwater.

"On the steep, winding drive up to Mayview, I had to slow down. The road's too narrow to pass a white Cadillac, and really, it didn't exactly seem right to pass Sabra's father—like it wouldn't be good manners.

"Then he noses right in between a Jag and a Chrysler, the hood pointing at the pool. He's still getting out when I jump off the sickle. I grab the saddlebags, throw them into the back seat of the Cadillac convertible, and when he turned, I was running up the bank to the pool.

"Sabra didn't even look up at the noise of my boots on the tile. But when I touched her, it was like I was a spark. She raises up just enough for me to get my arm around her, and I pick her up and carry her down to the Cadillac, her father turning on the path to the pavilion by now, his cigarette wilting in his white mouth. The towel got caught on a thorn bush and the lotion bottle fell in front of me and I nearly broke my neck stumbling over it. She shakes off the drowsiness of the morning in the sun just as I get to the car, pitch her in, and leap over her and land behind the wheel. I didn't *know* the keys would be in it, but there they were. That's the way everything happened right on to the morning we boarded the ship in Miami.

"But right then, she rears up and screams and throws a fit. I got the car on the road back down, at sixty miles an hour, taking those curves. I met the manager of Tweetsie just around one of the sharpest. In that Volkswagen of his, faced with my Cadillac, he decided on the trees.

"Sheriff Odom pulls out from in front of the post office, siren squealing, light flashing in the sun about a hundred yards ahead of me. I stopped for a light like any citizen would and as he ran through it, I waved and gave him my best grin. All this time—every bit of forty seconds—she's screaming and screaming, her hair batting the breeze.

"Out on the open highway, Sheriff Odom caught up to us. Know what I did? I stopped the car, grabbed her wrist and held her until I saw him in the rearview mirror get out and walk toward the car, then I give it the gun in reverse before he can get his pistol out of its holster, and ram his car so hard it rolled back down the hill and plowed through a roadside stand that sells—or sold—junk pottery and lawn crap made of Paris plaster. Then I shot ahead, swerving to miss the bastard, even if he did slug me in the lobby that time, and her just a-bellering.

"But she changed her tune somewhere near Charlotte and the screaming sounded more like playacting, like it wasn't the first time those lungs ever got a workout. And I guess it kind of got her, the way I fooled every highway patrol car that took out after us. I didn't have to plan any of it. I just used the tricks that came to my head from dusty old reels of chapter plays stored in the back of my mind. You know, all those wild, impossible ways of dodging the law you see at the show. Any one of them can get you killed. None of them did that trip.

"So I reckon she got to studying back on some of those antics, because I stopped on the highway somewhere along the coast to look at a wounded sea gull on the road and put it off on a dune and she didn't even *look* like she wanted to jump out and run—to this family that was lying on the sand with the surf on their toes.

"But she looked at me, and a hundred miles down the coast, I caught her smiling, and a little later she reaches in the glove compartment and I draw one of the toy pistols on her, and she pulls out a bottle of lotion and smiles at me as she pats it on her brown shoulders.

"'Where are we going?' she asks, and it sounded damn rich.

"'I thought we'd see what's going on at Monte Carlo.' I looked to see how she's taking it. It hits her just right.

"'You mean it?'

"'Sure do. I got a hat full of dough.'

"'Stolen?'

"'Voluntary contribution.'

"'Enough?'

"'How much it take?'

"I told her to look in the saddlebags and she dumps the money on the seat between her legs and plops the hat on her head and counts it. Then she looks up with a pout under the brim of my hat.

"'How much we lack?'

"'Lots. Just lots.'

"To put it short, I robbed a filling station with those toy pistols. She counted the take, and I robbed another one, and she even asked me my damn name before I did the third.

"'Jesse James,' I says, and she laughs and says hers is Marilyn Monroe, and I believed her. I believed her even more when she got done kissing me for holding up a roadside tavern outside Saint Augustine. She was Catholic and said she'd been forced to read Saint Augustine in convent school, and the more she saw of the world, the more she was sure the City of Gold was on this earth, and I told her I didn't know who the hell Saint Augustine was, but if it came to a choice, I'd pick her over any city in the world. She says get her over to Monte Carlo, one of the best, and I can have her till doomsday.

"Sometimes, listening to her talk, I got cold chills. She goes for everything new that's made: new cars, especially foreign, so her old man was a 'square' with his 'Cad convert,' as she puts it, and all the new fashions and fads and dance steps, and she even rode under the moon with her head in my lap, talking my ear sore about how she'd be the first beauty on the moon and set up a monopoly on the roulette racket. Just like the wind we stirred up down those highways, she took my breath away.

"So we made it to Miami, with the white Cadillac looking like a skin't coon, and we're sipping champagne in our cabin on a ship to Monte Carlo and she's tickling my ribs with her green toenails when come a knock at the door and she tells them to go to hell. But they busted in, and the cop had to carry her off the way I did before, to get her off the ship.

"They broke us apart at the station, and she says, 'Good-bye, Jesse. See you on the moon. You get the first spin free.'

"I didn't say anything. I'd been saving it for a good time, maybe as we entered the Mediterranean, but I couldn't say I loved her with all the cigarette butts on the floor and my own butt riding pretty low. Some low-down trash talks like it was just one big sex orgy, but here's something only you and me know—I'm what you call a damn virgin.''

Coming out of the Pleasure-Dome, I asked him, ''Where is *she* now?''

''Momma said she saw her yesterday at noon spreading suntan lotion on her legs by the pool. You ought to hear some of the wild things my momma says about her . . . But I don't regret it. I didn't get what I wanted— But I got the memory of a good try. Maybe they just don't make Jesse Jameses like they used to.''

''Oh, I reckon there's some of the old breed up in the mountains who'll get the papers two months late, and they'll put you to song.''

''But it didn't turn out right. A puny ending, ain't it?''

''How does it look for you?''

''Nobody gives me the hope of less than ten years in a string of prisons—to go with the string of states I robbed in. Did Jesse James ever get caught?''

''Oh . . .''

''Did he?''

''Look, Hart, wouldn't it be better if you forgot all that about Jesse James? Maybe you had him pegged right the first time, when you saw those chapter plays and didn't cotton to him.''

''Aw, that was phony. Don't you get it, Lucius? I put some flesh on those old buried bones. Feel.'' Hart grabs my hand and claps it to his ribs. ''That's the blood of us both beating.''

''Hart, you've got to forget all that stuff. You've got years in prison to serve. You can't keep it going in your mind, laying on those prison cots. It'll—''

''What kind of bull you slinging at me? Didn't you—''

"Yes. God, yes. It's *my* fault you're in here. It's *my* fault, those ten years ahead. And if it gets you sucked under, this goddamned myth I pumped into you, that'll be my guilt, too. You only did what I—"

"Wait just a damn minute, none of that *your* fault stuff. Don't *you* try to hog in on the credit, Lucius. It was *me* — I did what I did. Now you can go out and do what you want to, but keep your hands off what I did. I ain't got Sabra. But I got that. The memory. Do you think I'll just be another punk in that prison? Wait till they find out how I—"

"Hart, they'll laugh, they'll—"

Hart frowned, cut deep. "Lucius . . ."

"Hart, it's fine, it's the only way to *see* the world, but you can't go out and make it real and then live on it. You have to have control. You can't let it control you."

Not that I had achieved control myself yet. Except when I held him willing captive awhile in the Pleasure-Dome. But Hart's gesture bore witness to both the fruits and the risks of the vicarious impulse.

When Hart said, "What you talking about? I don't understand," I knew it was too early for him, to even bring *up* the subject, much less go *into* it.

But I did say, "Look at Miss Ransom. Look how *she's* ending up."

"They told me. The bastards! I know how she feels now. I wish I hadn't listened to Momma about her. She might have told me, someday. Called me inside, instead of making me stand on the back porch, and told me—"

I took a firm grip on the bars, said, "Okay, Hart, goddamnit, *I'll* tell you."

"You already did."

"No! I mean the damned *facts*. It was all the way

she told it — except the end. Jesse James chickened out. He didn't get the girl. He—"

"Shut up!"

"Now, listen, I've got to tell you—"

"*You* don't have to tell me nothing. Get gone, Hutchfield, get gone, get gone."

"Okay. But you *do* believe me, don't you?"

"If she's the one told the rest, she'll have to tell the end."

"She can't come *here*. She's confined at the old folks home. You hear me, Hart?"

I yelled for Georgia to unlock the door. As I go out, Hart calls down to her, and she goes gladly up, and I don't even pause to watch her climb the stairs.

# 31
## The Wreckage
## of Dreams

The other daughter and the sheriff's wife were drinking Pepsis and the baby lay on a tow sack on the floor and a swarm of flies lay on the baby. The woman and the girl sit on the glider, gliding, the springs sound like a saw cutting wet pine. Their eyes look up at me where I pause awkwardly in the doorway.

"I wondered if you could tell me how to get out to the old folks home?"

"Who you know outsyonder?"

"Miss Ransom."

"Momma, ain't that the one Daddy's out looking for?"

"Looking for? What happened?"

"Ain't nobody seen her since noon. They went in the dormitory to call her to lunch and she was gone and wasn't nowhere 'bout the premises."

"Thanks."

"My husband's over at the Blue Goose now, poking around. I told him he mize well come on in and eat his own meals. Out on a wreck, come in, out again on a lost person before I can get it on the table."

It took a while for me to sell the hubcaps for a few gallons of gas and drive to Sweetwater, imagining her hidden in the tree, among the roses and pine needles and the wasps.

The bulldozers were parked on the clean-swept cliffside, looking on their work as though slightly in awe. I parked among them.

In the middle and along the sides of the road and up the hotel drive, trucks and cars are parked crookedly. Sheriff Odom's car showed its polish in the moonlight, despite patches of dust.

"Yonder he comes a-walking!"

Men ran off the porch and leaped over the rail, and one jumped out a window.

I saw a man in overalls and a ball cap standing on the hood of a produce truck point down the road in my direction, and he yelled again.

Sheriff Odom appeared at the end of the drive below the hotel, a beam round as a melon in one hand, a gun in the other.

"Okay, Hart. Up with those hands. Run you ragged, didn't we?"

As I raised my hands, it was as though my thumbs had flicked switches: four flashlights nail me to the road in cross beams. "So he broke loose and beat me over here," I said, laughing.

"That don't look to me like Hart Woodring."

"No," says Odom, "but I seen him som'mers before. Can you see, Billy? He got blond hair?"

"Dirty blond, if you ask't me."

"Hey, you— No, keep them pea-pickers in the air— Was you in the jail a while ago?"

"Only the Shadow knows . . ." I tried to laugh like the Shadow.

Another light came up to the group. Men were running down to the road from all around the hotel. A few flooded me with headlights, cutting on their brights as they coasted down the drive.

"A few more lights," I said, "and you won't be able to see me."

"I see you good, boy!"

"Sheriff," one of the men said, "they ain't *no*body in that place. Nothing but dust and dead flies."

"Okay. Start into them woods, men. Fan out! Flush him into the valley. Some of you take the creek. Hey, you men in the red truck! Race down to the highway where those woods come down the other side. Hobe, watch this man."

"Now look, Sheriff. I left my produce on the streets of Boone to see some action, not guard no prisoner."

"Well, bring him with you, then. Just keep that gun on him. He's slippery."

As the sheriff turned, the flashlights turned with him, and followed him away from the end of the drive toward the woods.

"Come on," said Hobe, and shot his light into my face.

We moved through the trees where the lights flashed, the beams chopped and deflected by the trunks and splintered by needles and fine-leaved ferns.

"Hell's bells," said Hobe, quietly, "I followed that boy in the newspapers right on, and to tell the God's truth, I admire the fool out of 'im. You help him break out?"

"I locked him in."

"Stop!" Hobe gripped my arm, and we stopped so close I smelled him—the man I helped to carry the basket of potatoes into Mayview Manor. "Hear that?"

"What?"

"That running."

I listened. The others had stopped, but their lights jerked viciously, along the ground, into the trees.

"There he runs!" a man yelled, shrilly.

"Where?" Sheriff Odom's voice boomed, fully, in the woods.

"In the trees yonder!"

"Where?"

"*I* saw him, Sheriff."

"Shut up, Cait," somebody said.

"*You* shut up, you— Damnit, I can't see 'im now."

Hobe and I come to a path. "Let's see where this leads," he says.

"In the moonlight, all paths lead to romance," I said, bitterly.

I heard springwater. Around a bend, I saw it. But as I stepped off the path to drink, I see a man on a rock ledge at the mound where the path dips down the other side of the mountain. He wears a suit and a hat and the moonlight glimmers on the barrel of the pistol in his hand at his side. The hat shadows his face, and for a moment the light on the gun is on a watch chain.

"Who's that on the rock?" asks Hobe.

"Who the hell's askin'?"

"Hobe Keely, by God."

"You the damn leader?"

"Now, now. I just wondered what you's doing standing there in the full of the moonlight on a ledge like a damn target a blind man could shoot between the eyes . . ."

"Well, if it's any of your damned business, I ain't never been up this high before and I suddenly come on this view and I was a-looking at it. But *ain't* none of your business, mister . . . He's not *in* these woods anyway, if you ask me."

The man's last words pacified me, as though he were Frank James, the one with good sense. I bent over the natural fountain where the water sprang from the rocks. But before my tongue could taste the water I smelled, a limb cracked in the silence among the trees. Very loud.

All the lights got still, a few seconds. But I, standing rigidly by the fountain, felt the rapid movement of blood in my veins, pounding in my chest, in my neck.

"Wonder what that was?" Hobe asked.

The sound of a human voice at this moment sickened me. "Shut up."

"You telling me—?"

"Shut up, Hobe!"

I ran into the woods.

"Stop! Halt! Or I'll shoot!"

The cliché in all its sterility stunned me.

"Don't shoot!" someone near the pine-rose tree yells. "No use to now!"

The flashlights swoop over me again unintentionally when I reach the bewilderment of pine needles, thorns, leaves, vines, and roses. The man who'd stood on the ledge, gazing at a view from the heights, had found Hart. A swarm of wasps rasped and droned inside the entanglement. A booted foot sticks out of the foliage.

"Never seen anything like *that* before," the man says.

"Is he—?"

The foot moved.

"I saw her, Lucius." The voice inside sounded as though it, too, had fallen through thorns.

"Lie still, Hart, I'll—"

"No. Don't you get near me. I ain't dead. I'll live, and I'll kill you, if you touch me."

"But Hart, those wasps— Hey, help me get him out of there."

"Some other time," the man of the romantic view says. "I've heard tell of a body not recovering from Japanese wasp stings."

I plunged my hands and arms through a foot of tangled needles and briars and forced an opening close to the ground. My hand left blood on Hart's boots as I gripped his ankles. The man's hands nudged one of mine loose and he pulled on one leg as I pulled on the other.

Hart tried to keep from moaning. The man and I keep pushing back the briars as Hart's shoulders work through. Wasps get caught in the briars, enraged, trying to get at me and the man.

"What the hell is *this?*" Sheriff Odom said, kneeling beside me, panting. When he sees what I see—the boy in the oversize overalls, his bare shoulders and arms and neck and face covered with swelling red welts and raw scratches—he doesn't say anything else. He puts the gun in its holster and clicks off the harsh light.

"Little bastard fell out of the tree like Humpty Dumpty, huh?" says a man who just caught up.

Odom, still looking at Hart, says quietly, "Somebody shut that man up." Then he tells someone to go down for a truck and to pull it up to where the road runs to weeds. "Can you stand to be picked up, son?"

Hart lies there without moving his head, looking up at me. "You hear me? I saw her tonight. I knew she'd be there—I felt it in my bones. 'Specially when I heard she run off from the rest home. I told her who I was, and she didn't say a word. She just hugged me. She hugged me for a long time and wouldn't turn loose of me. And I asked her was it true, did he chicken out, and she said, no, no, no, he didn't. And she— and then—" His eyes closed, but his mouth was open. He made no sound.

"Did he say— Billy, pick up the boy and carry him to the road— Hey, you, did he say he talked to Miss Ransom?"

I said, "I didn't hear him."

"Well, *I* did. Good Lord, what a day. Let's go, men. She's in the hotel som'mers."

"Why don't you leave her alone, Sheriff?" I said, in a tone meant to convey my awareness that he wanted to.

"Boy, how come *you're* in all this?"

"Can't you let her stay there till—?"

"Till when? Till the bulldozers climb that drive tomorrow morning like Patton's tanks?"

"It'll kill her."

"Not ever'body gets to die all at once."

I followed them under the trees to the road where a pickup truck was parked. The bed was full of manure.

"You're not going to—"

"It's soft and it's fresh. Good for corn, good for a corn-fed outlaw like Hart Woodring. He wouldn't mind."

They laid Hart in the bed of the truck and a man got in and sat beside him. Then the truck backs all the way down the steep road past the Blue Goose Hotel, its headlights bouncing over the faces of the men who walked back down the road, flashlights extinguished, guns dangling at their sides. The truck turned in a space between the blades of two bulldozers, and its red taillights fade into the misty glow of the moon.

"Reckon he'll live?" Hobe asked.

"Likely to as not."

"Ripped up, looked like."

"For life."

# 32

# *Nothing Dies, but Something Mourns*

Cars dropping down from the main highway dipped a moment into darkness, then their lights leaped across town, over the arched backs of the caterpillars, and spread weakly over the windows and walls of the hotel, dipped again, and shone on the backs of the crowd as the cars climbed the hill. Many were parked on the road already, and tourists and local people walked among them with an air either of having everything under control or of being frankly bewildered at their ignorance of what was going on. I saw a girl in shorts who probably rode Tweetsie earlier in the day write her name with lipstick along the side of a bulldozer: MILLIE BICKERSTAFF, CHAGRIN FALLS, OHIO.

The sheriff's men collected around him and waited for him to speak. He leans against the front of his patrol car where Hart smashed it, white paint force-smeared on the grill.

Now that they knew Zara Ransom was in the hotel, this congregation of strangers behaved just like the townspeople several weeks before.

Sheriff Odom tilts his hat over his eyes, bends his head in meditation, and flicks the flashlight on and off.

I'm sure Zara Ransom was watching us from one of the dust-powdered windows. Finally, Odom pushed off from the bumper.

"Don't nobody move. This is *my* problem."

He starts up the sandstone steps. But midway, he stops, steps backward down one step, and removes his hat.

Zara Ransom appears in the doorway of the glassed-in porch. The crowd on the road and the drive below hush.

She wears the same white dress, and what the noon sun did for it, the midnight moon now does differently.

I look at her, the question itching my tongue. She stares into my eyes as though sticking a needle into a button, and then I know for a certainty that though Jesse James may never have touched her, Lucius Hutchfield *did*.

The silence began among those under her gaze at the foot of the steps and spread slowly, steadily, to the edges of the crowd. The lights of some of the cars parked among the crowd shone bright on the porch. But when she appeared in white in the moonlight, headlights went off. Even at that distance, the crowd seemed aware that a legend was bodied forth on the porch, that the figure, which *demanded* no respect, deserved it, reminding them perhaps that those who do not remember the past are doomed never to relive it in the imagination.

Caught in her eyes, I half expected Zara Ransom to fling the three hundred-dollar checks at my feet. I saw that I was not, like the others at my back, a stranger. I had known her, I had ravaged her, and the dust on the hem of the virginal dress, like the stingers in Hart's body, seemed to testify to that act. If the ravishment had occurred in time, it had occurred in a past that had never changed for Zara Ransom and would now never change for me.

I wished the sheriff would speak. But he stood there like one of the telephone poles that would come down tomorrow.

A man jerked at the straps on his overalls, as though pounding himself like a post into the ground. Having never been to Sweetwater before, he had the look of a man who would never forget that he once had. Its eyes uplifted, the crowd seems to be waiting for a sign from the porch, perhaps an order, or a revelation.

She opened her mouth as if to answer them, but a long space ticked between the expectant silence and the sound of her voice.

"I will come with you in a moment, sir," she said, to the sheriff, I suppose, although her eyes remain on me.

I knew that if I turned away, or even averted my eyes, I'd never turn again in the direction of whatever salvation remained for me. No one followed her eyes—they must have seemed to look at nothing.

"I came back to get something that belongs to me and Jesse."

I flinched. She steps back and a shadow falls across her eyes before she turns.

And she knew that privacy was a thing she'd never know again. She knows what I knew even more clearly and differently, that her story is in the public mails, that I had committed her privacy to the eyes, if not the hearts, of the readers of *Harper's Bazaar*. For the first time, she had made it public herself. Now I knew, with a sick thud in my chest, why Zara kept the money. She felt that she'd earned it. She had, in her own genteel way, arrogantly pronounced the name of her situation.

She disappears behind the wall of panes, the white of her dress dissolving in and merging with the moonlight that flows through the warped squares of glass.

Sheriff Odom jumps up onto the back bumper of the patrol car, claps a big hat on his head, and holds up his hands, palms out to the crowd, like the victim of a stick-up.

"Ladies and gentlemen, may I please have your undivided attention. Please! This is very hard on Miss Ransom. I ask you, as good Christian folks, to get into your cars and drive away. Hart Woodring has been captured and took to the hospital. There's no more here to see.

"Miss Ransom is just gonna get together a few things and I'm gonna drive her over to Fair View Rest Home. And that's all they is to it. So do her this one favor," he says, assuming that everyone knows her, even though most of these people are summer residents and tourists. But they're responding.

"Don't make her have to see your faces when she comes out . . . I see a few folks are getting into their cars. Good Christian folks that know how to act. So . . ."

The sheriff continued to talk to them, his deep, resonant voice getting lower, more soothing, as they turn, some with hands in pockets, some flipping cigarettes over the cliff, toward their cars. He remained on the bumper, watching them.

Between the starting of motors, I heard jar flies. An elderly lady in one of the tourist station wagons rolled the window up in front of the pug face of a barking Pekinese.

I couldn't move. I waited for her to come down. Maybe I wanted to see her up close, to see and touch the sharp edge where the virginal white dress, the past, and the gray hair and wizened face were separate. Tainted now, she might look upon me with at least a glint of compassion.

The red taillights of the last cars pass between the bulldozers lining both sides of the road and they're blinking on the rise to the highway where the rail fence and the population sign once were, when I see a glow of red on the side of the sheriff's patrol car.

On the bumper, Odom turns and lets down one leg in the same motion. Seeing me, he says, "What the hell *is* your name, boy?"

"For want of a better name—Bob Ford," I say, wondering where the red glow is coming from.

"Well, if you ain't out of sight of this place in two shakes, I'll make hell for—" He stops, his eyes on the porch.

Hearing behind and above me a sound like the rising of the stage, I turn, expecting to see her stepping out onto the porch. The glass panes are red.

The crowd returned with the fire engines, which came from Blowing Rock and Boone over the imminently obsolete highway.

I stood in the crowd and watched the Blue Goose Hotel burn and the long, thick whips of water lash the crumbling timber.

The multipaned front had turned me and the sheriff back from the pulsing heat, and we'd tried to raise the windows facing the porch, which encircled the hotel, but the force and suffocating density of smoke had made us turn our backs, stagger to the rail, go finally over the rail, and writhe on the grass amid flying sparks.

We listened for a human sound from the rooms.

An ambulance came.

Between the driver and his assistant sat a young man in a T-shirt. "What's the story?" he asks me, his glasses doubling the burning hotel. "The old lady in there?"

"I don't know," I said. "Why don't you go in and see for yourself?"

"Ha!"

"False alarm for *you*, ol' boy," the driver says to the young man. "Reckon the questions you raised in your article will just have to dangle."

The driver and his assistant, with the young newspaper reporter between them, their cheeks and ears red, turn and go away, the sheets white and neat through the window.

At dawn, when the men arrived to operate the bulldozers and other wrecking equipment, the flames were out. Smoke rose in thin, isolated, curling streams from charred and dripping planks and beams. The fire engines had salvaged a structure that still turned a few white walls toward the morning sun.

I remembered a photograph of muddy houses on the front page of a newspaper I'd delivered on Clayboe Ridge. As I gestated in my momma's womb, the Tennessee Valley Authority forced families, sometimes physically evicted them, off their farms in Anderson County, and the year I was born they started constructing Norris Dam, and in 1935 covered the vacated land with water. Ten years later, when some of the same families were being forced off land to make way for Oak Ridge and the bomb, there was such a hot spell that the waters of Norris Lake receded and the old town, its stores and houses and sidewalks and telephone poles, installed not long before the deluge, rose, and the mud baked in the sun, and thousands came back, some from Florida, Canada, New York, Detroit, California, and Baltimore, to gaze in wonder at their old houses in the little town. Then rain fell for days and the town sank, and the people went away. As if I'd really been there, forgotten, then suddenly remembered, that scene on the shore of the lake often came back.

A man in a red sporting cap stumbled into town from

the woods above the hotel, his shotgun broken over his shoulder, his game bag flapping loosely at his side, and asks me what it's all about. Before I can tell him anything, the sheriff calls to us across the ruins.

"Hey, you two men! How about helping us look in these ashes? Help us find her. These men have got to get going."

The wreckers are sitting on the machines, smoking, talking quietly.

The hunter and the sheriff and his deputy and several other men and I move carefully among the ashes, trying to keep clear of the walls still standing, that chance alone supports.

With a stick, I poke into smoking mattresses and black upholstery, afraid each thrust will send back into my hand the vibration of a bone. But I was still hoping to find something that would give me the truth. The compulsion to complete the factual picture nauseated me.

Her body's somewhere near. I can smell it. When I look up and see one of the wreckers looking down at me with distaste on his mouth, I know that I'm closer to the machines than any of the operators are. In me, the inanimate, conscienceless monsters have found a will.

When the hunter found Zara Ransom in the ashes, her bony wrist was caught in the charred coils of the bedsprings, three coils away from what was once a packet of letters. A kerosene lamp lay, black, at her feet. Around her head lay the fragments of the glass chimney. It had shattered like the dome of her imagination.

The fire appeared, then, to have been an accident. That depended on whether, as the years pass, I will believe my own eyes or vision from another source.

The hunter asks me to hold the letters while he

works loose the old woman's hand. Strange that the man had extricated the letters first. I went down to the creek, away from the smoke and the stink, away from the human, living faces. Were the letters from Jesse James or from Davis Woodring? Did one of them tell her where to meet him? Did one of them—?

I didn't want to know. What I'd seen in the old lady's eyes had solved the really important mystery: the nature of my own guilt. Is guilt what makes the world go round?

I crumpled the charred packet in my fists and sprinkled the flakes of paper into Sweetwater Creek. Leaning against a birch that the shoulders of animals and men have rubbed smooth, I realize that the way to any palpable punishment—the checks—had gone up in smoke with the love letters. But how sweet would be the caress of handcuffs on my wrists, this instant. It's subtler forms of punishment I dread.

The motors starting up startle me. I'd expected the wreckers to eventually turn and go away. A final, belated gesture of respect. But if they were going to do it, I'd have to watch. I was, I knew, the supervisor on this job.

Only the wreckers and their machines remained. They climb the drive, gravel and grass sputtering out from under the mammoth, smoking rubber tires. Other machines bounce along the creek below, heading for the houses that have already been pushed over the edge, their windows opaque with dust and smoke, to finish the wreckage.

"Let's get this job done quick, boys," the foreman yells, "before the place swarms with curiosity seekers!" But something else makes his voice quaver shrilly.

Ashes like charred skin cling to my sweaty palms,

but I don't wipe them off. Standing in the midst of the whirling dust and the concatenation of machinery, the smell of the charred wood and the exhausts of the machines in my nostrils, I feel something deeply for the first time besides nostalgia.